Praise f

"[O]riginal and highly immersive."

—*Good Morning America*

"Brazilian American Rogers's debut novel is polyphonic, raw, and a revelation . . . Through that darkness, glimmers of love, hope, and redemption shine through Rogers, by turns, shocking and brutal, effervescent and delightful tale. . . .Young people will be moved by Daniel and Lucia's plight, challenges, and choices."

—*Booklist* (starred review)

"Rogers debuts with the riotous and tragicomic story of a Rio de Janeiro family in turmoil over lies, infidelity, and parental abandonment . . . Rogers's plot sizzles as much as the Copacabana Beach where the party's fateful events play out. This packs a powerful punch."

—*Publishers Weekly* (starred review)

"With a tremendously powerful voice and a commanding hand, Harold Roger's *Tropicália* shoots us out of a cannon from page one . . . With riveting and fearless prose and moments of tension so thick they make your spine tingle, *Tropicália* weaves us in and out of the Cunha family's past and one inextricably linked week in their present that will force the siblings to decide if it's possible to escape fate and what it means to define ourselves on our own terms. This book and the humanity, humor, and, yes, even rage, these characters made me feel, will stay with me for a long time."

—Xochitl Gonzalez, *New York Times* bestselling author of
Olga Dies Dreaming

"A bacchanal of familial entanglements, as beautiful as it is brutal. This is a story of what happens when love is the midwife of destruction, trauma the cousin of redemption, and fate the absentee mother of us all. I loved this book in all its parts, but as a whole, it left me awestruck."

—Jamie Ford, *New York Times* bestselling author of
The Many Daughters of Afong Moy

tropicália

a novel

harold rogers

ATRIA PAPERBACK

NEW YORK   LONDON   TORONTO   SYDNEY   NEW DELHI

ATRIA
PAPERBACK

An Imprint of Simon & Schuster, LLC
1230 Avenue of the Americas
New York, NY 10020

First Atria Paperback edition June 2024

ATRIA PAPERBACK and colophon are trademarks of Simon & Schuster, LLC

Simon & Schuster: Celebrating 100 Years of Publishing in 2024

For information about special discounts for bulk purchases, please contact
Simon & Schuster Special Sales at 1-866-506-1949 or business@simonandschuster.com.

The Simon & Schuster Speakers Bureau can bring authors to your live event. For more
information or to book an event, contact the Simon & Schuster Speakers Bureau at
1-866-248-3049 or visit our website at www.simonspeakers.com.

Interior design by Kyoko Watanabe

Manufactured in the United States of America

1 3 5 7 9 10 8 6 4 2

Library of Congress Cataloging-in-Publication Data
Names: Rogers, Harold, 1997- author.
Title: Tropicália : a novel / Harold Rogers, Jade Hui.
Description: New York : Atria Books, 2023.
Identifiers: LCCN 2022053220 (print) | LCCN 2022053221 (ebook) |
ISBN 9781668013878 (hardcover) | ISBN 9781668013885 (paperback) |
ISBN 9781668013892 (ebook)
Subjects: LCGFT: Domestic fiction. | Novels.
Classification: LCC PS3618.O4587 T76 2023 (print) | LCC PS3618.O4587 (ebook) |
DDC [FIC]—dc23/eng20230206
LC record available at https://lccn.loc.gov/2022053220
LC ebook record available at https://lccn.loc.gov/2022053221

https://locexternal.servicenowservices.com/pub
/?id=cip_data_block_viewer&lccn=2022053220

ISBN 978-1-6680-1387-8
ISBN 978-1-6680-1388-5 (pbk)
ISBN 978-1-6680-1389-2 (ebook)

for my family

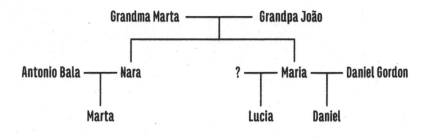

part one
purgatório

quem sabe de mim sou eu

—gilberto gil

december 29

CALL ME DANIEL, I was telling the american girls. Mateus met them this morning and asked me to pull up, thinking I needed a rebound after his cousin dumped me. So the four of us were out here chilling under the hard sun, the sun mean like it was trying to scorch us into order. The turista girls shining pretty, soaked in the day's slow progress. Our kiosk watched by the bronze frozen gaze of Princesa Isabel, the statue the police were all posted under, cradling their machine guns like gifts for the people. Sweeping the beach with their military stare. But how could you sweat that? With the pigeons all plump, plopped weary on the calçadão cobblestones, with those malandra vultures circling their black spirals in the sky, with the kiosk cover band batucando nice?

Copacabana was bustling!

The muvuca all crowded around to hear the band go into País Tropical. Eu moro! num país tropical!

And I couldn't help but think of my Leticia. Who wasn't mine anymore. Because she dumped me yesterday. For cheating. Or not listening. Or something.

3

Anyway, I asked the girls where they were from.

Rachel, who had ferocious green eyes and was smiling at me in a way I could get behind, said, We're from Pittsburgh, we go to college around there.

Her sister Olivia said, No we're not. We're from like forty minutes outside of Pittsburgh.

I said Pittsburgh so he would have an idea! You can't expect him to know our geography.

But don't lie to him!

My geography is pretty good. I lived in the States. That's why my english is so much better than Mateus's.

Vai se fuder porra!

Rachel said, What were you doing there?

Living with my dad.

What happened?

He died so I had to leave.

Oh my god, Olivia said, I'm sorry.

It's ok.

Rachel said, Our mom died too. Well, not too, but. She died eight years ago.

Of what?

Cancer. How bout yours?

She seemed breezy enough with death, so I said, Guess.

Suicide?

I started cracking up, Jesus!

You told me to guess!

It was a car wreck, so close, I guess.

We both started laughing. I took a long drink from the beer in front of me. We were strangers who just hit a nice laugh. I had to temper this moment so her high fun expectations wouldn't crash on me later.

Olivia asked Mateus, How did you and Daniel meet?

Futebol, we played juntos over there by the Palace. He pointed out into the distance. Daniel was so bad. Pernas de pau we say here, wooden legs.

I flipped him off and said, Fuck you, in his accent.

We moved here mermo tempo.

Same time. Summer 2006. We were both a little out of place here, so we bonded quick.

Tell them about the license plates.

There was this dude who used to hang around the fields running these little schemes. And we would help him out. Mateus started first but he was scaring turistas off, couldn't get nobody to trust him. So I started helping out because I got a friendly face, you know. We would walk around with these Rio vanity plates and we would say, Give us half the money now and then tomorrow we'll meet you with whatever you want written on it. And then you just didn't show up. It was easy. Until one day these french fuckers I scammed ran into us, demanding their money back. And Mateus in a courageous enthusiasm punched one of the dudes right in the face.

Wow! And then what happened?

They beat our ass and got their money back!

Mateus and the girls cracked up. Mateus hawing and slapping the table.

But after that we were like best friends.

Verdade!

The table got quiet.

I waved over another round of beers from the kiosk guy, thinking about when this shit used to be a lot cooler, cheaper. When me and Leticia were real young and haunted these places. You had the dudes back then who actually owned and ran their own shit, every kiosk a solid blue or green or yellow with the flimsy plastic chairs out in their orbit on the calçadão. Coconuts studded on the kiosk roof like it was jeweled up.

Now you couldn't even get a coconut broke open! They drilled a bullshit hole in it and sometimes even poured the water into a plastic cup. Lame! The best part used to be when you were done. You'd take it to the dude and he'd get that big butcher knife out and split it in two, giving you the halves and a little husk spoon you'd use to scrape the meat off. Now the kiosks were all owned by Nestlé or some shit. So we almost always dipped without paying. Our little rebellion against the state.

Rachel's purse was splayed out on the table, tossed all strewn like she stole it.

She grabbed it and pulled out a pack of Marlboro Reds.

I would die for a cigarette right now.

It doesn't have to be that serious, she said, handing me one and a lighter.

The beach breeze hit, bringing that fishy maresia and the gaivota smell, cooling the sweat on the back of my neck. I leaned down and cupped the cigarette close to light it and took a deep inhale. My mom used to smoke Marlboro Reds, so that smell was embedded in the cramped and hot walls of my memories from the Ilha. That loud little house. That loud, violent little house.

So why'd you guys come here? I asked Olivia, trying to spread the conversational duty.

Our step mom is from Brazil. She said it would be cheap and hot.

Certainly cheap if you got dollars.

Your mom carioca? from Rio?

Mateus said Rio in portuguese, it flowed from his mouth easy. I americanized it when I spoke english, drawing out that R, like I was climbing over a hill.

I don't know. I don't listen to half the shit she says. She's the worst.

Don't say that.

What Rachel, now you don't think she's a bitch?

Some real tension sparked up between them, like Rachel wasn't defending the worldview they agreed to present to the public. It got awkward. I just smoked my cigarette and drank my beer, looking out at the green hills in the distance and the pulsing sea. Wishing this miserable heat would let up. I needed another drink.

Olivia pulled out her phone so she wouldn't have to talk, a big iPhone she shouldn't be flaunting around. I pulled my phone out too, uncomfortable resting in the silence. I scrolled through whatsapp. There were some guys that stayed sharing the goofiest shit, just spamming. Like this nerdy hermetic kid that I hadn't talked to since high school, Kleber. He sent a video captioned with horrified scream emojis, and I clicked it. My morbid curiosity winning over my tact. It opened up on a dude in a red sunga, standing on the roof's edge of the hotel right next to the Marriott, right over there by my grandma's place. He was clinging to the edge, precarious as hell. The camera zoomed in, slowly swaying back and forth. Suddenly he takes a big olympic style leap, arms out and everything, right off the building. The guy filming it goes, Meu deus meu deus meu deus, and runs toward him. The video ends.

I closed out of it quick, my breath tight, hoping nobody saw me see that.

Like it was something dirty. Something rotten in Copacabana.

The despair was thick these days. People without shit to do, no job, no purpose.

Like I was one to talk.

But jumping off a building?

Grandma used to say that a suicide would relive the moment of their death again and again and again until the end of time. That it was the worst hell you could imagine. Peeking down at that interminable abyss. Your body cutting through that light air, feeling no resistance. Until the ground stopped you dead. Over and over and over. Good reason not to do it. Grandma stuck working at the supermarket bagging groceries all day, newly widowed. All her daughters gone. I wondered if that's what kept her around, bearing time and those brutal scorns, knowing that the undiscovered country she's heading to might not be filled with light but with endless misery. I could see why you'd do it. It looks like an answer. No more grunting and sweating under this heavy life. All your problems solved. Like magic. Gone.

Grandma, grandma, grandma. She hadn't even called me since

grandpa died two days ago. Well, why would she? I hadn't been home in weeks. She probably thought I didn't wanna hear from her. I only got the news because my sister Lucia texted me. I didn't respond. But her birthday was yesterday, and I was feeling the pangs of being a bad grandson and brother and all that, so I texted her. So our text chain looked like

grandpa died

happy birthday

with no responses in between.

Mateus was going, Daniel, ô Daniel!

I must've zoned out. The girls were looking at me. Rachel with those eyes.

What's up?

As minas wanna do things.

Oh yeah? Wanna go see the Christ?

Rachel got quiet and looked away. Olivia kinda mumbled something.

Mateus said in portuguese, Dude, an american family got killed there like two days ago.

How bout the Pão de Açúcar then? It's a hundred percent safe!

Cobrinha's working.

Perfect. We can get in for free. How does that sound?

Rachel said, Sounds good to me.

That smile of hers!

I was the only one who asked for another beer and as soon as the waiter set it down, I chugged it. I think Olivia was gonna do the same thing with the last drops of her drink, but as her hand reached for it, she knocked it over, splashing beer all over Mateus's jersey. The sacred Zico jersey his father had given him right before he died. To make matters worse, Flamengo was in the world championship today. All Mateus had to do for them to win was keep the jersey clean and not watch the game. Porra! His relic on the day of the world championship, tainted.

But Mateus never lost his cool.

Ahh, he said. Merda.

Olivia was apologizing profusely and trying to dry up the mess with the weak and useless table napkins, but it was like trying to towel yourself off with a plastic bag. Mateus said, It's ok. But I knew in his mind he had let down his dead father and Zico, and that this was a terrible omen portending a Flamengo loss, if not worse.

Rachel threw in an apology too.

It's ok. Tá tudo bem.

Let's fucking vambora. Grab your stuff. We're gonna run.

The girls rounded up their things in a hurry. The lone waiter was busy taking out the trash, everyone else distracted by the band.

Go! I yelled.

We took off across the street, toward the bus stop.

MY FLIPFLOP came undone while I was running so I was fixing it hop crossing the street. One bare foot hot on the asphalt. The military police were set up makeshift right out front of the hotel. They watched us as we crossed, making sure we weren't dangerous, wondering why we were running. Police had always been everywhere, but not like this. We were drowning in them. And since it was two days until New Year's Eve, they were ramping it up. Like they were expecting some shit to finally pop. For the lid to blow off this carioca pressure cooker.

So they couldn't leave a corner of the city ungripped by their brand of safety.

My flipflop was working again by the time we got to the bus stop. Everyone standing around waiting, waiting, waiting. That patient Sunday crowd derretating in the heat. This shit would get too hot one day. The sun would incinerate Copacabana. Scorch all of Rio. Leave a pile of ashes of all the generations that stepped foot here and the rain would come and batter us. Make us a part of the soil. That's what I was thinking while the girls were standing around kinda sheepish. Not talking much and not on their phones. Probably wary of the bus stop crowd.

I asked Rachel what was good.

I'm a little nervous about taking the bus.

We never take the bus back home, her sister added.

Rachel was wearing a Pittsburgh Pirates shirt that she threw on over her bikini. Olivia's shirt said Franciscan University. They looked very american in a way I reluctantly found attractive. Something of a confused saudade in me for that seven months with my dad. For that cushy, seasoned life.

I mean, worst case scenario is that we get robbed or kidnapped or die in a fiery accident.

Mateus laughed. Don't assusta them!

I'm playing. I've only been robbed on the bus once, on the way to a Vasco game. But that's the 473. It happens.

Vasco's his team. Uma merda, they suck. Not worth getting robbed over.

Rachel laughed a little.

Our dad just told us it's dangerous.

Well, these drivers are bored lunatics. I mean stewing in this heat and traffic all day would make anyone crazy. One time I saw a guy standing too close to the street, and the bus came and clipped him, mangled the dude.

They looked at me.

Which is to say we're probably safer actually riding the bus.

That ended that conversation, leaving us quiet. Standing around sweating. There were probably ten other people waiting with us. One guy was looking at me. Staring. Tall with a thick black beard and dark eyes. Looking like a portrait of Cabral come to life. Come back to re-conquer this country. Or looking like. Nah, nah, couldn't be. But he was just staring at me. In a way that made my stomach go cold. I had to turn the other way before I did something that would put a stop to our fun.

After a dead twenty minutes, the bus pulled up. Mercy! Because we could've been stuck here another hour easy, and that would've sundered all our built up momentum with the girls. Exhausted all possible conversation.

I guess Mateus was up on the fare increase and let the girls know because they had exact change ready. Meanwhile I was held up for ten more cents, 4.30! Ridiculous.

This greedy city and its little catastrophes.

Bora turista! Mateus yelled.

The driver gave me my change and I went to the very back. Mateus and Olivia had slid in to one pair of window seats and Rachel had slid in to the other side, leaving a spot open for me next to her. The driver sped off and I knocked into Rachel. She laughed and helped me balance as I sat down. No AC on this bus so it was tomblike. Our death suspended here in the stagnant passenger smell. But the closed grave heat made the window breeze feel like a blessing when it hit your face, like the air wanted to personally relieve your misery.

Rachel pulled out her phone and started scrolling through instagram.

I was willing myself not to sweat through my shirt.

What's your IG?

Don't have one.

Why?

Well, my mom left like six years ago, and she was always trying to hit me up after that. But I didn't want anything to do with her so, on a whim, I deleted everything. Couldn't stand her trying to talk to me.

Where did she go?

Ran off to the States to marry some fool. I don't know much about it.

Sorry. That sucks.

It's how it goes. Some people can't wait to get outta here, take any chance they get.

Rachel wanted to cut my drearytalk short, so she said, I love it here so far, Rio is one of the most beautiful places I've ever been.

I wanted to say, You'd get used to it fast. You'd be begging for a break from this infernal city in two weeks tops.

But I just said, Yeah, it's really pretty.

Do you have a girlfriend?

Nah, no. I don't.

Now's the time when I should probably tell about Leticia. Leticia! She dumped me yesterday. Which is a bummer because she's Mateus's cousin, so I'll have to see her all the time. They live together with Leticia's mom, the incomparable Dona Isabel. Who let me sleep on the floor of their tiny thirteenth floor apartment every other day for the past few years. It had been every night lately, which meant I didn't have a place to stay now.

But she'd take me back. She'd take me back.

Leticia!

I mean, we'd known eachother since we were kids, since we were nine years old. The day we met is my favorite memory. The summer I moved here. Me and Mateus were at a festa junina at the Santa Teresinha church, right by Rio Sul, playing a crushed up can game. Barefoot in the courtyard, flipflops for goalposts. You know how it is.

I was trying a Ronaldinho elástico to get around Mateus, and all of a sudden I heard a voice that stopped my heart in the gap of its beat.

Can I play?

And there was Leticia, dressed caipira with a polka dot shirt, cheeks all jestly freckled, a straw hat barely capping her wild lion's mane of hair, always untamed.

Her dark brown eyes hit me like lightning.

That's my cousin, Mateus said.

She joined our game and I've been in love with her ever since. The day before I left to go live with my dad, we went to the beach and shared a joint. She kissed me in the water. My first kiss. Iemanjá giving us her blessing. Then I came back and we'd been dating on and off ever since. She even got me going to college with her, UERJ, which because of the bankrupt state and the constant strikes, neither of us might ever graduate from. Which sucked for Leticia. I mean, I probably wasn't gonna graduate anyway, but she was smart. Crazy smart.

Leticia!

Anyway, she dumped me, not for the first time.

But now she was pregnant, so I needed to fix this.

I was sure she'd take me back.

The bus was stopped at Rio Sul, near the church where I met Leticia. I gazed at it longingly, looking past Rachel who was also peering out the window. And when I looked up there was an old couple walking to the back of the bus. A hunched, withered woman and a man who looked exactly like my grandpa, with a wrinkled, sunbeat face and soft eyes, shuffled slowly to the back of the bus. Exactly like my grandpa would shuffle around our house in his late stage cirrhosis. I remember when it was just me and him all alone in that haunted apartment. He'd be asleep and I'd go to the edge of his room just to stand there, listening to see if I could still hear him breathe, listening to make sure he was still alive. I was always waiting for that last moment. That last grating gasp for breath.

The woman helped the man down the steps, slow, slow. She was sturdier than him, betraying her hunch. But just as he barely set a foot safe on the ground, the bus took off, the door still open. The man yelled, Porra! exactly like my grandpa if Vasco had just got scored on. It was like I was a child looking in the room where he sat putting away beer after beer while I watched this woman hug the rail with one arm and hold on to her husband for dear life with the other. He was dangling off terrified, shoes scraping the road. Everyone on the bus was screaming and so the driver finally stopped after having dragged my grandpa for about a hundred meters.

If his wife's grip had slackened an inch, he would've been flattened dead.

She was breathless after the bus stopped, trying to compose herself. But my grandpa with newfound mental and physical vigor stepped back on the bus and yelled, Vai toma no cu porra! to the driver, and then stepped off with his wife, the two of them clutching eachother tight.

Someone yelled, Idiot!

Another yelled, Psychopath!

And we were back on the road.

But I was shaken and troubled by what I had seen. How much that looked like my grandpa. The anguish on his face. I looked around at the people who were with me, having forgotten they existed. Everyone looked bewildered. Mateus said, Caralho mano.

That was that. We went on.

Rachel, in her fright, had scooted close and grabbed my hand. Which was good. But this was the second terrible omen of the day. If I had been alone I would've stepped right off this bus, but I didn't wanna look weak to these girls, to Rachel.

Besides, my time was meaningless. I had nowhere else to go.

WE WERE the last ones on the bus as it drove through Urca trafficless and pulled into the Pão de Açúcar lot. You could see those two big hills connected by cable cars against the blue backdrop of the clear beach sky. The Vermelha beach sitting tranquil in between. The sea, the sea, stretching out endlessly. The whole vision looking like a postcard.

But the lot was empty. The beach was basically empty.

Not once had I ever pulled into this lot where it wasn't stuffed full of turistas and paddle boarders and people out here chilling, checking out the maritacas and turtles. But today, nobody. A few soldiers out front of the inescapable military barracks doing their exercises, practicing their shouts, but that was it.

Is it open? Rachel said.

Yeah. Probably just empty because of the game today.

I didn't believe what I told her. I was disturbed.

Maybe that family getting murdered at the Christ had scared all the turistas off. I never heard of that happening before in such a famous public destination. Maybe it sent out a signal to these outsiders that their mere presence poked the open wound of these disparities. You couldn't just have all this shit around people who didn't have shit and not expect any consequences.

But really, I didn't have a clean explanation.

We stepped off the bus, the soldiers watching us. As we walked up to the uncrowded entrance, hearing the birds singing and the soldiers counting, I felt like I had missed the rapture. Like this place was bustling and teeming just moments ago and then suddenly the saved were plucked up, leaving we the damned behind to taste the remnants of their last breaths in the wind. I looked to my left and had to keep myself from yelping horrified at what I saw.

In the middle of the parking lot, cooking, baking under the impossible sun, was a dead turtle. A big turtle, the type that would swim right up to you at this very beach, leave you smiling for the rest of the day. And there it was, splayed out, defeated. Like it had tried to crawl toward freedom and failed. Leaving a flat husk as the last mark of its life, covered with ants, getting sniffed at by the parking lot pigeons until an ugly vulture flapped in and scattered them.

No one else saw it and I was silent.

Mateus's cousin Cobrinha was waiting for us at the entrance. They weren't actual cousins, but that's what they told everybody. He slithered over to us languid and cool, his usual mode. He dated Leticia in one of our off periods. Cobrinha was very good looking, charming, and very nice. Plus he had tattoos on his face and they say he killed a couple dudes back in the day. Which made me feel shitty about myself. Not that I wanted to kill someone, but it might have added some different kinda credence to my life. Some different kinda credence to the man I wanted to be. I couldn't help but think that Leticia wouldn't have dumped me if I was a cool handsome murderer. Cobrinha dumped her because he realized he was gay.

And he was so tactful about it!

Which infuriated me, knowing how much courage and courtesy I lacked.

I tried to be a serious criminal once. When I was about fifteen, a couple years before my aunt Nara went to prison, at the peak of her and my uncle Antonio's business. Me and Mateus were selling weed for them for pocket money. Antonio didn't really want us doing it. He always drilled into my head that his life wasn't an exemplary one, but it was hard not to admire. He was rich, he had swagger. He was a big time drug dealer and people did what he said. He had respect. And my father was dead.

How wasn't I gonna look up to Antonio?

But so Mateus came across a gun he didn't really wanna use or buy ammo for so I said let's put it to some use in an easy way. Tranquilo. We went out stalking around Rodolfo Dantas late, waiting to see if somebody would come up the back way to the Palace.

Sure enough a few hours later here comes this couple talking loud in english. We creep up behind them until they turn the corner and then I make the move. I put the gun on the guy's back and say, Money now! Mateus is backing me with a little knife in his hand. The couple turns around slow and calm and the woman starts rifling through her purse saying she's gonna get the money. But instead she pulls out a can of pepper spray and nails us. We go down. They kick us and run off. I told Antonio about it and he chewed me out. I wasn't cut out for that life, and I got pissed that he recognized that softness in me. So I avoided him after that. Participated in my mother's doom rooting. Saying they weren't shit and that it would all come crashing down. Which I felt awful about after the police raid, after everything that happened.

Fala molecada! Cobrinha said. He gave everyone a hug, the girls a kiss on each cheek.

Mateus said in portuguese, Why's it so empty?

I don't know man, weirdest day I've ever seen here.

Mateus shrugged and Cobrinha started talking to the girls in his basic school english, which really might've just been portuguese, but like Mateus, he had a supernatural ability to chat it up with people regardless of language, regardless of where they came from. In seconds, he had the girls cracking up. They didn't include me in the chitchat so I looked around.

It turned out we weren't the only people here.

There was a family at the ticket counter. At first glance, I thought it was Cabral from the bus station, those dark eyes, that black beard. But then shockingly, he transformed into somebody else. I swear I felt like my grandma sometimes, seeing ghosts. But I never believed that spirit stuff, that silliness was for Lucia to indulge. It was just my eyes playing tricks on me, because this dude was blond, clean shaven.

It had to be a german turista. With his wife and some strudel ass kids who were making faces and stomping their feet while their dad tried to talk to the ticket lady in some common language of commerce. They were all wearing ridiculous I ♥ RJ shirts. I mean, when were the brasilians making this shit gonna realize that nobody outside Brasil associates RJ with Rio de Janeiro? They're just gonna think these fools love some motherfucker named RJ!

One kid caught me staring and stuck his tongue out. I felt some violence flare up. But I was probably just sensitive toward any germans since that terrible, terrible game. The seven to one. I remember watching it in my grandparents' room, the summer after Nara got arrested and my mom left. Watching it on our lone, tiny TV when my dad's house had four. Me and Lucia sitting on the floor, my grandparents on the bed with my little cousin Marta laying in between them. After the fifth goal Lucia and grandma were crying and my grandpa got up and pushed the TV over and broke it. Without Nara there to buy us a new one, we didn't watch nothing for a while. That game was like a turning point. As if Germany's goal scorers dead stopped Brasil's whole growth and knocked us into a regressive crumbling spiral. But maybe kicking this kid's ass would make up for all that.

Ô Daniel! Mateus was saying. They were all looking at me.

They almost caught me making a face to that little asshole.

Bora ou não?

Let's go!

We walked through the lobby museum. Black and white pictures of old Rio, people standing proud next to rickety cable cars. I couldn't believe they not only charged for this, but actually convinced people to ride! I'm sure some people died, trying to heft it together, but this was an international attraction now. So what if it took some blood! Who cares if you gotta sacrifice some brasilian bodies! As long as we can get turistas frolicking up in our space.

We made it to the bondinho boarding zone. There was a ticket girl bored on her phone, but she lit up as Cobrinha came through and let us in no worries. He dropped us off and said goodbye, he had some work to do. He kissed the girls on both cheeks and did the same to me to get a laugh, and then he was off. Of course, we had to wait a moment for the german family who came bumbling through, bickering in their gruff language.

We all boarded the bondinho. There was probably room for twenty more people, I mean, this thing was as big as Dona Isabel's apartment. But it still wasn't big enough to keep away those nazilooking kids who were buzzing around like dengue mosquitos. The boy who stuck his tongue out at me had his face pressed up against the window, slobbering against the glass. I knew street dogs who behaved better. No son of mine would ever act like that, me and Leticia would straighten his ass out. Me and Rachel met eyes and caught sight of the girl laying on the filthy carpet throwing a fit while the dopey father took pictures and his wife looked at her phone.

I hate kids, Rachel said. What's worse than being a mother?

But isn't the whole point of this dumb thing to kinda keep it going?

She looked at me.

Or not.

So what is there to see up there?

For one, micos. These thieving little monkeys that live up there. They'll come right up to you and take food out of your hand. They're too cute.

Mateus heard that and said, São malandra demais!

Now I'm excited.

The bondinho rose higher and higher as the day wound down in the city around us. The sun dipped as we rose, floating over the dense forest that looked sinister as the day changed. Everything was looking sinister to me. But the sun enveloped Rio in a way where it really did look noble, like this city really was marvelous.

Mateus was playing tour guide, showing the girls all the sights and whatnot, making them oooh and ahhh. I was standing in the middle of the bondinho, not looking at anything, thinking about how long it had been since I'd been here. Probably not since high school.

The first time I ever came here, we were still living on the Ilha. Dad was in town on one of his rare trips to visit us and he rented a car so we wouldn't have to take that long, dull bus ride. Lucia stayed home. Like she usually did. So it was just me, mom, and dad. By the time we got to the second hill, they got in such a savage screaming match that the cops had to come break it up. They kicked us out. My mom told him to go fuck himself and we took the bus just to spite him. Well, she was spiting him. I was just an extension of her will.

The german kids were having a screaming contest as we pulled into the first hill.

Right off the bondinho, the first thing you see is an H.Stern jewelry store. In the window they got these tacky, expensive, decked out toucans and maritacas and papagaios that I couldn't fathom attracted any customers with voluntary control over their actions. So of course, testing the limits of free will, the german family strolled right in, cooing at how pretty the birds were.

Rachel and Olivia were standing around like where to? The sun was gonna set soon and I knew a place where the view would be serious. This little manmade bamboo grove where you could cut through and be free on the hillside. I found it by accident when I was a kid, wandered over there while my parents were fighting. Years later that's where I would take girls from school, or girls I was seeing extracurricularly.

Leticia had never come up this way with me, she was too special for any kinda tricks.

Well, damn, maybe I should've brought her. But it's not too late! Follow me, I know a spot.

We walked down a big ramp into the shadowy grove where we could hear low chirps of birds and bugs and micos, buzzing together like a Pixinguinha samba. I could hear brusk quibbling not far off, and I knew those pesky germans had followed us. We walked until there was a clearing, looking over the hillside at the wide expanse of the Botafogo beach. The sun was dropping, coloring the few clouds in late day pinks and reds.

Rachel said, Woah, catching the view. Olivia was speechless.

I sat down on a rock and looked out over the abyss.

The city looked immense, and I was panged with pride by its enormity.

But we were loose up here, a deep drop if we slipped. Despite the thick trees and the natural hillside ledges, if you fell, you were probably fucked.

But then I saw something truly amazing. Perched there on the hillside, barely noticing our presence, was an enormous bird. With a bright red color and a huge curved beak.

Meu deus!

It flew off, wings beating against the air.

That's an ibis, I didn't know they could get this high, Mateus said.

Is that a good or bad sign?

I don't know.

WHEN THE kid showed up, Rachel was taking pictures of Olivia. Me and Mateus were leaning against the rocks, chilling. I heard some rustling in the bamboo, and who else would it be but the german boy? Looking at us like it was no problem he was invading the private space we'd made with our presence, like it was no problem he was altering our whole environment. No, he belonged here. No family trailing him. Alone.

He climbed out to the area adjacent to us where the rocks jutted out, dangerous and unstable. Kid being teimoso, precarious as hell. It was late and everything was getting dark. A big tree that grew from the abyss hung over us, draped in shadows, its mute branches twisted around like ominous warnings.

We all stopped, just watched him, tense. As if a snake had snuck up on us. And then his family showed up. His mom walked to the edge of the bamboo and started scolding him, motioning him to rejoin them. But he wouldn't even look at her.

I heard stirring from the dark tree.

I looked up and it was a mico! Against the blood red backdrop of the falling day, the sun crowning his head like a saint. Climbing out on the branch, chirping, squeaking, real cute.

I said, Look! And a gasp rose from the gathered group. The babaca father emerged carrying an H.Stern bag, but as soon as he saw the mico, he dropped the bag and pushed past his wife to get a picture.

The mico regal as the city on that high branch.

And then! sprouting like fruit from within the tree, six or seven of his subjects went to join their solitary king on the end of the branch, on the edge of the abyss. The whole court coming out to confront us like we had landed on their shores, unwelcome. They were nearest to the kid who was walking out closer and closer to the tree, closer to the abyss, close enough to where he could reach out and touch one.

The air around us congealed into a thick, hot tension. He swung his backpack around and started digging through it, his movements the focus of our collective gaze. With a nefarious look, he pulled out a banana. The banana glowing golden in the sunlight. Like a treasure for the micos. They stopped chirping and stared. We were silent. I wondered if maybe I had misjudged this kid, if he was about to offer some benefaction to the true residents of this mountain.

But no. He started waving the banana around taunting their attention, and then he fake threw it off the cliff as if he wanted the micos to jump for it and fall to their deaths. Those malandra micos didn't budge. Instead, the kid lost his balance, stumbled, tried to catch himself, failed, and we all watched as he tumbled over the cliff, becoming a fading amplification of ahh!

Olivia screamed first, and then his mother.

The rest of us were just looking at eachother, jaws dropped aghast. And my stomach churned cold with nausea at the thought of another death weighing on me. The kid's mom ran out, almost knocking down the foolish father who was catatonic with indecision. For a second, I thought she was gonna tumble off too and the rest of the family would follow until there was a pile of clumsy germans at the bottom of the cliff. But she held her ground and stood there yelling, Leo! frantic.

The moment hung in the air, all of us hoping hard he wasn't dead.

The micos were looking down at us like, Yeah, but what about that banana?

The kid's mom got down and crawled to the edge yelling his name like she could see him. And then he yelled back. Alive! and we could hear him crying. My worry subsided. He deserved it. A proper cosmic judgement for messing with those poor innocent micos. He got lucky. Very lucky. Usually when people fell off here it was a search and a half just to recover the body.

The girl and her mother were trying to communicate with the kid while the dad stood there and cried, the camera slung around his neck. I was kinda thinking, Pussy, maybe you deserve a dead kid. But I took the thought back.

It was getting darker and darker by the minute. And the police could sniff out a fallen turista, so I was a hundred percent ready to vambora. But I realized the girls were invested in this rescue. Mateus was with me, but Rachel was crouched with the mom trying to talk to the kid and Olivia was standing right behind her.

I said, Rachel. She looked over and I made a motion like, Let's go! She walked over.

He's probably hurt. We have to help!

I'm not a fucking fireman, what am I gonna do?

She looked at me for a moment with those green eyes like maybe she noticed I wasn't the guy she thought.

Yeah, you're right. Let's get help, Mateus! We'll be right back.

She smiled and went to rejoin the bereaved.

We walked out of the grove and told some workers hanging around that a stupid german boy who was taunting the micos and being teimoso! had fallen off the cliff. The workers ran to get the firemen who hustled over worried frantic about a growing foreign body count that would surely clamp their wallets tighter. Neither of us were keen on the rescue, so we posted on a bench and lit up one of the joints that Mateus had brought with him. We sat there smoking and swatting away the initial mosquito assault. The lights and the bugs had woke around us, morning time for these nocturnal life cycles.

The weed was making me sad and silent. I was thinking about Leticia and my ruined future paths, veering toward despair. But then I reassured myself. Everything was gonna be cool. Anyway, this Rachel liked me. If the kid got saved and I played my cards right, I could get laid tonight. Mateus was playing guitar at a bar in Lapa. We could take them to see the show. I would teach Rachel some samba. Everything was gonna be fine. I just needed to get out of here and get a drink. Fast.

We heard a cheer rise up in the distance.

I killed the joint and stomped it out with my flipflop.

When we got back, the firemen were on the last stretch of their heaving rope pulley rescue. The air had changed, lightened. Relieved and hopeful was the mood. Rachel was chatting with the kid's mom and when she saw us return, she gave me a big hug and said, Thank you so much for getting help! This family is so lovely. They're from Belgium but they speak english.

Belgium! even worse.

Olivia was talking to the notdead kid's sister. Their moronic patriarch was sitting on the ground staring blankly, as if he was some sort of victim. Maybe of a spoiled vacation.

The firemen yelled, Porra! and with one final haul the kid emerged over the edge, Young Lazurus on a stretcher. The emergency flood lights the firemen set up gave him a dead pale look. Apparently he hadn't run out of tears because he was still crying. His leg looked fucked up and his clothes were covered with dirt and mud.

We all cheered.

The firemen picked up the stretcher like pallbearers and led our funeral procession out.

Rachel was walking next to me, and she reached out and held my hand.

We rearrived at the main area and I saw trouble. Two military police officers uniformed up, walking our way. An older one with a pastel swollen belly bursting out of his shirt, and a short dude about my age, with a walrus mustache. They stopped right in front of us. Smiling like leopards. The short one's badge said Cunha, my name. The glutton was Grunewald and he took the lead, real polite.

Boa noite. What happened here?

A kid slipped and fell. He's ok. You see him. I pointed over his way.

But what were you doing out there? I thought nobody was allowed?

I don't know. I just followed the turistas.

Cunha took stock of Mateus. Looking him up and down. His old school Flamengo jersey. His bleached buzz cut and old flipflops.

Are these girls with you?

Yes. They're americans.

He smiled and addressed them in english.

And then, as if he had a sixth sense for petty crime, he said, Can I see your tickets?

Rachel seemed calm. She said, We threw them away.

I said, Yeah, I thought we didn't need em.

But Olivia, who was visibly nervous, goes, Someone snuck us up here!

Me and Mateus and Rachel all looked at her like fucking seriously?

The officers let that hang in the air.

You think that's ok? Grunewald asked Mateus. You think it's ok to do whatever you want? Tromp all over this country and go wherever you want without a care in the world?

Mateus said nothing and stared straight ahead, not looking at anything.

Cunha grabbed his face and forced him to make eye contact.

Attention moleque! He's talking to you!

Look at his eyes, Grunewald said, He's high!

Have you two been smoking weed?

I said no. Rachel who had been poised and composed started to fluster. Olivia was freaking out. Grunewald told Cunha to search Mateus. He shoved him to the ground, and sure enough, they found a bag with two joints in his pocket. Grunewald asked me, You got any on you? I said no but he turned me around and searched me. He didn't find anything but when he was done he punched me in the stomach and said, Sorry. Cunha couldn't help but laugh.

They started cuffing Mateus who was silent on the ground. I could feel his anger from here. They would keep Mateus overnight and it would take a bribe to get him out, a few hundred reals. Turistas with two joints would get off on the spot.

They stood him up and Olivia started to cry.

Rachel snapped at her, That's not helping!

It's gonna be ok, I said.

Cunha, who was walking behind Mateus, leading him, said, There's only one more bondinho going down, if you want to get on it, you better move.

So we followed, silent, as the officers perp walked Mateus to the bondinho.

We boarded. The germans looked at us exhausted and confused. Grunewald made a smoking gesture and said, Drugs, in english. The useless father looked at us disappointed. His resurrected kid, who had finally stopped crying, was laying on a stretcher eating a popsicle.

We took the slow ride down the mountain together in the dark bondinho. The firemen and officers chatted about their respective heroism. Olivia was distraught. Rachel was worn out and clinging to me.

Suddenly Cunha said, Yes! Flamengo lost in extra time!

Mateus goes, This day keeps getting better.

I couldn't help but laugh. He started laughing too.

Cala boca!

We all shut up.

We finally made it down and out the entrance. An ambulance was waiting there parked behind the police car, both their lights echoing off the dark empty air.

It was a hot ass night and there was nobody else hanging around the parking lot.

The germans and the firemen went left to the ambulance.

Our group went right to the cop car.

Sem problema cara, you'll be out tomorrow.

Porra fudida, Mateus said, demure.

Olivia put her hand on the window in solidarity. Rachel had her arms wrapped around me. She was warm and smelled good.

The police left first and the ambulance followed. We were alone under a dim streetlight. The only sounds were the far off waves splashing and the bugs and night birds singing their sleepy songs. We stood in silence for a moment.

You guys tired?

Olivia said, I'm going home.

I'm not, Rachel said.

Do you wanna go out?

I could use a drink.

Olivia said, I'm going home.

Ok. Let's head to the bus station.

No. I'll call an uber.

BURUMBUM! I woke up grieved and troubled thunder shaking the room thin light peeking through the hotel curtain oh god dark snoring mass in the bed. Rachel. Burumbubum! heart beating fast. That nightmare woke me up quick. I hadn't had a nightmare since I was a kid. Never had any dreams. But there I was, standing in the middle of Nossa Senhora getting hit with a terrible storm and the water rising higher and higher. I was knee deep in it, frozen, watching the building in front of me get wrecked by fire. The rain poured on the flames but the burning wouldn't stop.

I could hear my grandma and Marta and Lucia screaming.

I knew they were burning up and I couldn't save them.

And then I heard my mother's laughter drowning out all the noise.

My heart was pounding like the thunder.

I shouldn't be having any dreams. That was the point of blacking out! You sleep until the next morning, untroubled. I caught my breath and stood up. Shorts right there on the floor. Put them on. Walked over to the window, headache burgeoning. Rachel's shit spilled about like a shipwreck. I peeked through the blinds. There was my slice of Copacabana.

Of course it was the Marriott. Where else would she be staying?

Burumbum! I was startled by the thunderclap and the lightning that flashed, cutting through the black ceiling of the sky. It looked like my dream. I might've screamed when the thunder hit because Rachel yelled groggy, It's too early!

My phone was lying on the floor next to me. Dead.

Do you have a charger?

She didn't say anything.

I realized she had an iPhone anyway so it wouldn't do me any good. The room was a mess, like Rachel had a grudge against maids. My mom cleaned rooms at this hotel for a month. Until she was fired.

My head hurt so bad! I needed my shirt and my flops. I poked around for them and ended up finding a pile of twenty dollar bills. Eighty dollars. I stuffed it into my pocket. Something caught my attention on the wall, something written. I got closer and looked at it. It said Daniel and had my phone number written in permanent marker. Seems like something I would do. Except the number was way off. Which definitely seems like something I would do.

Be quiet and come back to bed.

Sorry.

I spotted my shirt on the floor. Damp and crusted in puke. Fuck. I was gonna have to get another shirt before I went to see Leticia. I guess I could go home. My grandma's apartment was literally a block away. No. No. The last thing I wanted was a reunion. I was gonna have to slog through this rain shirtless. Porra!

But today was gonna be a good day!

I was gonna get Mateus out of jail.

And I was gonna get Leticia back.

—LUCIA?
—Yeah. It's me.
—Oh my god. Hi. Is, um, is something wrong?
—Grandpa died.
—No. How?
—He had cirrhosis for the last five years. What did you think was gonna happen?
—I'm sorry.
—Why? You didn't kill him, liquor did.
—Lucia. Be kind.
—That's all I have to say to you. Goodbye.
—Wait! Is there going to be a funeral?
—No, he's getting cremated today.
—Maybe, um. Maybe I should come down. What do you think?
—I don't care what you do.
—I'm coming. I can be there by New Year's Eve. You can count on it.
—Whatever.

—I miss you. I miss Daniel.

—I have to go.

—Wait Lucia I lo

I hung up. I hadn't heard my mother's voice in years, and despite how strong I thought I built my defenses, it immediately retransformed me into the fifteen year old Lucia, who begged and pleaded to tag along to the airport where, with a saccharine goodbye, mommy would close her heart to me for good and fly off to marry some strange american dolt. No, I didn't even get a goodbye. Because when I went to the bathroom to expel a malevolent pastel that my mother always warned would turn me into a beastly blob undesired by men, she vanished. I came out wiping bile and the traces of a smile off my lips and realized I had no mother, no money, and no ride home. I begged the last bus driver to let me on, fareless and deflated, and I sat in the very last seat, abandoned all alone, soaked in sobs and stagnant heartache.

Little Marta burst into the room, unkempt and unslept, wearing her faded schoolshirt.

—I'm late! I'm late again!

—Did you eat?

—It's too late for that Lucia! I'm gonna get in trouble!

I grabbed my bag and we hustled out the door and down the stairs, my flipflops clomping in the narrow spiral. We didn't even look to see if the elevator was working because there was no chance, even though it had been the building manager's first priority for the last two years, but it wasn't a big deal because we lived on the third floor. Until this week. On Christmas. When grandpa. I was sitting in the kitchen with Marta when grandma came home from work. I thought he was just napping. I should've been more attentive. She went to check on him and called me in a weary panicked tone. I walked in and he was laying there unresponsive. Eyes in deep sleep suspension, sputtering and sneezing, slobbering all over himself. Wheezing like a tropelated street dog. Dying. Marta ran out of the room as soon as she saw him, went to hide like I used to as a kid when the adults were scream bashing eachother.

Grandma called an ambulance and they made her jump through hoops and said forty five minutes. We tried to lift him, impossibly, desperate to exhaust all efforts to prop up the final whimpers of his spirit. We called Seu Zé the doorman and he came to help, and Regina, our neighbor, who happened to have a wheelchair, heard the commotion and rushed over. We heaved his dead weight into it, trying to show as much care as we could. As if it mattered. His whole human experience whittled down to a carcass in his underwear with a bulging herniated stomach, radiating an old hot reek. It was more than sad, seeing his failed life in its last vestiges, and I was too weak to even look at him, the last dregs of grandpa being dragged down the stairs and I was looking away, trying not to smell the staircase stink.

The plan was to get a cab we couldn't afford and take him to the hospital, but by the time we toiled his wheelchair out the door, the ambulance arrived, curbside. The paramedics hopped out mute and rude. They grabbed my grandpa and tossed him onto a stretcher like a sack of trash. I held his hand, a useless final gesture of kindness and love I wasn't even sure he deserved. He puked a little blood on himself and the paramedics shooed me as they closed the door. That was the last time I saw him alive. He died yesterday. Maybe I should've elaborated all that excruciatingly for my mom. She hated him, right? She would want to hear it. Maybe through his bloodpuked grimaced anguish she would feel how far she put herself away from us.

Grandpa used to loom fearsome in our lives, so it was odd to see him blip out so puny. Marta never got to experience his raucous rage nor his nice funny turns, he was just sick, just a death ticking clock. Like a pet fish. No. Marta already suffered so much in her nine years. Her dad dead, her mother in prison. What was another cold vacancy where love and warmth should've been? She was so good and sweet, I was worried the world's wounds would leave her calloused and mean. That's what happened to my grandpa. His wrongturn life left him prone to these scary drunken snaps. We'd all be in the kitchen, the windows open to let in the heat and bugs, sometimes a lost hummingbird you'd have to lead free. He'd start screaming in mom's face. One time. Suddenly. Grandpa what did you do! Her teeth on the ground like bloody chiclets. Mommy he headbutted you. Mommy. Shut up, Lucia!

—Lucia!

Marta was tugging my arm hard. We were in the lobby. Dona Dalia and Dona Celeste were leaning on Seu Zé's station. The Donas were old ladies who lived lonely, bored, on the seventh floor, so they haunted the lobby, eternally gossiping. They were staring at me.

—We were telling Zé about the murders at the Christ. Did you hear?

—No.

Marta was pulling me doorward.

—Oh my god! These favela kids murdered a poor american family.

—Not just murdered! They decapitated them! A mom, dad, and their son.

—Oh.

—So you americans better be careful!

Big laugh. That was their favorite joke, that me and Daniel were american because of our father. Though I never went to the United States and had no desire to go, and our absent father never wanted anything to do with me. He bought this apartment for us in 2006, to placate my mother for his sins and separate life, and he was probably turning in his grave knowing I lived here with Nara's daughter and still referred to him as my father.

—We're joking Lucia! You're too young to be so serious!

—Let's go!

Marta led me out the door, fast, into the hot loud street swell, past the supermarket where grandma was bagging groceries, and across Nossa Senhora and Figueiredo in one diagonal shot. It was our usual unlanguid school rush where we didn't have time to stop and linger like we liked with the pedestrians and dogs whose commutes aligned with ours. In our hurry, we scattered a flock of pigeons, and one flew up and smacked a guy's face, sending him stumbling, astonished, into honking traffic. That made me and Marta laugh so hard we nearly had to stop.

Soon we were at the mouth of the Siqueira Campos subway. It was overflowing with military police, stationed here to stamp out the insidious infection of homeless people just living quietly, lounging in their cohorts, ruinously impinging on the image of Rio as a turista pristine paradise. There was a feeble old man, a neighborhood staple, with an overgrown tumor bulging out of his neck, whom I never spoke to, regrettably, I would just pass and look and smile, as if my forced attention was any salve, but this man refused to leave, bravely, so the police beat him bloody, while I watched, uselessly, and I never saw him again. What could I have done except feel bad for him? Worthless gestures. The accident that I was me and he was him. That my random accumulation of matter configured itself into whatever this Lucia is and his left him so fully doomed. Well. Grandpa in the oven today. Grandpa died, grandpa wasn't buried, grandpa returned to dust. I am dust. I will be dust. We would all get evened out. Maybe.

We walked down the broken escalator into the cavernous station.

—Who were you talking to earlier?

—When?

—This morning, Lucia. Duh!

—Oh. Um. Aunt Maria.

—Aunt Maria! No way! Is she coming to visit?

—Yeah. She'll be here in a few days.

—What? You didn't tell me that!

Marta was beaming. I shouldn't have said anything because I didn't know if it was true. I didn't trust my mother, and she hadn't visited once since she left six years ago. Why would her dad's death, a man she never showed any affection for, finally lure her back? I didn't want to see her. I turned twenty one years old today, and I was fine. Grown and fine and happy. Without her. Yet there was still a small part of me that longed for her, in low moments of heartbreak and disappointment where, even though my grandma was wonderful, not having my mother made every sting feel sharper, and made my aloneness much more acute. The only reason I hoped she would come was because Marta had a ravenous appetite for anything related to her mother, and having her mother's sister in town to tell stories and share her facial features would be a rare joy.

Marta and I hustled trainward through the dank, dark station that stunk of animal bodies and impatience, swaddled the whole way by the snug blanket of police stretching from corner to corner, ensuring by the threat of death that no poor kids would ride the train for free. I heard the train pulling in and we ran down the steps and made it as the doors were closing. A woman held it for us and we shoved our way in, crammed like we were bodystacked in a morgue. A man rose to offer Marta his seat. She sat. Her beat up sneakers nearly touched the ground flat. She was getting so tall. No matter how close you watch, time passes without you. I was leaning over, looking at her dark eyes, my grandma's eyes. She sighed. Her impending aunt visit smile scrunched into a grumpy clump.

—What is it?

—I don't wanna go to school.

—I don't wanna go to work, garota. Join the club.

—Ugh!

—Tell me what's wrong.

—There's this mean girl, Ana.

—Why is she mean?

—She's a bully! I don't like her.

—You gotta deal with mean people sometimes. That's life.

—I'm tired of it though!

—Ok, next time she's mean to you, bite her.

—Really?

—Sure. I bet she'll never mess with you again.

I didn't know if that was good advice, but why not? Words weren't free. People needed to learn that there were material consequences for what you tossed in the air. Marta sat quiet for the rest of the ride, plotting. We got off at the Botafogo stop, went up another broken escalator, and walked out into a bustling market. It was Saturday, a day her school added to make up for the constant teacher strikes, and the big Flamengo game was tomorrow, so it was crowded, all the barracas up, covered in jerseys like trees with red and black leaves. We were very late. Her class started at noon and the street clock said 12:32.

By the time we made it to the school door, I was sweating. Dona Marielle, the vice principal, was waiting outside. She was Marta's favorite person at the school and she looked like Nara, two facts that were probably not unrelated, even though Nara had a matchless elegant poise, but I liked this woman too, she was the only faculty member who tolerated our tardy faults and didn't have a wayward word to say about the lurid lives of Marta's parents, and since this was a private school where Marta was kept on scholarship, we needed her internal support.

—Do you know what time it is?

—Sorry.

She shook her head sympathetically, and I was about to leave when Marta yelled.

—Wait!

She dug into her backpack and pulled out a folded piece of paper, a card, with a smiling sun on the front and HAPPY BIRTHDAY LUCIA! written in block letters, my name scraggly small because she ran out of space. On the inside there was a drawing of stick figure me, her, her mother, and grandma, floating around like we were in heaven, holding hands and smiling. The card surprised me, there were tears in my eyes. I bent down and hugged her.

—Have a good day garota.

She went inside and I ran off, late, late, late.

THERE WAS a bus stop by the school that was dilapidated and dangerous, but serendipitously, my bus arrived right as I did, so I didn't have to wait. I sat in the back and pulled my notebook out of my backpack. Blank page toward the end. I started to write. Claudia was born on the Ilha do Governador during the dictatorship. I crossed it out. No style! Boring! Claudia wasn't the name at all! I was trying to write something about my family, but nothing was clicking ever since my story was published.

There was this magazine that my coworker Gilberto wrote for and edited, revista pau brasil, which was actually run by Daniel's girlfriend, Leticia, who had briefly been one of my best friends. She was a grade below Daniel, and I skipped a grade, so we ended up in the same class around the time Daniel went to live in the United States. I knew they knew eachother, but it was unthinkable that we could share something, so she was mine, until he returned, whitehorse glorious, and reclaimed her. Now we rarely spoke. Anyway, I submitted a story to her magazine and they accepted it. The issue was coming out soon. Not that it mattered. Only writing the next thing mattered. I closed my eyes for a second, and when I opened them, the bus was at my stop.

My boss, Mario, was waiting for me at the restaurant entrance.

—They should call you Late Lucia!

—Sorry.

—And you show up wearing flipflops!

I hadn't even realized I put on the wrong shoes.

—You're lucky we need that pretty face around here.

I walked to the back. Pretty face. My mother endlessly proselytized the value of being beautiful, as if that was the important project in life. Really, until she left, I was unattractive, a situation she lamented openly, discussing strategies, workouts, creams, serums, nose jobs, injections, willing to risk anything to have her daughter walk alongside her worthy of gawks and leers. I did what she suggested, and it didn't work. But like a year after she left, I suddenly became everything she ever wished for, a fact I flaunted and fostered, but now I was tired of vanity, of my unwon ornaments, I wanted to figure out what was true of myself beyond that. In the back of the kitchen, Gilberto and Rita were waiting with big smiles. Rita was holding a green magazine with yellow lowercase letters, revista pau brasil. Rita's smile made my heart flutter. She handed me the magazine and gave me a hug.

—Parabéns Lucia!

I gave Gilberto a hug too.

—That story is dark as fuck, girl!

My story was called The Possessed, from a line in The Passion According to G.H. The narrator is this guy whose mother moved to São Paulo with a new man after his father died. After biding his fury for a few years, not speaking to her, he decides to invite them back to Rio for a carnival reconciliation. When they show up, he poisons them, and everybody dies. It's a little Hamlety. I flipped through the magazine. Leticia had two pieces. A poem called Response to Ana C and an essay, Prison Abolition and New Leftism. What did she ever talk about with Daniel! She was brilliant and interesting, and he was apathetic and lazy. She was organizing a protest on Monday, and I would bet my life he didn't even know about it. All he was good at was taking things away from me. In a frightening coincidence, my phone vibrated, and it was him, texting me happy birthday. We never texted. Right now our thread looked like

grandpa died

happy birthday

Daniel. He was languishing in college right now, fruitlessly, jobless while we paid his phone bill and gave him money and he never even came home to thank us. I wanted to go to college, but the whole thing seemed like an expensive waste for both of us, one of us needed to make money. If there was an opportunity in this family, it was going his way. I'll never forget when dad came back for the last time. You're taking Daniel to the United States? Why can't I go? Why? Grandma, what did dad mean when he said?

—Get to work, people!

I deleted the message. I started working at this restaurant, Mario's, in high school, back when Globo was doing reports on it being the epicenter of a Rio food renaissance. Since then its fame had only waned, but the pay was decent, I liked my coworkers, and I liked disappearing into the servile nature of the work. Lucia didn't have to exist while she was here. She was just a mindless vessel for customer whims and wants, a severely desiccated version of whatever Lucia was outside these walls.

And I met Marcus here, the year after my mom left. I was sixteen and he was twenty seven. He was involved in some business somethings, bouncing around Rio and SP, down here for months at a time. He was tall and gorgeous, educated at the best american schools. He knew about literature and he would bring me books, back when I was still infatuated with the United States, he would feed me american writers, Toni Morrison, Gayl Jones, Marilynne Robinson, Emily Dickinson whose book of poems still sits in my room, absurdly worn. Maybe my favorite he ever brought me was Mary Shelley's Frankenstein, and I got obsessed with her, all her private pain. She was drenched in death. Yet she transubstantiated all the cruel arbitrary exigencies of life into a profound artistic vision. It was thrilling. Reading those books was so much work, with an english to portuguese dictionary right next to me, copying down words I didn't know, saying them out loud again and again. It made those books feel sacred to me.

But I was done giving those english books my attention. My language was portuguese. My people were brasilian. I don't know. Machado de Assis read in english. So did Guimarães Rosa and Clarice. I don't know. What was the point of integrity with a language? Integrity with an identity? Marcus's books were piled in a corner, collecting dust, along with some Daniel stole for me from bookstores, in his brief moments of clearheaded kindness, terrible ones, Paulo Coehlo and Dan Brown in translation. Right now I was only interested in national writers. Beatriz Bracher, Lygia Fagundes Telles, Hilda Hilst. I don't know. Any pure standard was disastrously misguided.

Marcus was entangled brightly in my artistic beginnings, but that was a dark time for me. Grandma warned me gravely that there were bad spirits in my aura, and though I was skeptical of her spirits, she would often pull a premonition from the pit of my worries and send a shiver down my spine. When I was with him, I was drinking and smoking everyday, doing coke at dead end parties until dawn, throwing up all my meals to keep myself rail thin and pert, and then he would go back to the States, and I would oscillate between bedbound depression and wild nights spent letting Rita, strangers, anyone use my body because I needed to be loved, desperately, all the time. When he would return I would tell him everything, and he would scream and call me a slut, and we would fight viciously until we were too tired to speak. Reenacting every relationship my mother ever had with a man.

One day he proposed to me, right after I turned nineteen. He wanted me to live in the United States and stay home and be a wife and rear his children. He wanted to save me. I said no. He begged and grabbed and screamed and I said no. I didn't want a savior. I didn't want to be my mother. She needed a romantic attachment to define her, she could only be in reference to a man, a gross and easy fate. She would never have to learn about Maria because she could just be Daniel Gordon's wife, Mrs. whatever the new fool's name is, safe and sound, saved from the pyre. Not me. I wanted to figure out who Lucia was and I knew Marcus wouldn't help me, and so I broke with him quickly, cleanly, I shed him like an old husk, and I never saw him again.

My shift was easy and boring. I served americans from California, americans from New York, americans from Louisiana, an american from Texas who hit on me, a portuguese couple from Lisbon who gave me a very generous tip, an english couple from Liverpool, a french canadian who stiffed me, which I made sure to complain about to Rita and Gilberto and tell them about the fanny pack he was wearing tucked into his pants, and they threw me back complaints about Mario and the cook, and then I served one more table of americans from St. Louis, where Marcus was from, and the lunch service was over, it was time to pick up Marta.

I said goodbye to everyone and left. I walked three blocks so I could get on a bus that would go right through the tunnel and into Copacabana. I was tired and sweaty, and I was dreading coming back to the restaurant for the dinner service. The bus stop was packed. Across the street, I saw a woman moving fast. I wouldn't have noticed, but from where I stood, she looked stunningly like Nara, the same exact graceful gait, but she looked terrified, sprinting scared. A man caught up to her.

My throat got tight. He grabbed her arm and pulled her toward him, so harshly that she fell to the ground. Now she was down and he was standing over her, screaming belligerently, and as he leaned in, his furious spit flying all over her face, she smacked him, staggered him back. Just then the bus pulled up. I felt cold and sick and I thought I should do something, but my bus was here and they were across the street, caught in their private chaos. It wasn't a situation I could step into. Was that true?

I got on the bus. I slid into a window on the opposite side and stared at the shopfronts and pedestrians as the bus drove off. The couple across the street made me think of a fight between my mother and Nara, back when I was a kid. Nara was living in Cantagalo with Antonio, and I wasn't allowed to visit, even though Marta had just been born and I was desperate to see her. My grandpa was grief stricken over her birth. My granddaughter born in the favelas! How far this family has fallen! He and mom would sit in the kitchen, showering them with sardonic scorn. I never understood why my grandpa acted the way he did toward Nara, but from what I gleaned from grandma's stories and some rumors, my mother was jealous. She used to date Antonio, and then he met Nara and ditched her, and she was bitter.

But who knows what the fight on this day was about. I remember me and Daniel and grandma were sitting on a stone bench, sipping cane juice and talking to Nara, one of my grandma's subversions, keeping her in our orbit despite my mom's decrees. Nara, out of nowhere, gets yanked to the ground by her hair. There's my mother, standing in the sun's way, seething. Nara gets up and grabs her, ably, and they start fighting in broad daylight like it's a capoeira demonstration. Me and Daniel were silent, enrapt, frightened. Grandma was crying. Finally some street vendors came by and broke it up. Nara stormed off, and my mother flocked us home, nose bloodied, and we had to listen and nod as she cried and excoriated her sister's slatternly lascivious ways. My mother. She was coming back. My mother.

Borges has this short story, Three Versions of Judas, about a theologian who argued that everything we know about Judas Iscariot is wrong. He offered three differing views. One, that Judas intuited the divine purpose, and so he betrayed Jesus for the greater cause. He sacrificed himself to reflect Jesus's sacrifice. The second was that maybe Judas was like a monk. A monk renounces everything for the greater glory of God, and Judas, through an extravagant and limitless asceticism, renounced honor, peace, happiness, and heaven, and committed the worst act possible. Lastly, Borges's theologian proposed, the scripture says that the Messiah will be the lowliest of all men, and people think this refers to the crucifixion, but it's blasphemous to ascribe the deeds of Christ to one afternoon on the cross. The Messiah could've been anyone, Alexander, Caesar, Jesus, but God chose Judas. Judas was Christ, and his true sacrifice was enduring eternal damnation. This conclusion gave me chills. It's a good story. But is that Judas? He was responsible for his friend's brutal execution. Why did he do it? I see the silver in his hands. A sick smile on his face. Betraying someone he was supposed to love because he was jealous. Maybe the Gospel of Luke is right, maybe it was simpler than all that. He just did it because the devil was in him. But it took an evil person to do something like that. You couldn't throw around that accusation unless you knew, unless you knew for sure. I put my head against the window and closed my eyes, sleepless, until I arrived at my stop.

WHEN I got to the gate of Marta's school, obviously late, the principal, Seu Getúlio, who in a canny misfortune was named after the first dictator of Brasil, was waiting outside with her. The afternoon sun was starting to change, casting shadows around his face, contouring him ghoulish, making him look uglier and sterner than he was. Even though he was already thin necked and bald, like a metempsychosed vulture, and he spoke with a weird, stilted formality. A breeze swept through the street, carrying the smell of palm trees and soon dusk, and a cold that made me jolt. His arms were crossed, his eyes boring a hole in mine as I approached. Marta was at his side, droopyheaded.

—Senhora Cunha, you are tardy again. This is becoming unacceptable!

—Sorry.

—Anyway, we need to discuss Marta's delinquency.

—Did something happen?

—She bit her classmate Ana. Her behavior is becoming intolerable. And it is certainly unaided by your being late bringing her to and from school.

I started laughing.

—Do you find this humorous?

—No. I think this is very, very, very, very serious.

—Good. If Marta doesn't shape up, you will need to find her a new school. For now, she will serve a two day suspension and she is required to write Ana an apology. Additionally, you should consider getting her some counseling.

—Yes sir. I appreciate your concern.

I did not appreciate his concern. Marta was an excellent kid, prone to mood valleys, yes, but she was loudly high spirited and smart, and a suspension was outrageous. Whatever Ana had done, she surely deserved a bite. I knew this girl, I knew her parents. They lived in a magnificent apartment in Leblon, which I only knew about because I saw pictures on facebook from Ana's birthday party that everyone in class was invited to except Marta, so even if her indiscretion today wasn't so egregious, she had it coming. Seu Getúlio was done speaking so he turned and walked away. Marta and I headed down the street toward the bus stop. She was hunched in a guilty and contrite posture. For a moment I considered being serious, but I couldn't even pretend.

—You took my advice, huh?

—Are you mad at me?

—No. But the school is, and you're gonna have to write that girl a letter.

—I'm not sorry though!

—So? You better say you are. And no more biting! You're not a dog.

She snorted like a pig and laughed, and then sank back into herself. We kept walking. I was feeling happy in the bright afternoon, holding Marta's hot sweaty hand, a quick peace before being pulled back to my restaurant torpor to feel my life tick away. The sky looked gorgeous, limpid blue melting into lavender, an impalpable array of colors swaggering as the sun dropped, and the low flying gaivotas squawked lazy toward the beach to snag a late fish lunch. There were so many Lucias who felt the same heats, heard the same traffic and animal and pedestrian chatter, but in different afternoons that were dead to time. It was my birthday. What had all my amassed experiences left me with? Marta was muttering grumbly next to me.

—What is it?

—It's what Ana said. You didn't even ask why I bit her!

—Why did you bite her?

—Ugh.

—Ok, don't tell me.

—She said that mom and dad. Well, I was talking about dad because everyone was talking about their dad and I was like, You should've seen my dad he was better than all of yours. And Ana was like, Well, he's dead, and everyone kinda laughed. I told her to shut up and she said that dad was a criminal and the police killed him. She just told everybody. So I grabbed her arm and bit her really hard. I couldn't just let her say all that!

—You can't let her bring you down, Marta. Have you seen her? You're so pretty and smart, she must be exploding with jealousy!

Engendering envy, a cheap consolation.

—Ugh.

—What?

—Do you think she's right though? Were mom and dad bad people?

—No, I don't think they were.

—Then why did the police get them! I don't get it, Lucia.

—They loved you, garota! They loved you more than anything, and they were good to us, always. They were doing something that's against the law, that's true, and they got punished for it. But just because they were doing something illegal doesn't make them bad. They didn't hurt anyone, ok? They were good people.

She didn't say anything. Whenever her parents' plight arose, either she found my explanations unconvincing or she was too sore to speak, because she never said anything. It was a situation I struggled to grasp too. After they moved into that lavish penthouse in Copacabana, which my mother spoke of with such green wrath that if she could've snapped her fingers and burnt it down, she would've, they kept a room just for me, and I was basically sleeping there every night, so I thought about it often, that while they treated me with so much love and care and curiosity, treated me like a real daughter, attention I hadn't received in any of my ostensible homes, they were running a lucrative drug operation that left addiction, death, and broken families in its wake. Objectively, that wasn't good. But my experience with them left me with nothing but unmitigated delight, full good, so how could they be bad? What did it mean to be a good person, and how could you become one?

The day after the raid, Nara's imprisonment, and Antonio's death, my mother and my grandpa sat at the kitchen table and talked about how they deserved what was coming to them. Deserved. That word was batted back and forth like a peteca. They were criminals, so they earned their downfall. Nara's father and her sister talked about that right in front of me with such snarky glee, after the darkest day in our family's story, while Martinha, now an orphaned child, the poor locus of all that warranted justice, slept all day under our roof. Grandpa and mom were good people, but Nara was a bad person? That didn't make any sense to me. Justice was never meted out fairly, almost nobody got the end they deserved. Salvation and damnation were fickle, roving contingencies lurking dormant in every choice, and they could strike anybody, anytime. You might get lucky and be plucked away by a foreign dunce, or a police officer's bullet could put an end to your history.

A gloomy silence descended over Marta and me as we walked toward the desolate bus stop across from the Aterro Park. Honestly, it would've been a better option to take the train back. This stop was very sketchy and deserted because it was right next to a tunnel, which went under the highway to get to the park, where people were robbed constantly. Whatever earlier happiness I was feeling vanished, and now me and Marta were both slouched in a spiritual pout, and I remembered that my grandpa was dead, but nobody at work knew that yet. I could use that as an excuse and call off from my dinner shift.

—What do you say we get some ice cream and watch a movie tonight?

—Don't you have to work?

—Maybe I'll take the night off.

—Oh my gosh Lucia, yes! And grandma will be home tonight, she can watch with us!

Marta's new joy was reverberating in the afternoon, and I was thrilled that my idea cheered her up. I pulled out my phone and called Mario and told him with a quake in my voice that my grandpa fell and we were taking him to the hospital and the situation looked extremely dire, but while I was talking, I caught, out of the corner of my eye, a kid shiftywalking toward us from the tunnel. He was wearing a tattered Fluminense jersey and he was barefoot, head low, hands in his pockets. I thanked Mario for his kind condolences, and hung up the phone. I held Marta's hand tighter, trying to check myself against bad prejudgements about the world, but knowing I should trust the dangerous feeling in my stomach. Like a flash of memory, I thought of the day my father came back to take Daniel to the United States. Mom and dad screaming. Lucia sitting there. The cold tile on her feet. The picture of Jesus that watched you as you moved, those menacing blue eyes. I'm taking my son with me, Maria! My son, you hear me? What about her? She's your daughter! Why don't you owe her anything? My daughter? Ha! She's fucking black, Maria! I know how you are. Parading around with your brother in law. You're just like your sister, a no good slumfucker! Grandma what did he mean? Grandma what was he talking about? The kid was right in front of us, and I had the nauseous certainty we were about to get robbed. He pulled out a small knife and demanded my phone and my backpack. Marta was trembling. I was terrified too. This kid was so young, and I tried to find some softness in his eyes, behind all that hardened youth. I spoke calmly.

—You really wanna do this? My phone's cheap and there's nothing in the backpack.

—Hurry up, porra!

—Here's twenty reals, that's all I have on me.

—Give me the phone now!

He pushed the knife closer to me. Marta was clutching me tight, burying her head against my back. Suddenly, out of the tunnel, a man materialized, and immediately ascertaining the situation, this big sweaty man holding a basketball in his hands yelled, Hey thief! Go fuck yourself! Our assailant turned to look at the man, who in two big strides got close, and in one swift motion, impressive and startling, hurled the ball overhand. It hit our assailant flush in the head and woozied him, and as he reached up and checked his face for blood, bobbing rickety, our savior dropped him with a punch to the jaw. I was stunned. I didn't like how the situation had escalated.

—Are you guys ok?

He stood in front of us heroic and proud, with his hands on his hips, blocking out the sun. Before I could say anything, the kid, who I had almost forgotten about, sat up and stabbed our sweaty savior twice in the side, hard. You could hear the gush of his insides as the knife plunged into his wet, real body. Me and Marta both screamed and our assailant fled as fast as he could. I should've just given him my phone! Now this man was on the ground, whimpering, writhing in pain, as a small puddle of his blood pooled on the dirty concrete.

—Help me, help me.

There was nobody else around. Nobody to see what I did next. What if he died? Was I supposed to call an ambulance and wait here as he bled in my arms? Endure questions from the police for the rest of the night? There was nobody else around. He would be fine. It was just a small wound. It wasn't his heart. He wasn't going to die. I didn't ask for this.

—Help me, help me!

I grabbed Marta's hand, and I said vambora, and we ran.

—No, don't go!

We flew down the street, ran for probably ten minutes straight until we made it to the train station. We were both panting heavily, and I walked us around the block to catch our breath, meanwhile looking at every face, paranoid and guilty, knowing I made the wrong choice, knowing I should go back. There was still time. We got on the train. Marta curled next to me, silent. I put my arm around her and embraced her, and I whispered sorry into her ear. She looked up at me.

—Is he gonna be ok?

—Yes. He'll be fine, don't worry about it.

—Why did we run?

She said it in such a low voice that I pretended not to hear her. I sat there sounding a gentle shush, hopelessly inadequate as a guardian and a person. What did being good mean? Now I had a partial answer, it wasn't like that. I was failing miserably. Marta whispered to me.

—Hey Lucia? Can we, uhm. Can we still get ice cream?

THE ICE cream place was closed. We walked home in mutual dejection, not even holding hands, the streetlights shining on our sweaty, frizzy faces. The doorman in the lobby was Seu Edson, who sometimes worked the night shift, barely worked, really, because he was usually so cachaça stuffed he couldn't even open his eyes to look at you, much less open the door, so he kept it cracked open, perilously, to the dismay of many of the residents, though nothing bad had happened yet. We walked in and mumbled oi, he grunted something back, and we walked up the stairs. We were in front of our door, 302, the 30 gilded fake gold and a chalk outline where the body of the 2 had fallen dead, so long ago I couldn't remember when the numbers were all up, and I dug through my bag and realized I lost my key. I knocked and grandma answered the door.

—Girls! Ahh que saudade!

She had a big smile on her face and I could smell something baking, a rarity in this last year where her spirit dimmed into what seemed like a final reticence, where her raucous stories and rollicking laugh, her inspired confections and incessant displayed affections all fell away like flippancies in light of the grave work of preparing for death. So it was exciting to see her looking so lively. Marta and I hugged her and walked inside.

—Weren't you working tonight, Lucia?

—I called off, I didn't feel like going in.

—Well, this was going to be a surprise, but I made a cake for you.

She opened the oven and I saw my favorite chocolate cake, and the smell was so delicious that I was overcome with a wave of remorse, that grandma would do something so nice for me when I didn't deserve anything, when I was as awful as anybody I ever disdained, and the pangs of guilt and helplessness were so piercing that I started to cry.

—What's wrong? Come here.

I wanted to tell her about the man who tried to save us, and who, because of my negligence, might've had his life light burn out, but I couldn't talk about that, I couldn't talk about anything. The three of us sat at the table. The windows were wide open, allowing fruit flies and mosquitoes their inandout ambulations, wafting in the street racket of sirens and late night roguery. We chatted about nothing. Marta told her about the bite and grandma laughed and scolded her benevolently. When the cake was done, we slathered chocolate icing and sprinkles on it, and they sang me happy birthday while I sat there with a sheepish grin. While we were eating slices of cake, I decided I needed to talk about it.

—I called my mother today.

—You did?

—I thought I should let her know about grandpa.

—What did she say?

—Nothing. She was sad, you know. It was a short conversation.

—Did she say she was coming to visit?

—No.

—Good. I think that's for the best, Lucia. I know you miss her, but we know how she is. She's my daughter and I hate to say it, but just having her around would make everything harder.

—I don't know, grandma. Talking to her today, it felt. I don't know. I always feel like a little girl when I talk to her. You know I spoke to her in english? Isn't that weird? It was like portuguese would've been too close. And I'm sure she hasn't been speaking much of it. I guess I didn't wanna hear her grate and stumble. I get so discombobulated when it comes to her.

—I know what you mean, darling. But we're fine here without her. We don't need her.

I wondered if that was true. It was definitely a quieter life without my mother. There were no knockdown dragout fights, no smashed bottles projectiling around the kitchen, no dark fervors nor screaming frenzies. Sometimes I thought I would take all that back just to have a mother again. Even though she absconded from the duties of the role as soon as she plopped me out. Just to have a shape to point to, just to be able to say, There, that's her, sometimes I felt that would give me a wholeness I was lacking. And it was difficult to remember that the reason she wasn't around anymore wasn't that I chose to break my ties with her, no, it was her decision, and it seemed like she was happy with it. But if she wanted to come back, even as a dim glim of my ungraspable family fantasy, I would welcome it, even though I didn't have the guts to tell grandma that right now.

—I'm gonna get Marta ready for bed. Thank you for the cake, grandma.

Marta was so cake weary, she looked green and dizzy. At least this made up for my broken ice cream promise, and maybe it took her mind off the tough day. She took a shower and put on her sleep clothes, tried to skip out on brushing her teeth, but I caught her. She lay in bed and I read a few pages to her from Brás Cubas, which I was rereading right now. She asked about watching a movie, but I said it was too late, she had to go to sleep.

—Why did you tell grandma Aunt Maria wasn't coming?

—I want it to be a surprise.

—Oh. I thought maybe you didn't want her to know.

She was too keen for her own good.

—It's time to go to bed, let's pray.

Before she went to sleep, I always made her say a short prayer, not because I believed in prayer and its manifestations, I was pretty sure I didn't, but because my great grandma, my namesake, made it up. I thought it was important to keep passing it on, even though everything that I heard about my great grandmother was unflattering, she seemed like a mean woman, parsimonious with her love, who died painfully of a brain tumor, and I never received a good explanation for why I was named after her. I thought maybe it was a small hope of the future redeeming the past. Though my mother was not that sentimental.

—Com deus me deito, com deus me levanto, com a graça de deus, e o divino espírito santo. Essa prece quem me ensinou foi a bisa Lucia, boa noite bisa Lucia.

I kissed Marta on the head and turned the light off. I walked back into the kitchen, where my grandma was sitting in the near dark. The sink was cluttered full with dirty dishes, and grandma always said that leaving them overnight would attract bad spirits to the house, so I walked over and started to clean them, doing what I could to stave off any more apartment haunting. Grandma turned to look at me.

—How are you, Lucia?

—I'm ok.

She was silent. She was waiting for me to say more, because there was more to say.

—I've been thinking a lot about Antonio today.

—You have?

—Yeah, grandma. What do you think. About. I don't know.

—What is it?

—What if he really was my father?

She grimaced, and it took her a moment to respond.

—I don't know. It would mean he knew, and that he chose never to tell you. If you ask me, that makes him just as bad as Daniel's father.

—What do you think? Do you think he was though?

—No, I don't think so.

—But you know what my dad said. Why would he say that if it wasn't true? Don't I look like my mom? I know me and Daniel don't look that much alike, but it's not crazy, we look like siblings. I just don't understand why my dad would've said that.

—Sometimes you have to pay for other people's mistakes. Life is unfair that way.

—But whose mistakes did I pay for? My mom's? Would Antonio really cheat on Nara like that? He just didn't seem like that kind of guy.

—Probably not. But you don't know what goes on in someone's heart. Especially in a marriage.

I didn't say anything. From what I knew, grandma was always totally transparent with me, but I had the feeling that she was hiding something, that there was something she wasn't telling me. I went and sat down across from her. The picture of Jesus was on the wall, watching me creepy like it always had, his eyes supposedly focused in graciousness, but I saw different flickers, he looked like a bloody bearded Cabral.

—Is there something you're not telling me?

She recoiled at the suggestion and shook her head.

—I don't know who your father is, Lucia. I think it's awful that the american brought you into his problems with your mother. He used you as a bargaining chip. He never cared about you as a person, you were just something he could throw at your mother to hurt her. So we might never know what's really true. But I do know sometimes people do things they regret. Horrible things they can never take back. That reverberate in ways they could never expect.

—Like what?

—Nothing. I'm just talking.

—Whatever it is, grandma, you can tell me.

She took a deep breath and looked at me. She stared right into my eyes like she was gathering the courage to say whatever it was she needed to say, but I could see that she couldn't do it, whatever it was, it was too much.

—There's nothing to say, querida. I'm tired. I need to go to bed.

She stood up, kissed me on the head, and walked out. I went back to the sink and finished washing the dishes. I had never spoken frankly with her about my father, or asked her who he was, except for on that day, ten years ago, when he renounced me openly, right in front of me. Maybe I would never get an answer. I didn't know what piercing comfort it would provide to even know. Both men were dead, so even if I found out now, it wouldn't matter. My mother was the only one who could give me an answer, and in a few days she would be here, maybe, and maybe now, after all this time, she would be ready to tell me the truth.

Still, something bothered me. I knew my grandma very well, and I never saw her act in such a furtive, avoidant way. There was something she wasn't telling me. It couldn't be about my father, if she really knew the truth, she would tell me, but that fact was solely my mother's secret now. What was she keeping from me? I thought it would be simpler to be an adult, out of the murky chaos of childhood where feuding giants rule by whim and don't take questions, but everything became more complicated, it became more vital to clutch your lies close, and the only way to function was to navigate the roiling waters of deception as best you could. But I loved grandma, and I trusted her. If there was something she wasn't telling me, it was for the best. You didn't have to know everything, even about the people closest to you. Though I wanted to know everything about the people I loved, but there was that fear, that, what if you did know, and it was more than you could bear? I left the kitchen. I took a long shower, a warm respite from this very bad day, put on my pajamas, and crawled into bed. My thoughts weren't going to let me sleep tonight, but I could at least pretend. I closed my eyes, and I stayed awake, listening to Marta breathe.

AS I SIT here on the first day of this final week trying to airplane medicine into your weak mouth, as if you were a sick kid or a street dog Nara brought home, as I sit here with the ghosts of this kitchen, in this apartment I told Maria I never wanted because I wanted to die in that corner of Ribeira where I had spent my whole life, but no, she let her rich american with his vanquish hungry eyes uproot us from the soft Ilha soil and plant us here in this hard asphalt, gnarled and fruitless while life rots away from us, and as you sit here, biting my hand, refusing this medicine with your bottom lip pouted like one of our girls pleading off school, I think of that day I met you on the rainy bus I hardly ever took, sitting sleepy in the back with my head against the window, weary from the strictures of my life, when you got on and walked right to me, as if some cosmic light was showing you the way

—Is this seat taken?

and I said no of course not, as soon as I saw you all dressed up, dripping from the rain, those unmistakable green eyes staring at me, your crooked teeth peeking through a nervous half smile, and as the bus bumbled on through the rickety roads, we sat next to eachother, so silent we could hear all the raindrops, how young you were João! our legs touching, both of us stealing shy glances when we could, fearing what would happen if we boldly looked into the other's eyes we hungered for, and suddenly you held my hand, and my heart rose and I felt like I was free for the first time in my death battered seventeen years, I saw life, and it looked like you, and I knew that what Gloria said about how spirits are tied together for eternity, helping eachother find salvation, was true, because I needed you to save me like you need me now

—No no no

refusing this medicine, and I can't let you die now João, though you will die, and I've seen it, and I'll weep for you and all the suffering your spirit will endure, because we're never finished purging ourselves of our sin and failure, even though we were brought into this incarnation to help eachother and what help have I given you? letting you rot, letting you drink yourself to death, what good was I to you? when you lifted me out of that miserable shack where I lived with my mother and her miserable ire, her constant reminders that I would never be anything, that I was worthless, that I was a witch, and just when I thought the world was about to swallow me whole, there you were, shining like eternity on that bus, our hands intertwined like our next fifty five years were engraved in the stone of the earth, and you stood to get off and snuck a kiss on my cheek

—My name is João
—My name is Marta

and my face got so hot that I cried because I hadn't felt that sort of tenderness outside the scant silhouettes of memory I had of my father before he died when I was nine years old and it was just me and mom and little Fernando, living in a mansion in the neighborhood where all the military officers' families lived, and my father went off to the United States for some military exercises, and I was excited because everytime he left, he came back with presents and candy and would say

—Marta, meu bem! que saudade!

and would wrap me up in a hug and whisper to me how I was his favorite, and I would eat his gifts of foreign candy with enamored awe while my mother looked on with that green anger of hers, but the last time he left, he sat me and Fernando down with a weary reticence in his eyes and he said like he always did

—Fernando, if something happens to me, you're the man of the house

and he kissed us both on the head and smiled and walked out the door into the stifling swamp of our Ilha but

a week later, an officer appeared at the door

and my mother started wailing

dad had a heart attack, diving off the coast of Maryland

and my mother looked at us

pure hatred burning in her eyes

and she screamed and walked out the door, leaving us in that great big house all alone with our grief, and when she came back, she had withdrawn the last echoes of our money from the bank with a plan to go to the United States and give her husband the funeral he deserved, and so she left, me and my brother, tiny with this overwhelming pain, not knowing what to do, we just held eachother and listened to the radio and whenever a Pixinguinha song would come on, that samba my father loved, we would cry and scream and beg the sea to give him back, and when my mother finally returned, two weeks later, she was trailed by piles of american clothes, shoes, and sunglasses, and nothing for us, not even a last remembrance of our father's face, not even a simple

—Marta, meu bem! que saudade!

those words I heard reverberate in my ears, and I didn't think anything of it until I started seeing a man around the yard and I would say

—Mommy, who is that?

and she would scream

—There's nobody there Marta, shut up!

and I didn't know what to do because the man would be looking right at me, in his dark suit and sunken eyes, approaching me, and I would run from the sight, consumed by terror, and I would tell Fernando and he would say

—I don't see anything Marta

and I would tremble from fear hearing my father's voice reverberate in my head as if he was right next to me, as if he was saying his last goodbye all over again

—You're the man of the house Fernando

and other voices too, desperate ones

—Help me please help me

—Tell my mother I miss her

—Go see Gloria go see Gloria

and I would tell my mother, whose rage at this point was in a constant overflow, having to move us out of that mansion and into a shack in a noxious neighborhood, a shack that hardly had room for all her clothes and jewels she slowly started selling off because she didn't want to get a job and my father's pension wasn't enough, crying that she had to feed two ungrateful kids even though me and Fernando tucked into the house's corners and made ourselves as invisible as dust, and I would tell my mother

—Mommy I'm seeing things, I don't know what's happening

and she would always say the same thing

—You're a bruxa Marta! Leave me alone!

and I would go down to the Engenhoca beach all alone and sit in the sand crying, the waves biting at my feet, and I would watch the turtles and the gaivotas play until one day I decided to swim and from then on I would swim way out until I hit a little island where I could explore, feeling powerful in the Guanabara waters, my body like it was a part of the waves, and I would hop on boats and see if they had snacks I could steal, or I would just sit in the boat and pretend it was mine, hearing my dad's voice

—Ahh minha Marta, minha fofa

and another voice constant, telling me

—Go see Gloria go see Gloria

until one day I asked around

—Who is Gloria?

and people told me

—Oh Gloria Macumbeira, she's dangerous, stay away from her

but one day I wandered into her little house, a few blocks away from Seu Zé's botequim, and there she was, waiting for me

—Are you Marta?

and I wasn't even twelve yet, scared and looking for answers, and I told her about the voices, the things I was seeing, I told her that people called her a macumbeira, a bruxa, and that people called me a bruxa too and she looked at me with dark kind eyes

—You have the gift Marta

and from then on I would go to her house everyday after school, Fernando would walk me there and go drink guarana at the botequim on Seu Zé's dime because neither of us wanted to go home, neither of us wanted to endure my mother's rage, her utter stagnance, and Gloria would read to me from Allan Kardec's books and teach me about the soul and Jesus and what it took to save ourselves, how to finally achieve God's grace

—Outside charity, there is no salvation

and she would explain to me where that word came from, how the latin caritas came from the greek agape which isn't charity the way we think about it but an indivisible love, a love that transcends these petty conditions, these petty ascriptions, a love for the eternity of the soul and how it reflects God's divine perfect presence, and that no matter what anyone did to me, I would have to love them, I would have to be good to them and endure anything, but I would tell her about my mother, about how much she yelled at me, how mean she was, how she hated me

—No matter what she does to you, you have to love her

—I have to love everybody?

—Outside charity, there is no salvation

and Gloria taught me how to channel those voices that lambasted me constantly and how to write the messages they were bringing me and soon I was writing letters for people I didn't know, writing things I couldn't even remember writing, in handwriting that wasn't mine, and Gloria would tell me to take those letters to people and they would cry reading them, they would weep, and I didn't know what to say

—This is my mother's handwriting, oh thank you oh thank you

—I miss my brother so much, oh I'm glad he's ok, can I pay you?

and Gloria would tell me to say no, no, you can never charge for the gift, and word got around the Ilha about what I was doing and my mother found out

—You're not allowed to see that dirty macumbeira anymore!

but she couldn't stop me, I had someone to talk to, Gloria would give me books to read and I never had any books, I would go to see her after school, and then after dark me and my brother would go swim and explore the sand banks, the little islands on the bay in the pitch dark moon bright night, and we would lay on the Engenhoca beach and look at the stars and it was all so happy until one night, we went out on the cold windy beach, and the next day me and Fernando were both coughing, we both had fevers and mom called the doctor and he said we had pneumonia so he told my mom to boil up a pot of scalding water, and she poured it on our backs, I was thirteen and the water tore up my flesh, left it red and raw, and I had to sleep on my stomach for weeks as the raw skin congealed into scars that I can still feel when I trace the lines on my back

but poor Fernando

the water didn't cure me but I healed

the water didn't cure Fernando

and he died, coughing his last breaths as I watched

and we buried him in an unmarked plot and it was just me and mom now, all alone, my older brothers long gone, moved out of the state and out of the wrath of my mother, and from that moment on, I became the Bruxa da Ribeira, everyone would laugh as I passed

—Olha a Bruxa!

—Haha! Haha!

—A dead brother and a dead father and she sees ghosts!

—My grandma died twenty years ago Marta, can you tell her I said hi?

—Haha! Haha!

and I would ignore them and read my books and feel my body grow stronger, fighting the Guanabara waves and playing volleyball in the Engenhoca sand and I knew that they called me those names because they were angry, because whenever there would be a swimming competition, I would win, whenever there was a prize at school to be had, it was mine, and they couldn't handle being beaten by a poor witch

but oh I was so sad, I longed for someone, I longed to be out of my mother's grasp

and you João, with those soft eyes, so cloudy and faded now

—No no no

when you kissed my cheek

—Is this seat taken?

when you held my hand

—My name is João

and I thought, it will be through him, it will be through him.

But we were so young João! do you remember that? do you remember anything? those early nights in our hot refuge, finally free from our bonds, from the hands bursting out of graves to pull us earthward, I had never been with a man before you João, I was so young, and your body was so beautiful, I remember I would sit with the other girls and watch you and your friends play ball on the beach, your sweat shining, the girls around me saying,

—Wow, look at João

and I would smoke quiet and proud that that body was mine, and it felt like my only path was you, I had given up on school, and whenever an ambition would rise up in me, whenever the books felt like pathways out of the Ilha, into some freedom whose contours I could barely sketch, I would remember my mother's exhortation

—You're ugly and you're poor Marta you can't be anything

and I felt like my mother's words, they burrowed deep into my heart, but when you were with me the bemtevis would sing, when you would put your lips on me in that stifling room, where we could hear the capivaras playing outside our window, and our bodies would be entwined in the midst of the owl hoots and distant crashing waves, when I had you I had everything, I had the freedom I wanted, I had the love I wanted

and one day I felt a change

I never thought I would be a mother, because I couldn't see a future past your eyes, past your body glowing in the Ribeira sun, but you were so happy João! and I basked in your joy, I was willing to give my life again and again for you to be that happy, and you said

—If it's a boy let's name him Fernando

and I was stunned because I had never told you about my brother and that's when you told me about your brother and your sister and we stayed up all night trading grief, memories of dead fathers and mean mothers and curt burials, I knew from then on, unequivocally, our spirits were bound together, that you would never leave me and that I would never leave you

and I had Fernando

he was so little, too little

oh João! maybe we cursed him

with that name

what's in a name João? eleven days, eleven days, eleven days in his small gorgeous weakness, I can still see him lying on our bed coughing, shivering, and I can see you crying João, demanding some explanation from me, from my God, and I didn't know what to do, I thought of calling my mother, I thought of calling the doctor, and we should've but we were so young and foolish, we didn't want reality to spoil our sanctuary

and we were empty again

the darkness that had trailed us for so long swept its way through our house

and we were empty

Fernando was buried with the rest of our dead family

and I couldn't look at you from then on João, you would go to work, your horrid jobs, cleaning barracks and schools, refueling planes, selling knickknacks on the street, I don't even remember which job you had, I just know that I would leave and go spend my days with Gloria asking her how, how was this possible? why would this happen to me? and she would give me empty answers and I would nod my head and agree and then go swim for hours, furious at the senselessness of the world

it's funny to me how angry I was

how lonely I was

when now I sit in this house with you, emptied of our children once more, Maria who looked so much like you, and Nara whose name you can't even remember, the first word gone in your dawning senescence, and I remember years after our son was gone and we excised his name and his memory from our life, when it looked like we would have some peace, some happiness, with two toothy giggly girls with pigtails, even though you were drinking everyday and couldn't keep a job, and the money was so bad that one day you said to me

—We need to go visit my sister

a sister I didn't even know existed, who apparently lived in a Copacabana mansion with the General's friend, and I knew nothing of Copacabana, just the name that sounded like movie stars and presidents strolling in the sun, and so you packed us up, me and our daughters, and we took a long dull bus ride into Copacabana to go beg your sister to relieve our poverty for a moment, and the girls in their new Sunday dresses were so excited, playing and laughing the whole way there while you said nothing, nervous to see a sister I knew nothing of

and I'll never forget the sight of your sister's mansion, right on Avenida Atlantica, now with a vacant lot in its place, the last mansion to get torn down in Copacabana, boarded up to keep out vagrants, and somehow in fate's cruel cosmic contortions, here we live, not two blocks away from it, not that you could stand to walk those blocks, you would die in the sun and collapse on the concrete, but back then you were fierce, in your suit and tie and your tight bound grimace, as we strolled right into the most beautiful house I'd ever seen

your horrible sister waiting there with her maids and her fat oaf of a husband, and she greeted us with abject distance, cordiality drenched in condescension and nausea, as if she couldn't believe that this was the poor stock she sprouted from, and she gave us a tour, every room more lavish than the last, our girls' eyes shining like silver and gold, sparkling in the midst of the high ceilings and the museum art on the walls, and finally she took us into the last room, a huge room filled with cages, forty or fifty of the most beautiful birds I had ever seen, macaws and papagaios and maritacas of every color you could imagine, all squawking and rattling, illuminated by the enormous window that poured in light from the beach, and our little girls, all pigtails and milkteeth, gasped, and Nara reached in to touch one of the birds, those depressed miserable birds, and your sister barked at her

—João tell that mulata not to touch anything!

and you pulled Nara away as you looked at me, my throat tight as that word echoed in the room, that word as if it had snatched away the delusions we were smiling under, and after that, we had to endure a dinner while you sat there stewing the whole time, avoiding my eyes, with an anger apt to burn right through you, not saying a word to dissuade your sister from ranting and raving and barking at our daughters, and you got your money to hold us over for another month at least, and on the bus ride home I tried to talk to you and you said

—Don't pretend it's not true

and turned away as our girls whispered amongst themselves until Maria finally mustered up the courage and leaned in to ask

—Mommy, what did that word mean?

Maria and Nara looking at me, sadness and loneliness and curiosity mingling in those young eyes, and I couldn't tell her how I felt, early in those days after we'd lost our son, I couldn't tell her that I felt sundered in your sight, João, fruitless under your shadow, I felt like the jaca tree that spilled fruit into our yard that our neighbor cut down in angry spite, because my salvation was slipping from my hands, your glittering nobility was dimming away, and all I saw was a craven heap, and so one day while I was swimming all alone and you were wasting your day at the bar, I came out of the water and there he was, not João, gleaming, shining, more beautiful than anything I had ever seen

—So you're the Bruxa da Ribeira?

—My name is Marta

—My name is Marcelo

and we sat in the sand and he talked and talked and made me laugh in a way that felt foreign in my tearhoarsed throat, and when he asked me to come back with him to his house, I did, his humble little house up on the hill, where he lived alone and slept on a cot, but he had a record player, and he would play me João Gilberto and Nara Leão and Dorival Caymmi records and my heart would swell and float with the music, and we would smoke and laugh in the sticky heat, and I never wanted to go back to you João, the thought just made me sad, and Marcelo made me so happy, Marcelo who would make me feel things I could hardly understand but I'd remember what Gloria said

—Outside charity, there is no salvation

and I would think, Is what I'm doing really love? leaving you all alone at home to drink yourself to death, letting you disintegrate into a shadow of yourself when I felt like I owed you eternity? and so I told Marcelo

—I have to go back to him

and I did and I gave you Maria, who we named after your dead sister

though I warned you it was a curse

but Maria lived and she had your eyes

the curse would come back to us

but she was beautiful

and I was unhappy again, all I thought of was Marcelo, and you would stagnate at home drinking and yelling at me as our money slowly dwindled, and because of your laziness, I had to go work with a baby not even a month old, I had to go work in some disgusting lawyer's office answering his calls and letting him talk down to me, and I thought, Forget João, he doesn't deserve me

so I went back to Marcelo

and we gave eachother our bodies

but the guilt encroached on me again, about what I owed Maria, about what I owed to you, I owed you my life, I owed you my freedom, I believed that, I believed I owed you those things forever and still do and so I came back to you

but I was full when I returned

and when you asked me what her name should be, I said Nara, a small rebellion, a small memory for me of those hot nights and Marcelo and that music, and you never said a word as Nara grew up, even though people whispered about you all over town, they laughed at you

—A cuck and a witch!

—Haha! Haha!

—Oh João's a nice guy, he lets his women do whatever they want

—Haha! Haha!

oh, I betrayed you João! and my sin grew roots in our home, as soon as we got off that long dull bus back from Copacabana, unhappiness descended on our lives like a cancer, like that tumor that would grow in my mother's head as she forced her way into our house so she would have witnesses to her death, my mother sleeping in that bed with Maria while Nara slept on a cot in the kitchen like a maid and you would say nasty things in your cachaça haze, about your own daughter

—Well, she's a slum girl, that's where she belongs

and I would be so angry at you and our little girls would cry as we screamed at eachother and you grabbed me by my throat and I'd spit on you and my mother, her head bulging from the tumor, would walk into the kitchen and say

—We get what we deserve Marta

and I was so unhappy, I was so angry! with nowhere to go João, because Marcelo didn't feel like safety anymore, I would see him drunk and sloppy, stumbling around on the beach with none of that grace that inspired me like fire, and I would realize this is just another João, that's why it doesn't matter where Nara comes from, they're all João, they're all not João, I just filled their names with what I needed, I drew outlines of the words in the dark sand and I would fill them in with João or Marcelo, whoever looked beautiful to me at that time, and that's not love

is it?

and you're not João

are you?

not anymore, not as you sit here in front of me reeking of urine and fetid ends, and how can I be angry at you still? when I resigned myself to love, I resigned myself to endure all the pain and all the grief because this is a transient state, and I know how marred and haunted your soul is, but isn't it the same soul I once loved? even if this João is of no use to me now, this João can't be taken to task for his sins, there is no atonement for this João in this life

. no atonement for the man who headbutted our daughter in the stark light of our kitchen in front of her own children

no atonement for that man who gloated, who cheered when the daughter he'd excised from his life with a paltry figure of division was thrown to the ground and chained

no atonement for that man who called his own granddaughter a slum girl and laughed at the murder of his son in law

but those men aren't João, João suffers now

and I have to love him

—Outside agape there is no salvation

because my soul is not clean, I carry the reverberations of my own sins, but our salvation depends on eachother, our salvation depends on eachother.

But what's left for us here João? what's left for me? to suffer my memories in this house where I have to see Nara's eyes and her face in my granddaughters and conceal the truth from them because I'm too weak, where my grandson who was inscribed with the name of Fernando until my daughter allowed some brute king to brutely reappellate him Daniel, so he could be marked by that americanness our Maria so wildly yearned for, and now he won't even come home, he doesn't want to have anything to do with me or you, or even his sister, wonderful Lucia, whom grace has touched

even though when I heard her name a shock went through me

it seemed like a purposeful hex from Maria, Maria who slept with my dying mother for that whole year while she was emaciated down to bones and bulging pain struck eyes and her unbearable stench seeped into the bedsheets, Maria slept with her while Nara slept on a cot in the kitchen like a maid, and when her daughter was born she told me

—I named her Lucia, like grandma

and I wanted to puke thinking of how my mother died in my house, lucid until the end despite the constant anguish in her eyes, my mother who after all the misery and happiness and toil and change her life had wrought, had nothing to give me at the very end except another dagger to pierce my heart

—I wish it had been you instead of your brother, Marta

and still, I put aside my fear and hatred and willed myself to love and I knelt down at her bedside and I prayed for her salvation as she took her last breath in that tiny room stuffed with the late December heat, and Maria next to me

—Is grandma dead?

and how could she put that name on her own daughter? but Lucia grew out and past it, she rose up, and her soul is strong, and when she was born I never dreamed of my mother again, not once, though I often dreamed of my father, but all those dreams stopped for years, the voices stopped for years, I felt like I lost the gift back when we were still on the Ilha and João exhorted me

—Never see that macumbeira Gloria again

just like my mother had said and I listened to him, I listened to him for years, until one day my urge to see Gloria was too great, I woke at dawn and walked over there and was stunned to see a fire burning through her building, razing the two buildings next to hers, all the Ilha firetrucks and police officers standing by

—What happened?

—There was a fire

—What happened?

—They cleared out the building, they didn't find anybody

and that's how I learned of Gloria's death, a bodiless disappearance told to me by a doltish fireman, and I never saw her again, I never cried for her, and I never dreamed about her, until last night, last night João was the first time I ever dreamed about her, can you believe that? she was standing in a flooded street surrounded by fire and she told me we would both be gone soon, I would see Maria one more time, and then me and you would be gone João

aren't you ready to be gone?

because I am, this isn't the life I wanted at my age, looking at the clock, knowing I'll have to go bag groceries for eight hours on Christmas Day as I worry about you here all alone, falling and dying without me seeing, as if having a witness to your death is what the whole point of living was for, but I want you to have a witness João, I want you to be ok as you die, as you suffer

but this isn't the home I wanted

I used to dream that we still lived on the Ilha, in a comfy house with a view of the beach, in a house filled with my daughters and my grandchildren, you sitting there, lucid, sober, happy, both of us holding hands, having made it past all the chaos and fights and strife, and we'd tell old stories that we knew by heart and we'd tell jokes and say prayers with our children, all our children smiling and well in a house full of love

but Maria's gone

and Nara's gone

and what Maria did to Nara burns my throat when I think about it

but I see her daughter and Nara's daughter together and I have some hope that maybe they can be better than all of us, Nara's beautiful little

girl that took so long for her to have and when she finally got pregnant
she told me

—I'm going to name her Marta, after you

and I cried for her and that unborn girl, and for all the beauty my
sins had inadvertently wrought, because I had sinned, I had betrayed, I
led Nara on a path darkened by the failures of my heart, because I didn't
realize how my actions were like stones dropped in the Guanabara Bay

the ripples that became Maria

the ripples that became Nara

both of them widowed and their children taken from them or
willfully abdicated, and it's my fault, it's my fault, my sin rooted itself
thick in that Ilha soil, but its branches grew and grew in ways I couldn't
anticipate, in ways I couldn't grasp

and I regret it all

but how beautiful my grandchildren are! how sad and lonely their
eyes!

I don't think I would take anything back if I could

though maybe I should wish to take it back

when I see that little girl with my name and with tangles in her hair
as if she's her pigtailed mother about to touch a papagaio in a Copacabana mansion

—Mommy, what did that word mean?

a mansion that I revisited only one time, long after the dictatorship
had fallen and your sister, João, was left without a fat oaf to dote on her,
left in that big mansion all alone, and by this time Nara was grown and
beautiful and she might've even gone to college, she might've made a life
for herself, and we took the long dull bus ride from the Ilha and paid
a visit to your sister and we walked in, the whole place reeking, black
cloths covering all those bird cages, unconcealing the death smell, and
your sister coughing, her maids all gone, coughing, sweating, asking

—Who's there?

and me and Nara walked over to see her, so she could see what Nara
had become

—Oh João's wife and the girl

—Rot in hell

and maybe it was some evil in us, piling animosity onto her death throes and laughing, spending the day on the Copacabana beach, thinking that was the only time we would ever play in that sand, play in that corner of the Atlantic, and two weeks later we saw a news report that said a rich old lady in Copacabana was found dead, all alone, preceded in death by fifty rare macaws, and that they were going to tear the mansion down, and at least you won't be like your sister João, because we're here for you, you have never been here for any of us, but if you fall we will lift you, if you stop breathing we will anoint your body and carry you to your tomb

—No no no

but I feel stupid, I feel senseless, as you refuse this medicine and the clock ticks me toward my supermarket grave, and I feel my seventy two years weighing on me like an unafastable yoke, but it will all be over soon, I feel the relief coming, the relief for both of us that a final heartbeat would bring, and maybe we'll find ourselves stuck in the deepest hell together João, away from all the fire and the clamor, and you could be green like your eyes used to be, green like those caged birds, and we could have forever to reconcile, to find that love and freedom we thought we found the very first moment you held my hand

—My name is João

—My name is Marta

that first moment you kissed my cheek, and I can't help but cry, as I think about all these nothings we cling to, your name, just a shape wrapped around a nothing, this love I've been so consumed by, just another shape wrapped around a nothing, and as I cry softly and quietly and think maybe I'll give up on this medicine, maybe I'll give up on this job and we can just both die right here and right now, Lucia walks into the room

—Oh grandma, you're crying

she says and embraces me

—Here let me do it
you take your medicine right away when it's Lucia
I wonder if you realize she has Nara's eyes
and now it's time for me to go, and Lucia says to me as she always does
—I love you grandma, have a good day
and I respond to her as I always do
—I love you Lucia
and I kiss your cheek João, like you kissed mine on that rainy bus,
and I say goodbye, and I walk out thinking, I do have love, I do have
love.

december 31

I BLACKED OUT again and woke up the next day rattled and shook to the sound of construction. Banging on and on like I was shaking off my first night in hell. Fuck. I sat up. Sand in my hair. This headache. I hated myself so much. I took a deep breath and stood. Holding on to a palm tree for balance. I started sweating cold and threw up all over the sunk sand that held the shape of my body. The construction workers saw the whole thing and started laughing.

Where was I?

I forced my eyes open past the daylight and looked around.

The Palace. Oh shit. How did I end up on the beach?

I felt better after puking though. I took stock of what I had.

No shirt. No flips. I patted my pockets. My phone was cracked and dead.

Great!

A construction worker and one of his buddies walked over to me laughing and said, Ô mano! New Year's Eve is today bro, you got that party going too early! They laughed and slapped eachother, delighting at my misery. I threw up again and they roared. It was New Year's Eve. Caralho. My days were falling away from me in a drifty haze.

Get back to work! I wanted to yell.

But I needed to make some moves.

I took a few lazy steps out of the shadow of the tree, but the sand scalded my feet.

I ran back to safety.

Fuck this day! Fuck this heat! How was this heat even possible? The sky was wide and clear but I felt like I was trapped in a tiny torture box. Or a sewer. The way everything around me stunk. The way I stunk.

I took a deep breath and in the name of action I took off for the calçadão.

Ow ow owing the whole way.

I made it!

But the cobblestones were too much for me. Those black and white rocks stabbing every which way into your soles. I was too soft. Everyday you saw people out here collecting cans, doing their thing all barefoot. But I was way too soft. I was bouncing up and down, grimacing, not sure what to do. I could see the construction workers pointing at me.

Do some work! I yelled.

And then I ran back to my puke covered palm tree shadow and formulated a plan.

I made my way toward the water, toughing out my foot pain.

The beach was just starting to fill up with the holiday muvuca, people posting up with their barracas and their families. I was weaving through the beachgoer set ups, looking for something easy. Some first timer I'm gonna take a quick dip in the water type of bundle. And as if Nossa Senhora was blessing me herself, there it was right in front of me. Flops wrapped in a shirt, lying unattended in a vacant area of the sand. Nobody really looking my way.

Burning. My feet burning.

I unfurled the bundle like it was mine.

The flipflops fell out along with fifty reals and a set of keys.

Yes! My size.

I was only gonna take the flipflops, but when I calced them and the fire on my feet settled, I was like, I could use some money. So I pocketed the fifty and grabbed the shirt. But then I heard someone yell, Thief! Thief! coming up from the sand, and someone else added, Ladrão! Ladrão! for good measure.

I took off like I was sprinting toward goal. Já era!

I was on the calçadão and across Avenida Atlantica in thirty seconds flat.

I was breathing hard, all that cigarette lung constriction manifesting itself. I opened up the shirt I took to look at it. It was about two sizes too big and it said You Don't Mess With Texas in big letters with a picture of the state in red, white, and blue. Whatever.

I put it on.

I was gonna wait in front of the Palace to catch my breath but some dude standing at the front told me to scram.

I crossed the street and slumped down by another tree. Feeling defeated. I stared at the Palace. Grandma told me one of Brasil's early presidents got shot there by his mistress. He survived, but four days later she was found dead. She killed herself, they said.

I wish Leticia loved me enough to shoot me.

That would be a wonderful way to be put out of my misery.

But nah, she just threw me away like an empty coconut. I was hollow and worthless.

I leaned against the trunk of the tree and closed my eyes. Listening to the Avenida cacophony and feeling the heat. When I opened my eyes I realized I was sitting right in front of Nara's old apartment building. Porra. Today of all days too. That sleek building, all black, mirrored, high class. Six years ago today they arrested her, in that top floor penthouse.

We were all there for a party too. The police flooded in like a dam broke.

Fuck, dude.

Six years. Antonio never even made it out.

It was a bunch of damn bullshit! How were you supposed to succeed in this world as a man? There was a minefield path to victory. And even if you got there, avoided all the traps and snares and boozy pitfalls, the police could pluck it up, fuck you. What kinda lesson was that? My life was littered with deadbeat dud debris. My grandpa was a drunk lout. My dad, ha. He was a pathetic excuse for that word.

But at least he had some real world success. He had money. Antonio had money. Now they were both dead. Who the hell was my example? What was I supposed to do? I had no prospects. I was a loser like my grandpa. I was lovelorn and dead broke. Who the hell was my example? My mother? If I was so lucky, I could just dip out and marry rich. But I couldn't do that. That was a power women had. Not some penniless, powerless boor.

I wanted to scream! What was I supposed to do?

I saw my life playing out in front of me, and I didn't like it. Maybe that's why my mom left. She read my palm and saw that I was destined to be one of these shiftless dudes, slinking around the city, cachaçing time down the hatch. As if she was any better. She was a fucking snitch, and a bitch, and she was dead to me.

I wanted to scream.

Leticia was right. How the hell was I supposed to be a good dad? What did I wanna be a father for anyway? To slough my loserdom off to another generation? It was so frustrating, knowing so clearly what I wanted. I wanted to be successful, and I wanted to marry Leticia and raise a family with her. And yet, all that shit seemed impossible. I was doomed.

Was I?

Maybe I just needed to go home, restart.

But that was just one more place I was inadequate. There was nothing I could do for my family, anyone. I remember the last time I tried to do something nice, I got me and Lucia and Marta tickets to a Vasco game. Our bus got robbed on the way to São Januario, and so we got there late and missed the first goal. Then me and Lucia got in a fight and we stormed out early, and out in the street we heard the singing stadium howl. Vasco won 2–0 and we missed both goals.

That was me though. I was gonna juggle fuckups and failures until the day I died.

But maybe not.

I wanted to scream!

I missed my family. Maybe home would be a good place to start. Maybe I wasn't stuck. Maybe with willpower and want I could change some shit. I could be the man Leticia and my family thought I wasn't.

Or maybe not.

Either way, sitting under that tree, I felt the pull toward home.

As I made to stand up, some dude walked over, no shirt, looking dirty, and wordlessly, right next to me, he pulled down his pants, squatted, and took a shit. Making eye contact with me the whole time and shrugging like, Life bro. I wasn't sure if that was a good or a bad omen, but it was definitely the world telling me to move.

I stood up and started walking aimless, unsure.

Maybe I would go home.

Maybe.

I had nowhere else to go.

I COULDN'T see Leticia today because I had tried that yesterday and it did not go well. After I left that Rachel girl's hotel, I went right to see her. Dona Isabel's apartment was in the last back street in Leme, near the ramp to the Morro da Babilônia. Babilônia, where Leticia and her family were all born. Now they lived in this tiny thirteenth floor apartment that her dad earned after being a doorman for like twenty years. I heard her dad had once been lively, vibrant, loud. But I met him in a different phase in his life. After he got his foot amputated because of his diabetes.

Leticia said he stopped talking, stopped laughing, sealed himself up. Was unreachable to his daughter and wife and nephew. Drinking got worse. And then he got cirrhosis in 2014. Same year my grandpa did.

He died last year. His death was horrific. Leticia told me every detail about it and asked me to never ever tell anyone else, the only time she ever made a request like that. So, I'd never tell anyone.

I think Leticia was almost relieved about it. His living was a reminder of pain and misfortune and how easy our lives could fail. But at least in death she could think softer about him, think of smiles and Sundays in the park. At least that's what she told me. Since he was dead, though, they were gonna get kicked out of that apartment soon. I thought, You know, why wouldn't we get a place together? Where we could raise our kid. Dona Isabel could live there. And Mateus could live there if he wanted. It made sense to me. We could be happy.

I needed to find a way to make money, but we would figure it out.

Anyway, I pulled up to her apartment shirtless, looking shipwrecked, drenched and battered from the storm I had to slog through. I'm sure if the doorman hadn't been my boy Chaves, I wouldn't have got let in the front door. I hopped in the service elevator to avoid residents. Because I doubt anyone who lived here would be too thrilled to see the ex boyfriend of the dead doorman's daughter malandrando around sullying up the place.

The elevator stopped at the twelfth floor and I bounded up the steps and stood in front of the lone door on the barely real thirteenth floor. I was shaking from nerves and shivering from the rain. I was nervous. Leticia said she didn't wanna see me ever again. And yet here I was, the very next day. Looking grimy and soiled and not really making a case for why she should welcome me back into her life.

But I knocked and knocked, and knocked again.

After a few seconds, she opened the door. She looked at me but turned away and my heart dropped to my stomach. She was pacing around, prepping to leave or something. I stood in the tight living room where Mateus slept on the couch and I slept on the floor. I was so overwhelmed by my feelings for this place and Leticia and by my own inadequacy that I wanted to cry.

I don't know if you heard, but Mateus is in jail. We gotta get him out.

She looked at me. What time do you think it is?

I don't know.

It's late enough that he's out. I appreciate the news, but me and my mom went there this morning. Now he's at Gilberto's house playing guitar. But thank you for your help. You're always there when we need you, Daniel.

Hearing her say my name broke my heart.

Leticia.

What do you want?

I just wanna to talk to you.

She didn't say anything. I walked closer to her. She turned her back to me.

I've just been thinking about things and I wanna talk to you.

I got even closer. I needed to feel her heat, needed to look at her. But when she turned to meet my gaze with a scornful look, like I was an insignificant speck, I turned away. Leticia is the most beautiful person anyone I know knows, so eye contact with her is impossible to maintain anyway. Like she'd turn you to stone.

I'm glad you've been thinking, Daniel, you've really grown since our break up.

Leticia, I love you!

She started to laugh. That's nice, she said, that's good. And she started laughing again.

I grabbed her hand. I love you Leticia, with everything, really.

She pulled her hand away and stood in front of me, regal and disdainful.

Look at me! I'm not some fucking thing you can project your delusions onto anymore. I'm a real person! I'm a whole person, and I don't need you. I'm done dealing with this shit. I'm not gonna be this girl you want me to be. I'm not gonna save you, Daniel! Understand that and leave me alone.

I know you! I know who you are! I want all of you. I've always wanted all of you. I have no illusions about you girl. None. I need you,

Leticia. It's me and you. That's what it's always been. Me and you. We could make this happen. Let's have this kid! Let's be a family. All of this is gonna be ok.

Tell me why I'd wanna bring a child into this world? To be raised by you! Why, Daniel? So we can be poor and angry and hate eachother? So you can run around and get drunk and cheat on me? Is that really what you want? You wanna keep this long line of piece of shit men in your family going? Make another woman endure that? I'm not gonna subject myself to your misery. Go make somebody else suffer.

It's gonna be different, Leticia! I'm gonna be different now! I swear on my life.

Leticia laughed, spent. She just stood there looking at me.

I wanted nothing more than her grace right now. Nothing more than for her to look at me and see something worthy of her attention, worthy of her love. But there wasn't the slightest glint of that old recognition. I started to cry a little, against my will.

Oh my god, don't cry. Look, Daniel, let me tell you something. I was at a protest downtown yesterday. Me and some people from school organized it and there were more than a thousand of us, closing down the street. It was beautiful. Everybody marching, chanting. And then the police showed up. They didn't even wait a moment, as soon as they saw us, they tossed tear gas into the crowd. I didn't know what to do, I couldn't see, I couldn't breathe, I didn't know where my friends were. My eyes were burning. I ran and felt my way to a curb and I sat down. In pain. Praying for relief, totally surrounded by chaos. And I felt defeated. I was depressed and miserable and I just wanted to go home. I wanted to go home and curl up with someone and cry to them. I wanted them to hear my story and listen to me cry and understand. And then I thought, I can't call Daniel. No way. Daniel is not that person for me and he never will be.

Leticia

You were special to me. I mean that. You were very special to me and I'm never gonna shake your influence on my life for better or worse. But

I'm done with your bullshit. I'm not gonna let you use me to become a real person. You need to figure out who you wanna be and how you wanna move about this world in a serious way, and I can't help you do that. I won't help you do that. And not to win me back! For you, Daniel. Respect yourself and take your fucking life seriously.

I'm, I mean, Leticia

Stay here as long as you want but I'm leaving. And I don't wanna see you. Period. I don't wanna see you. Don't come over and don't call me. I mean that.

Leticia

Goodbye Daniel.

As she was about to walk out the door I said, That kid's probably not even mine.

I regretted it immediately.

She looked at me and let out a single rueful chuckle, looked up to the ceiling, and then walked out. Not even slamming the door. Like it didn't mean a thing.

I sat down on the couch and wallowed for a bit, not crying but totally bummed.

Ok, crying a little.

But then I stood up and took a cold shower in their bathroom and put on some of the clothes I kept there. I grabbed the knife I kept there too, the little switchblade my uncle Antonio gave me for my birthday. He was Flamengo, but he got it made with a Vasco logo and my name on it.

I went to charge my phone, then scavenged through the fridge and found a plate of rice and beans with a napkin over it. I sat at the table and ate that cold. Washing it down with the rest of a little bottle of cachaça. There was a magazine on the table. It was all green with yellow letters and the front said revista pau brasil. I had no idea what that meant. Just one of those things that Leticia read and nobody else did. I flung it off the table, pissed off at everything that created a gap between us.

I finished eating.

I still had the eighty dollars I took from that girl's room.

I put forty of it on the table.

I washed the plate in the sink and left, a little drunk, with nowhere to go.

GOT ME thinking about when I told Leticia the story about what happened to me in the States. I was so fucking embarrassed about it for so long that I never said anything to anybody. You hold those private humiliations hard and that shame eats you up. But then, after her dad died and she told me how, she said, You tell me your story now. We were sitting at her wobbly plastic kitchen table. The table tucked against the wall in that cramped apartment. The only window open to the pitch black December night. The wet heat was squeezing us like an anaconda. I was shirtless, sweating, trembling with my dumb nerves.

But I told her.

The month before I turned fourteen, my dad showed up. Only the third time he showed up that I could really remember. My mom got all giddy, high strung. She prepared a feast like the king was coming through. I mean, I was only thirteen and Lucia was eleven, but even then we were looking at her like, chill out woman, he's not gonna stay. We were expecting it to be like the last time. Mom would stay with him at the Marriott for a month, we'd hardly see them, and then he'd dip. Leaving her deflated, unmarried, all tears and grief.

Leticia asked me, Do you look like him?

I didn't know. I didn't keep any pictures.

Grandma always said he looked like Pedro Cabral. A conqueror.

But anyway, he shows up and I'm immediately a little kid. Run up to give daddy a hug. He comes in, pops himself open a beer, and sits at the kitchen table. Me and Lucia were sitting there staring at him like he was a god come to life. I remember it was a chilly morning in August. My mom was kissing his neck, and he motions with his hand like he's about to speak.

My mom pulls away.

Maria, I gotta tell you something. I have a wife and kids in the United States.

My mom's face goes ghost white.

What? Is that true?

It's the truth. We've been married fourteen years.

She flipped out like I never heard in my life.

You motherfucker! You son of a bitch!

I got the hell out of there. I didn't wanna be around for no yelling. If it was my mom and my grandparents, sure, I didn't mind getting involved in a screaming match. But my dad? He's there for five minutes and he's already fighting? It was enough to break my heart.

I wandered around the streets. Just thinking. Like, duh mom, are you stupid? He was the ambassador to Brasil when he met you. You think some poor girl from the Ilha do Governador is gonna be his main bitch? There was no chance in the world.

I got back home and they had some news for me.

It was just my mom and dad in the kitchen, sitting there. Tensions cooled.

Lucia was nowhere to be seen.

My dad looks at me and smiles.

How would you like to come live in the United States, son?

I almost asked if Lucia was coming. But I wasn't stupid. My mom talked about him as our dad, but we knew how he felt. Lucia wasn't his. We all knew how he felt. The thing we wouldn't speak about.

I said yes. I didn't even think about it. It was like a dream come true.

Everything happened fast after that. The trip was set for the end of the month. I told Leticia and Mateus and they were shocked. They thought I was kidding. I mean, the week before I told Leticia I had a crush on her, and now I was leaving. I didn't care though. I wanted to ditch my life. My dad was more important to me than anything. He finally wanted me! I was gonna be rich! I was gonna have a future!

Everyone was damn morose the day I left, like I was dying. I didn't even sweat it. I hopped on that plane, and I was sitting first class. My first plane ride! I was the ambassador's son now. I was big time. He didn't say much to me though. When we landed in Washington, DC, he had a driver pick us up from the airport. This shiny black car, the type that would maybe last one day in Rio without getting its windows busted out and stole.

We rode out to his house. Out through the city and into the suburbs. My head was against the window the whole time, jaw dropped. I couldn't believe these enormous houses. White picket fences and trim lawns. It was like a movie. It was America! I made it!

We pulled up to this gated neighborhood, greeted the guard. I was being slick, nonchalant. But I had no idea any of this shit was a thing. I was a young prince on top of the world. The driver took us to the last house on the block. It was the biggest, most lavish. I walked up to the door like I was floating on clouds.

His wife was there to give me a cold welcome. She was imperial and frigid, nothing like my mother. Her first words were, Call me Mrs. Gordon. I was like, Ok bitch. Leticia was like, You never said that. No, I didn't. Leticia was surprised that she even let me come there. Me too. But my father always got his way. No matter who was involved. And he wanted a son. He had two daughters and a wife. But he wanted a son. And I don't think it's nothing that they had a boy there to do all their chores.

Leticia wanted to know about the daughters. I couldn't say anything. I said I didn't even remember their names. But really, I was embarrassed at how much I hated them. How they were fucking doted on endlessly, how they always got their family's full love. And I would stay up some nights wishing they would disappear, maybe even die. So I could be alone in my father's attention. Sole in that castle.

The first month there, I really felt like his son. We went to a baseball game in the city. Just me and him. Hardly talked. But he bought me a hot dog and let me sip his beer, and then we sat through three hours of the most confusing event I'd ever witnessed in my life. But it didn't matter. I was with my father. Every terse word he said to me was holy.

I was Daniel Gordon Jr. now.

I enrolled in school. My english was getting sharp. I didn't speak no portuguese the whole time I was there. So much so that when I came back, everyone was playing with me, calling me Daniel Americano, saying I had a sotaque. My mom would've loved that. If I lost all brasilianness for good.

Anyway, they enrolled me in a catholic school that fall. And that's when everything started to unravel. The magic started dwindling. The kids at school would tease me for being brasilian. And I didn't wanna be. At this point, all I wanted to be was american. I was desperate for it. But they would call me horrible names, and pick fights with me. And then I would go home and wash dishes and sweep floors, and Mrs. Gordon would bark and bark at me.

I missed Leticia so much. I told her that. How much I missed her and Mateus. How I didn't have a single friend. Even though I left them. And she didn't ask me, she didn't embarrass me by asking if I would've stayed for good.

I would have.

I would've traded my whole carioca life plus more just to stay in that shit misery.

It got worse. Now I'd only glimpse my father, briefly, on weekends. I got kicked off the soccer team and things plunged even deeper. I started hanging out with some kids from the public school. We'd loiter in parking lots, smoking and drinking all day. I'd come home late or not at all. High. Drunk. They were getting fed up. My dad would scream at me.

You're embarrassing me! You're the ambassador's son! Act like it.

The only times I would see him now were when he had to yell at me. Finally, six months in, they suspended me from school. They caught me smoking weed in the bathroom with three other kids, and I was the only one suspended. They were talking about expulsion, but it never came to pass.

This is what I told Leticia. I was home from school, suspended. I remember this clear as anything. Late February. I was sitting on the couch, looking out the huge frost covered living room window. The grass was chilled and stiff. The forest just past the yard was dark and snowy. It was just me and Mrs. Gordon at home.

The phone rings. Mrs. picks up, Hello?

And then she's just silent. Her permanent scowl gives way to the blankest, most vacant stare I ever saw in my life.

Then she drops the phone and starts to scream. I've never heard anything like that ever again. Her screaming. And then she starts crying and staring at me through her tears. Giving me the most vicious, feral look.

I say, What happened?

She doesn't say anything, just leaves the house. Leaves me there all alone, not knowing anything about what happened for twelve hours. I just sat there, confused and upset. Terrible suspicions clawing at me. I just looked out that big window, watching the daylight fade.

The house was pitch black when she came back. She had her daughters with her.

I asked, What happened? Please tell me.

She goes, and this is exactly how she said it, she goes, My husband died in a car accident.

I never went back to school. I went to the funeral and sat under Mrs.'s terrible gaze. She was looking at me like a wild, hurt dog. I felt like if I cried, she would've ripped me to shreds. So I just kept quiet, listening to people ask questions about me. And then I was on a long flight back to Rio. Alone. Sitting way back in a middle seat, crushed, sleepless between two strangers. I hadn't even let any of my friends or family know. I hadn't talked to anybody. They just shipped me back.

I landed at Galeão completely lost, pulling my little suitcase. I felt like I was six years old. Like the world was too big for me. I sat there for hours until my mother showed up. She saw me and hugged me. Quiet. Very quiet. And then we took a long cab ride home. Quiet. Very quiet. And then I came back and tried to go by Daniel Gordon and it was a disaster! Everyone calling me Gordão! Leticia laughed hard when I ended the story like that. Daniel Fatso, people called me for a second. Gordão.

But there was so much I didn't tell Leticia. So many lies. So many omissions.

I was so scared of the truth. So humiliated by it.

But I couldn't tell Leticia.

I couldn't tell anyone.

BUT ANYWAY. Yesterday, after I left Leticia's apartment, I went downstairs and headed to the calçadão. Hours had passed. The rain had stopped and the sidewalk was dry, though the street still smelled like rain. The hot beach breeze swept through the alleys bringing sand and maresia and it made the whole city feel reawakened, rejuvenated, and I was stumbling half drunk out of my ex girlfriend's house with nowhere to go.

I was finished, beat.

I walked to the calçadão and headed toward Posto 6. Feeling sorry for myself.

Everything seemed dreary to me. The kiosk bands sounded gray, the pigeons pecking and fusando and sleepy on the cobblestones looked like nothing but ratty birds. I heard the waves crash and I saw the foam jump up in the sun soaked afternoon, but the ocean just looked like a place to drown. But then I heard someone screaming, Ladrão! Ladrão! and I saw a kid running up from the sand, a young kid wearing an old Botafogo jersey with something in his hands. He was running fast, I could see the sand flying up behind him, and he was coming my way.

Ladrão! Ladrão!

He was coming right at me!

He leapt up on to the calçadão and without even thinking, I started chasing him. Weaving through the pre holiday promenaders. I was hauling ass, right behind him, my flipflops holding up sturdy. I chased him for six blocks!

He turned around to look at who was behind him and he fell.

I dove right on top of him. He probably wasn't even thirteen and he was holding a pile of cash. I held him down while he begged me to let him go. The people who'd been yelling ladrão pulled up behind me, also running, breathing hard. My adrenaline was pumping. They looked like dudes who rented chairs on the sand, that's probably what it was.

That kid had probably robbed them.

They saw me holding him down and yelled, Olha o herói!

A crowd started to gather around us and one of the chair rental dudes snatched the money out of the kid's hands. The cops came over. One of them tapped me on the shoulder and said, I got it. He flipped the kid over, pressed his face against the cobblestones, and arrested him. I stood up and everybody started cheering.

Eeiii! Hero!

I was feeling like they were right, I was a hero. I just stuffed out that robbery.

I was feeling pretty good!

And then from the gathered crowd I heard, Daniel? No way, Daniel?

Someone saying my name in english. I was sweating and my adrenaline was pumping and I looked over and it was Rachel! I walked over to her as people patted me on the back and as the thief, who was now crying, was led away by the military police.

She looked real good, the sun hitting her just right, standing there in her bikini, skimpy and yellow, looking real good.

Daniel! I guess you're a hero or something.

I like to do my part.

Someone yelled out, Buy the hero and his girlfriend some drinks!

Soon enough we were taking shots of cachaça at the kiosk while the band sped up their batuque and the day suddenly seemed brighter.

Rachel and I were sitting now.

She was like, It's been a minute huh? Haven't seen you since this morning.

We both laughed.

Where's your sister?

She's in our hotel room with some girl.

Some girl?

Yup.

No wonder she wasn't into Mateus!

We laughed and some caipirinhas magically appeared at our table. The kiosk crowd thrilled with the hero in their midst.

Wait, where did she stay when we were together?

We had separate rooms. But my parents are coming into town today so we moved into one. They're always trying to ruin my fun. So this is my last free day, she said, and took a drink. Oh! by the way, is Mateus ok?

Yup, I got him out this morning. No big deal.

You really are a hero.

I laughed, feeling very drunk and staring at her green eyes and her sun soaked body. I wanted her. She was touching my arm, giggling, her leg pressed against mine under the table. Another round of caipirinhas. She put a pack of cigarettes on the table and we were smoking them at will. The sun and the clear day and the ancient shade of the palm trees enfolding us. I was happy. I was drunk. And I wanted her.

I tried texting you. Your number didn't work.

My bad. I think I gave you a fake number.

You think?

I don't know girl, I was drunk! But hey, this is obviously fate.

She laughed.

After we finished our final drink, I said, Why don't we go for a walk?

Ok.

As we both stood up she looked at me, and I pulled her close and kissed her, feeling her heat, her soft lips. The kiosk crowd cheered.

Olha o herói garanhão!

And we walked off away from the laudant kiosk people, the two of us drunk, holding hands and laughing.

We walked about a half block and I stopped and pulled her close again and kissed her.

I said, You wanna go somewhere?

She looked at me like yeah.

We were right next to one of those underground beach bathrooms you gotta pay for so homeless people don't use it, so I said, You wanna hook up in the bathroom? laughing as I said it, like it was new and outrageous.

She laughed and said, Really?

I pulled her close to me again and kissed her nice, grabbing her ass.

It's clean and nobody's gonna come in.

She laughed and said, Whatever.

We walked down the stairs holding hands.

I said, Fala amigo, to the guy working the money desk down there, dude looking like a kid bureaucrat, too young for this big desk post.

Anyone in there?

He said nah.

I slipped him twenty dollars real sly. You wanna give us like ten minutes?

He cracked up and said, Tranquilão cara.

So we walked into the bathroom and he put up the cleaning sign.

We went back into the biggest stall in that deadly hot, admittedly cleaner than I thought bathroom, and we ended up fucking. Rachel pressed against the wall and me behind her, clutching her waist tight and kissing her neck, dripping sweat in that wild bathroom. I wasn't wearing a condom, and without meaning to, I came inside her.

When we were done she said, Did you come inside of me?

Yeah, my bad.

It should be ok.

She looked at me with a cute scold. And then she kissed me and we pulled our clothes back on and walked out of the bathroom. There was a big line waiting. We walked out holding hands. My main dude who was twenty dollars richer was laughing up a storm. The first lady in line yelled, Ta certo menó! gonna let these fornicators in and let an old lady shit her pants, nice!

We walked up and out into the real light, back into the real day.

I was feeling charged up, invincible.

But Rachel said, I don't trust you.

You don't trust me?

I don't. I don't think that's the first time you took some tourist girl in there.

Trust me girl, it is.

Hmm. She let go of my hand. Did you steal from me?

What?

I was missing like eighty bucks this morning.

I stopped and stared at her.

Rachel, I might be a liar, but I'm not a thief.

She smiled. I like how you say my name.

I smiled and said, Rachel, Rachel, Rachel. And kissed her on the cheek.

Look, I got somewhere to be, but why don't we spend New Year's Eve together? I'll give you my real number and we'll meet up. Watch the fireworks?

Well, my parents are gonna be here.

Fuck your parents.

She laughed. Ok.

I gave her my number and kissed her one more time, tasting only cachaça on her lips.

We said goodbye and I walked off, nowhere to go.

But I needed to be alone, and I needed to drink more, and I needed to figure all this Leticia shit out. But Rachel was really feeling me now, in a way that could turn into love. Right? That was a promising path. I walked back toward Leme and crossed Atlantica around Rodolfo Dantas and went into the inside streets. I walked into a jornaleiro and asked for a pack of Marlboros and a lighter. I was tapping the counter with my last twenty so the peruvian looking dude grabbing the cigarettes wouldn't think anything, and as soon as he set the cigarettes down on the counter and went to take the money, I grabbed the box and the lighter and took off.

He didn't even yell after me.

I walked to the Cardeal Arcoverde station and hopped a turnstile, rode the train to Cinelândia and got off and just wandered around the Centro. I was feeling aggressively alone in the arid heat, sobering up in the downtown wilderness, thinking maybe I should've just stayed with Rachel, thinking maybe I could go back with her. Maybe, you know, maybe Rachel could have my baby. I could have an american kid. I don't know. If Leticia really meant she didn't want me, I guessed it was the only option I had.

I walked, smoking cigarette after cigarette, sweating through my shirt, feeling ugly, until I ran into a little bar at Lapa and sat down to drink some more. After five big Antarcticas, I was trying to call Leticia. Nobody answered and when the voicemail played I hung up fast, realizing I had accidentally called Lucia. Shit. I drank three more big beers and was finally starting to feel like myself. There was a big dude next to me wearing a Flamengo jersey and talking loud.

Shut up!

What?

You're being fucking loud, I'm trying to relax.

I could feel the knife in my pocket.

He turned to his friend and laughed and kept talking at the same volume.

Hey filho da puta. Shut up before I shut you up.

He stood up and loomed over me, mean mugging.

Moleque, watch yourself. Just go back to enjoying your drinks. I don't want any trouble with you.

I stood up too. He was much bigger than me, much bigger than I had estimated, but I felt brave, feeling the knife in my pocket.

What are you wearing that loser's jersey for anyway? Didn't you catch the game Sunday? You lost mermão.

And without saying another word, he cracked me on the jaw and I dropped on the calçada hard, seeing stars, feeling like my face was bleeding. As I was laying there, he poured the rest of the beer right on my head. I breathed some up and started choking, coughing, disoriented like I just got rolled by a wave. The dude and his friend walked away from me laughing.

I can't remember much of what happened the rest of the night.

I know I tried to call Leticia. I know I drank more.

And I know I woke up this morning on the Copacabana beach.

AND NOW I was walking up the Avenida, trying to piece together every-thing that happened yesterday. Trying to remember, trying to remember. Maybe this drinking thing was a problem for me. And I couldn't even look at my phone to see if I had actually talked to Leticia. That would've been so embarrassing, to call her totally drunk begging her back after she spoke to me with such finality just earlier that day. After she laid that breakup talk on me thick.

But it was just talk was what it was, just talk.

Or was it? Maybe she meant it.

Nah.

I went to scratch my eye and as soon as I touched it, pain shot through me. It must be bruised. Great, I had a black eye. But I was gonna be ok, I thought, as I walked up the Avenida, and cut into the inside streets around Paula Freitas and turned up Nossa Senhora. It's gonna be ok because I got Rachel now. I was gonna hang out with her tonight. She could love me. She could love me. And who knows, I could use a change of scenery. Get out of this miserable city. See more of the United States. Where was she from? Pittsburgh? I could be a Pittsburgh dude. Little family out there. Kids playing in the snow. I could finish school there! Who knows! I could be a lawyer or something! Forreal. Rather than sitting here month after month getting scorched by this infernal sun with nowhere to go, nowhere to go, having to live with the fact that Leticia wouldn't ever want me back, wouldn't ever have my kid.

But I shouldn't give up!

All I gotta do is change! That's what she said.

I just gotta find some purpose. Make amends with some people maybe.

I was wandering toward home without even realizing it, well half realizing it, and maybe that was my path. I had to go home. I had to make amends with my family, and as soon as Leticia saw how I healed with my grandma and Lucia and Marta, she would want me back. She would think, Oh ok, this is a dude that's really dedicated to his family. I would stop drinking maybe, I would study maybe. She would think, Ok this dude is going somewhere. She'd think, Daniel is smarter than I thought! He read a book I read! I would read a book maybe. That would impress her. My sister had some books she could lend me. I could finally read The Da Vinci Code. I think I stole that for her one time. Leticia would be so impressed with me!

I was too quick to wallow!

Suddenly I noticed all the old landmarks around me, the signposts that would light my way home every night when I was a kid. I would tread this exact path home from late night pickup games on the beach, from the covert parties down by the edge of the water. The Pão de Açúcar supermarket. The vague boarded up building at the end of the block that replaced the strip club that provoked all my childish fascination. The Nossa Senhora church where the families slept and begged and looked after their kids on the steps. The park where the dudes played dominoes and cards from dawn to dusk. The same park where I fell off the swing when Lucia was pushing me too high and I landed and broke my hand.

I was going home.

They would welcome me back with warmth and shocked surprise.

I was going home!

Things were better than I thought! Now I had options. Leticia would want me back, and if she didn't, I would be devastated, but I would have Rachel. And now I would have my family to fall back on, my people.

It was going to be ok!

Tonight was gonna be fun!

I would charge my phone and I would call Mateus and call Rachel and we would turn up!

I picked up my pace and soon enough I was in front of the supermarket where grandma worked and I could see my building, 683 Nossa Senhora, and right out front was Seu Zé and the Donas bullshitting, gossiping. They watched me approach with flabbergasted faces and a shiver went through me, thinking of walking back into that building.

Daniel! Seu Zé yelled.

Oh my god, you look terrible! Dona Celeste said.

He must be back for the family reunion! Dona Dalia said and they both cracked up.

They were clowning me for being gone so long, so I chuckled.

Daniel, how are you? Seu Zé asked.

Good. How about you? Tough loss huh?

Yes it was, I loved your grandpa very much.

I said, Yeah. Embarrassed that I had been talking about the Flamengo game. It hadn't even occurred to me to mention gramps.

I moved to walk through the door and Dona Dalia said, Before you go upstairs! I forgot to tell your sister this! Did you hear they caught the favela kids who decapitated that woman at the Christ?

No. I didn't hear that.

Yeah, Dona Celeste said, they tracked them down to Alemão, the police had a nice clean operation but you know how those people are over there, they started shooting at them! And of course, the police had to shoot back! But they ended up killing the kids. One was twelve, the other was fourteen.

Ok, I said, thanks for telling me. Not knowing what to do with news like that.

Just wait, Dona Dalia added. I bet you these people come out full force for New Year's Eve. Get their revenge! You won't catch me dead on the beach. All those kids are gonna get together and start robbing and stabbing. You just wait! There's gonna be a big arrastão! You be careful tonight. I hope the police are prepared.

Ok, I said, wanting the conversation to end.

Don't forget to tell your sister, she reminded me.

And I walked through the door. Seu Zé called out, Good luck! behind me and I went right for the stairs, knowing in my heart that the elevator was broke. Anxiety was sprouting hard beneath my ribs and chest, making it tough to breathe.

I willed myself to walk up the stairs. It was time. I was going home.

Grandpa was dead and I was going home.

One step at a time.

I got to our floor and pushed through the loud swinging wooden door to the common area between the four apartments. I was delirious with apprehension. I felt the knife in my pocket. I wanted to scream, freak out, do something crazy.

I could feel the knife in my pocket.

I could feel the bruise on my face, the sand on the back of my legs, the too big shirt hanging off me.

I walked to the door, 302 with the 2 fallen off. I could barely breathe.

Behind the door I could hear voices. Tones and timbres I wasn't used to. Who was here? Or had I been away so long I couldn't recognize my own people? But I stopped thinking. Like submerging yourself in the late winter ocean, you just gotta do it, I told myself as I heaved my arm up to the door and knocked.

I knocked again and the voices stopped.

I could hear ankles cracking as she walked to the door. Lucia.

Who's there?

Daniel.

She opened the door and looked at me with a grim contorted expression that could've been a smile.

You actually came. I can't believe you came.

And then I heard her voice. No, it couldn't be.

Lucia, I said. Who's here?

MARTA, YOU CAME. I spent those first bleak hours poked and prodded and dried out like a codfish about to be stuffed into a cake, and I was sure I was in hell, but it can't be hell with you here, wearing that yellow dress you wore the day we met. But I'm in so much pain, these nurses must want me dead, tying down my wrists and ignoring my screams like I'm a caged beast! Back when I was young and stupid, I thought I beat all pain for good, the day I put on my hard shoes and my tattered suit and took a bus downtown to go look at the final carcass that abandoned me, my father, who I hadn't seen since I was a little kid. He only existed in a faded photograph of him and my mother on their wedding day, when they went down to the courthouse pressured and hasty on Saint John's Day in some frigid June. My father looked nervous and scrawny in an oversized borrowed suit and my mother stood next to him, leering devious like a leopard, the traces of a swollen belly under her white rag dress. And I would always ask, Mommy where's Dad? Why doesn't he ever come around? Don't worry about him! He's a nobody! He's poor and worthless and we're better off without him! Better off with her putting up a sheet in our dirt floor shack that stunk like a wet grave, a sheet that would separate us from the old lone mattress where she did things we didn't understand, and me and my brother and my sister would shudder in the corner like frightened toucans and pretend it was a game, the strange noises and shapes she made with every uniformed man in the city who would never be our father.

Though we hoped.

We hoped that one day, some gallant knight would stroll in and save us from our destitution, like in the story we always heard of our older sister, Otacilia, who was ten years older than me, fathered by some unseen blank when my mother was only twelve years old. My mother would sit up, still and quiet, when she told the story, as if she was reading from the bible. When Otacilia was fourteen, she was the most beautiful girl on the Ilha. And one day, while everyone was out on the street waving flags and cheering for President Vargas's parade, the chief of his security, the General, stopped and said, Her! I must have her! and my mother's eyes would flood with jubilant tears as she told us how, soon after, Otacilia was whisked away to live in a Copacabana mansion where she was dressed in the most lavish clothes and adorned with beautiful jewels. But where is this sister? Why can't we ever see her? We would never ask because if we did, my mother's warm remembrance would fade to fury. All we knew was that Otacilia had won. And that was the way to win, to be plucked away to plushness, or to be valiant and powerful like the General, who could salve away a woman's squalor by pointing his finger.

A stark standard, she made us understand, that my father never met.

My father, Marta, who on the morning I met you was lying cold on a metal hospital table, and I must have been the last name on a call sheet of the world that left him bereft because they called me down in the rain to look at the husked out skeleton of the me before me, and say, That's him, that disease worn rotten peel of a human who I only knew from rumors, rumors my mother spread so she wouldn't feel so bad dumping his life out with the morning trash, I had to say, That man who I never had a conversation with is my father. And after his death was notarized, I got on the bus to go home feeling hopeless, the world looking as desolate and fragile as my father's skull. Until I saw you, sitting there with that shy smile and those glittery brown eyes, striking me like savage darts, and I slid into the seat next to you despite the bus being as empty as a lonely funeral. I was twenty one, I had been with plenty of women, long drunken nights at the brothel until dawn, or neighborhood girls who, with a lie and a smile, you could get to sneak you through the window when their parents weren't home. I was blustering and handsome, with well worn tricks, but when I whispered my name to you, I was trembling. I knew you were different. I wanted to blow up my past and build a future on the rubble, a future devoted to Marta, Marta, Marta!

Everything fades doesn't it?

There you are looking at me like I'm an old fool in diapers, swollen and disgusting, nailed down to this bed like it's my cross, no, it's like I'm being spun around on a spit, roasted, I feel the hellfire nipping at me. I'm doomed, aren't I? Marta, I can't face whatever eternity has in store for me, I'm scared. I need a drink and I'm hurting and scared and these damn nurses, like the devil's agents! I wish they would untie my wrists so I could stroke your hair. Darling, darling. Do you remember our early days? My pulse would pound heartattack fast everytime you spoke. On our first date, I used a month's salary to take you out to dinner, wearing the same suit I wore on the bus, and we had the best moqueca in town and stared at eachother, too nervous to speak, but on the walk home, you reached out to hold my hand and said, You didn't have to do that, and you kissed me on the cheek. The only action I got from you for weeks! A peck here and there.

But I didn't care. Every other woman in the world stopped existing for me.

After ten dates you let me into your house, where your mother would hound us with her blistering rancor, and we would ignore her, close the door to your room, and lay on your bed, while you held me and rubbed my back, and the word love would creep into my brain and I'd recoil.

Because despite all I felt, I couldn't let go of my harsh days, all the early hardships you told me to tell you about, so we'd stay up all night, trading tragedies like it was relief. Nobody ever listened to me like that. I would talk so fast with my heart racing, crying, because I thought at any second you would cut me off like my mother used to and I would have to seal everything back inside and lock it away forever. I told you things I never spoke about again. Like how my mother would leave for days at a time, leaving my little siblings needy and hungry looking at me like abandoned owls. I didn't know how to take care of them. I would cook up tasteless rice and beans from the rations the nice neighbors gave us, and struggle to field their questions. When is Mommy coming home? Where does she go all the time? Until one day, my worst fears came true. I heard a knock on our door that was barely a door, it could only keep out big animals, capivaras and street dogs, it was useless against the rats and rat sized beetles. And I opened the door to the hot stink of the Baia and standing there like the devil himself was a cold gazed admiral with black eyes and a mouth screwed into a grimace.

Your mother committed suicide in Copacabana.

Was all he said, and left. My mother who despite everything, I loved so ardently, I would long for the moments when her ravage moods would cool and she would get quiet and whisper to me to come lay on her chest, and I would lay there as she stroked my head and sang. I forgot all her faults when I would hear that velvet voice and fall asleep comfortable and safe. To know it had meant so little to her! So little that she could choose to disappear from the world without a second thought. That she would choose oblivion over me, that she would leave me and my siblings all alone in the ocean of existence, her death like lead weights in our pockets. I felt like a hopeless little baby. How would I tell Fernando and Maria, who were laying on the mattress, still asleep after I got the news? I left home and wandered, lost, walking around Cocotá until the shadows on the trees got long, all the people in the neighborhood ignoring sullen João from the bad family. I thought about the paltry scraps of food left at home and what a nasty cruelty to have to mourn a dead mother on an empty stomach. But as I walked down our broken cobblestone road, I saw a pigeon hopping up and down the curb, flightless, feathers balding, with a crooked, swollen foot. I snatched it up, mean and hungry, and I snapped its neck on the street. I pretended he was me, weak and alone, and I killed him with pleasure and vengeance, and I went home with meat in my hands, sliced him up and tossed him into a pot with rotting mangoes and skinny onions and all we had left of our rice and beans. I told them Mommy was dead over our bad stew, and we spent the night huddled in the corner like sad sloths. When I told you those stories, Marta, it was like I was healed!

And my life started brightening dramatically.

I had you, and a month after my father died, I got a letter from a lawyer. He said to come to his office downtown, and it turned out my father had a will. He was bequeathing me his home in Ribeira and some money. A house! I was in shock, but I slowly came to realize that everything my mother told me was a lie. He left her. He never married again or had another family. He was a modest banker who just didn't want anything to do with his children. But in death, he was making it right. I went to see the house. It was five minutes away from the shack where we grew up. I couldn't believe it! This whole time, he was right there! The house was beautiful. It had two bedrooms and a kitchen and a little yard, bursting with wildflowers and strewn with jacas spilled from the neighbor's tree. I could've fainted from happiness, Marta. The first thing I did was run straight to you. Do you remember? I never let you see my shack because I was so embarrassed. But now! I had something to build my life on. I ran around town, but I couldn't find you at your house or at school or anywhere. And then I saw you coming out of the water after a long swim. I yelled, Marta! I love you! Will you marry me? You shouted back, Yes, yes. I will! How can that be the same João who lies here putrid and pissing myself, a garbage heap of a man, whimpering like a kicked dog? Life accumulates bitterly. You long for feelings that fleet before you can even catch them. You moved in and it was paradise, and soon we had a baby boy! One second he was fat and giggly, crying in the rickety crib we vultured from the trash, and the next he was coughing, quiet, dead. Marta, I can't, I can't

DID I fall asleep? You're still here. What was I talking about? Oh, my brother, Fernando. Did I tell you? How after my mother died I didn't know what to do, we needed money, so I started stealing. I would pickpocket on the bus and steal from stores, but I realized that having a partner could double my haul, so I taught my brother all my moves, everything, and we started going downtown with knives and taking purses from old ladies. It was bad, but it worked. For years it was all we had to do to get by. Until one day, when I was thirteen and Fernando was eleven. I took a wallet from this man, and he caught me, tried to grab me, but I took off running. Fernando was with me and he ran too. I turned right and he kept going straight. I heard a dull thud and brakes squeal. I couldn't stop though, the man was chasing me, so I ran all the way around the block and came back ten minutes later. When I came back, I saw my brother lying on the street with a bloody head, a crowd of people around him. I watched through a crack in the gathered crowd, as his chest gave one final heave, and he stopped breathing forever. Oh. Fernando. It's a mistake, isn't it? Naming children after ghosts? It's like pouring poison in a sapling's soil. They grow up, if they make it that far, already withered. After our boy died, the next day you were already different. Recoiling at my touch. Staying out all day. I didn't care though. I sulked and drank, drank until I blacked out and would come to in a brothel covered in drool and vomit and guilty fluids. I was so pitiful even my drinking buddies deserted me. I would go to the Dirty Foot, the bar I frequented like a church since I was twelve, and all my old pals would scatter like birds after a boom. And on an awful Saturday, barstuck by the rain, Ronaldo, the biggest loser I ever knew, who hung around the bar like a gnat, who had rotten teeth and a limp and a huge hanging belly, told me.

João, I saw her go home with him.

Who? Your wife. Marta? No, that can't be true. But he told me more and I realized I was living with a stranger. That there was some abyss separating the mysteries of your mind and mine. I thought we were everything to eachother, but I was wrong, wrong, wrong. I ran home and screamed and drank and broke bottles on the ground. I wanted to kill you. But it wouldn't have been killing you because the Marta I knew wouldn't have done that. She wouldn't have stuck a hot iron right through my heart. You humiliated me. I put us up in a beautiful house in a nice neighborhood and instead you wanted to go up the hill to some claptrap house to fuck some petty criminal. I'm sorry, forgive my language. Everything just hurts me again so clearly! This new lucidity bores a hole in my head, and all I can do is lay here and suffer. I'm dying, aren't I? Where will I go? What comes after, Marta? Is this it? Having to endure these memories like pitchforks pressed against my balls in this damn hospital room that's a cave where day and night don't exist.

Why do I have to remember everything now?

Like the first time you left me and turned me into a hopeless sobbing bastard who woke up suncrack early to open up a bottle of vagrant cheap cachaça and wander the house ranting and raving, sweating and smoking endless cigarettes, until it got dark and I would go to the brothel where the girls knew me, and they would say, Oh João, poor baby, and a different girl every night would rub my back as I slumped, weepy and pathetic, crying about my lost love. Did you know that? And that despondent cycle would've gone on forever, but you came back. On a sunny morning in June, when I woke up to a bed covered in cigarette ashes and spilled liquor and crusty shame, there you were, radiant. I was so happy I never asked any questions, and we fell into a second bliss, but deeper, because you chose me again, and you would never leave! I was on top of the world. I begged my job back at the airport, after I had sloughed off my duties in those wayward months. Even smelling those airplane diesel fumes was delicious knowing I had my Marta at home. And then you were pregnant! Which made us so apprehensive that we wouldn't even choose a name. But at the end of March, you gave birth to a beautiful girl, and I said, Maria!

A mistake. I should've learned my lesson the first time.

But I didn't want my sister's memory to disappear like she did. After my brother died, it was just the two of us. I never stole anything again after we buried him, in a meager plot marked by a stick and an old Vasco jersey. Instead I found hard jobs that kept me out from dark to dark, sweeping barracks and scrubbing floors. I would wake up in the middle of the night with my hands and feet cramping closed from the effort, but it was worth it, we had the little we needed, and I was even saving. I had a little wooden box where I would stuff the extra cash and Maria and I would stay up dreaming about all the things we were going to do with it. We were going to travel! Have a fancy dinner in Copacabana! Buy a car! But one day I limped home to our shack, and it was empty. Maria wasn't there even though she always came home right after school. Our paltry possessions were scattered as if the place had been ransacked. I looked beneath the pile of my few clothes where I hid the box. All the money was gone. My sister never came back. I was abandoned again! By my baby sister who I cared for and coddled, who'd gritted out life's harpoon wounds with me in a way I thought left us bonded forever. But no. She left me to learn about her life years later from a news report. She ran off to São Paulo and had a disastrous affair with a politician that ended when they poisoned themselves beneath a waterfall.

Fate lurks around like a shadow. We're just trains laid on invisible tracks.

But oh, Marta, I was so happy with our little girl! To watch her grow in those early days, every scream and laugh and diaper change was a new thrill because she was alive, we made her and she was alive! But everytime I would start to feel safe and happy, like we could make a sure life together, the rotten memory would creep up like a decayed tooth caught on an apple. I couldn't forgive you! I was never an angry man, but I started to scream. To grab you. Hate teeming through my hands.

And at least while I was drunk, my rage was loose and easy to express, but as soon as I sobered up, the sadness was so clear and immense I couldn't stand it for a second. I would die for a drink now, Marta, in this teetotaler hell, just a sip of that sweet cachaça, the sludge of erasure I slicked my life over with, but I have nothing to distract me now, I have to endure your stare like an inquisition.

These damn memories scald me!

You left again, Marta! How could you? You left me and a girl barely a year old. My lonely tamanduá nuzzled onto my chest. You abandoned us! I was so frightened, Maria burrowed deep into my heart like a mole, and I thought something terrible was going to happen, I would stay up all night watching her breathe, imagining a million deaths, diseases and car wrecks and villains prowling in the shadows, I would make myself sick with terror thinking about it. It was too much, Marta. After you broke my heart again, it was way too much. I couldn't fend off the despair. Days would pass without my notice, I was so deep in my grave pit of pity and alcoholic anguish. My mother and my sister both did it, so I thought, Why not? Why don't I end the thing too? Maria's eyes were my one tether to life. But somehow, six months after you left, you came back. I was so relieved to be unalone that I didn't even ask. Though the suspicions clawed at me. You gave me your long talks about God and forgiveness and the soul. But you had your growing secret. It would take me years to put the truth together. That you weren't brave enough to have a life with him, to claim his kid. Your mettle lapsed and you came running back. You didn't have the guts!

No! No! No!

I can't harbor hateful thoughts, Marta, after fifty years, when you're the only one at my bedside. It's goodbye isn't it? All this talk is wearing me down, I just need a drink, please, ask the nurses for something, to free me or feed me. I'm finished. Time passes. Life accumulates bitterly. The worst horror becomes as mundane as waiting room wallpaper. I lived, with a smile plastered on my drunk face, with two goofy, smiley girls in pigtails, while the dumb neighborhood yokels thought I didn't know. Always with the same joke mocking me and my parents. What do you get when you cross a pansy and a suicide? A cuck! As if I didn't wake up everyday to my glaring shame calling me Dad. Though for a while, we played house and it was nice. I liked it more than I let on, living in feigned ignorance with my girls. Those long days teaching them how to swim at the Engenhoca beach. We'd stay out laughing until the sun set over the waves, and on the way home we'd get ice cream and I'd watch the chocolate melt down their hands while they gossiped about their schoolfriends.

They were so funny, Marta! Do you remember?

But my laziness and my drinking started to tighten our lives like added notches on a belt. I lost my job. I started to lie and say I was out working, but really I was just borrowing money and accumulating debts. So I decided to concoct a plan. I tracked down my older sister, Otacilia, and I wrote her a letter. I asked her if she wanted to meet her nieces. I prostrated myself and told her about our meager life, appealed to her rich woman's sense of charity, begged for her gracious pity. She wrote me back! She said she would love to meet us! You were all so surprised I had an older sister, but I couldn't tell you that story, I didn't want to paint her as a glimmering faraway constellation because I would've been embarrassed for you to compare her to me, to think there was opulence so close in my bloodline. It would've been another humiliation on the heap that left me motionless, like a puddle pooling diseased mosquitoes. But we got all dressed up to go to Copacabana to endure a stuffy meal and spend the day at the beach, getting lambuzled with sand we'd track back on that long dull bus ride, our pockets stuffed with my sister's money.

Of course, it didn't work out like that.

My sister looked old and ugly. It turned out she hadn't married any General. Just some fat friend of his. They kept their distance and flinched from our words as if we had rancid breath. I was surprised. Why did she even invite us if they were going to act like that? But she pulled me aside and I found out. She told me that our mother had been begging to see her, on that awful day so long ago. Otacilia rejected her. She sawed down the family tree and wasn't interested in some humble stump. She didn't expect that our mother would. She couldn't even say the words. Nor did she have an apology. She just handed me an envelope full of cash, drenched in guilt. And then she gave us a tour. Her mansion was like my mother told it, a castle from an old story. Gilded walls, servants, and paintings. A room with fifty filthy squawking birds. Little Nara, who wouldn't avoid petting the mangiest street dog, reached out and touched one. Marta! My sister said that word, and I was done pretending. She salted the wound of my shame in front of everyone, and it changed everything. The retracted claws of my hate and anger were out. Nara wasn't mine and you were going to pay but

I CAN'T stay awake. Will you stay with me until the end? You almost look like Maria standing there. I remember, the day after we came back from my sister's, I took her out to the botequim. And we sat there and she sipped guaraná while I threw back shots, and I told her how you had abandoned us. How because of your lust and negligence, I almost killed myself! She was only ten, and she never looked at you the same. But now I had a companion in my ire. It became a competition. Your daughter versus mine. When your mother came to die in our house, and we had to decide who would sleep in the makeshift cot in the kitchen, it became a vicious brawl. I said that Nara should sleep there because that was what she deserved, a cot in a hot kitchen with no fan. I said awful things, Marta. Things all I can do now is regret, afflicted by this poor old boozy dying cough, betrayed by time and a bad fate that festered with the years. Everything feels so silly! It could've all been different. I remember when the girls were teenagers. I never told you this. I was at the Dirty Foot in the middle of the afternoon on a weekday. I lost another job and I was lying about it. I was alone because all my drinking buddies deserted me, it was just me and the bartender in the dim light of the bar, when another man walked in. He sat down, and we got to talking. He knew his soccer, he was a Vascaíno. We drank and drank and laughed about women and betrayal and the nasty luck that brought us low. We were at the bar for hours, and my stomach hurt from laughing so hard. I thought I found a best friend! And I realized I hadn't even gotten his name.

I'm João, I said.

I'm Marcelo.

It hit us both at the same time, like a gut punch. We pounced on eachother. We fought for what felt like hours. I smashed beer bottles into his skull and kicked his balls and poked his eyes and he pulled my thinning hair and stomped my ribs while the puny bartender tried to pull us off eachother. We ended in a bloody sweatdrenched huff, two loser cucks. I was gonna kill him the next day! But I needed to go home to rest. He must've sensed it because he skipped town, and on the way to São Paulo, a drunk driver did the job for me. And I had to endure you, Marta, wearing black and wailing like a widow. I was sad too! He could've been my friend, and in a cruel twist of fate, he was the man who ruined my life. No, no. I ruined my life, didn't I? Holding on to my meaningless pride and pointless bloodlines. I'm hurting now, and I deserve it. Time is slippery. Soon our girls were women and your hair was graying, and it was like I missed it all. Soon they were bringing men home, where I could see myself reflected. Maria brought home that american with eyes like the devil, who looked down on our life and yelled at her, and I asked her one day, while eating pastels from a roadside stand, Does he hit you? She just looked at me. Why do you tolerate that? She laughed and said, It's how I grew up. A dagger! It's an impossible job to bring up these kids, we're so poisoned with our own sins and faults that we infect them without even realizing it.

But, Marta, we could've been better. I could've been better.

Why did I let my anger ruin me? Because everything was fine. We had our girls, grown, healthy, beautiful. Maria gave us grandchildren, and that awful man was never around, until he came back to move us to Copacabana so I could die, marinated in the stink of Otacilia's and my mother's corpses. I'm bitter, but there we were, in a three bedroom apartment in a neighborhood near the beach, living with our grandchildren. And all I did was get meaner, sicker, drunker. All my memories like islands way out in the distance. There was that day I woke up, hung over as usual, and I went into the bathroom and looked at myself in the mirror, and I couldn't recognize João. The iguana skin drooping off his neck, and two teeth marks like a snake bite in the middle of his forehead. The image flashed through my mind of Maria standing there in front of me, saying something I couldn't remember. And I. Oh, Marta. Her face was bloody and her teeth were on the floor. I stared at an evil man in that mirror. Maria was my darling favorite. My true daughter! And I hurt her like that? I decided I would bury that memory forever. No apology, nothing. I would tomb it up in the recesses of my heart. I started to destroy myself. The cachaça was no longer a pleasure. I would drink thirty beers and my liver would throb so bad it would leave me breathless. I didn't tell you anything. I couldn't talk to you anymore. My mind was a muddy tumult of emotions and all I wanted to do was drown it out. I would smoke and drink and smoke and drink, hoping my heart would burst.

And now I have to lay here, suffering clear, a spotlight on my wickedness.

I deserve it. I'm finally dying, damned, like I thought I was years ago when I started to shit blood and my balls swole up and it was a daily agony. One day I passed out drunk trying to smoke a cigarette out the bathroom window and fell into the bathtub, and I thought that was it, but Daniel found me there, lying like a turtle on its back, bleeding out of my head, and he cared for me. You cared for me. You didn't give up. You didn't want me to die. You took me to doctors so they could bore me with their obvious advice I didn't listen to because I didn't want to stop doing anything. I liked feeling my mind deteriorate in my skull. My grandchildren became hazy. Everything started to slip away. Then Nara moved into a penthouse apartment the drug dealer bought her, so at least you didn't have to sneak visits up on the hill any longer to see

Martinha, the granddaughter I couldn't tolerate because she reminded me of your betrayal. Everything hurt too deeply. Nara would invite us nonstop for dinner, parties, days in the park, she even took me to Maracanã to see Vasco play Flamengo, so that I would have a chance to get to know her husband, but I thought he was ugly and arrogant and I interpreted everything he said as a slight. Flamengo beat us 2–0 and he cheered. Out in the parking lot, I said something awful and wrong and pushed him, trying to start a fight, and he just said, Oh João, embarrassed for the pathetic old man. I didn't want any love, I didn't want any kindness, I just wanted to be finished.

I'm a fool! A fool who would give everything to have life back.

It feels too fast. Is this really it? I'll never get to mend these ruptured threads. Narinha, Narinha, bananinha. I let her down. Her husband wasn't so bad, but he put her up in the most beautiful apartment I had ever seen, which was a direct humiliation because I could never provide for my family, and this damn criminal was rubbing it right in my face. I refused to go until that New Year's Eve, when you begged me like it was the last chance for all of us to reconcile, to live out what was left of our lives in some semblance of togetherness. The whole family dressed up and gathered for a feast. I'll admit, Marta, I was excited like a teenager. I put on a tie. You were dressed up and gorgeous, and I kissed you on the lips, the first time I did that in years. We walked over together, me and you and Lucia and Daniel and Maria. I thought, Is this what my life could be like now? We stood around the massive living room drinking wine and laughing, listening to music. The first time in forever that drinking was making me happy. And Nara pulled me aside. Dad, I'm so happy you came. I love you. When she said that, I loved her too! With all my heart. But I couldn't muster it. I couldn't apologize. I just said, Happy New Year, and touched her meekly on the shoulder. We sat down to eat and the intercom kept buzzing. Who is it? Who is it? Everybody ignored it. There was a sudden sharp bang on the door. It got louder and louder. Police! They started yelling. Everything was dashed in an instant. They threw my Nara down and handcuffed her, and all

I could see was my girl in pigtails building sandcastles. Marta! I didn't want any of that to happen. I didn't want him to be murdered by the police in front of his daughter. It was horrible! But the next morning while everyone sat around our apartment shocked and rattled, I laughed in your face because it was the final affirmation of my victory. You lost. Your daughter was a criminal! So what I headbutted my daughter and knocked her teeth out? I must've been a good father because your daughter was going to prison! I was wrong, I was wrong, I was wrong. We had our most brutal fight in years. You tried to tell me Maria turned her in. You blamed Maria for everything. It was our old war all over again. Your daughter versus mine. But they were both our daughters. Two days later Maria announced she was leaving, she'd finally found a man who would marry her and she was going to be with him. Are you taking your children? we asked her. No. They were our responsibility now. Why, Maria! Don't leave! I yelled at her. If you leave you're going to kill your mother! But really I meant she would kill me. I couldn't take it. Two daughters gone in the blink of an eye. You're a bad mother! A bad mother? she said. Don't you realize I'm leaving because of you? You ruined my entire life. I hate you. You mean nothing to me. Nothing. And she just walked away like what she said was true. I couldn't even tell you that, Marta. How did she grow so brutal and cold? Our girl who would lay on my chest and whisper that she loved me, who danced and cried with me when we watched Vasco win the championship and she was pregnant with Daniel. My coffin was nailed shut the day she said that. I watched her leave, her son's anger hot like a summer sun, and her daughter gripping on to her, as if by grabbing the brim of her dress tightly enough, she could get her to stay, and it was the scene of my abandonment that had been happening again and again since the moment I was born, betrayed relentlessly by women and time, oh Marta! I feel it now, my leaves have drifted from me, all, but you cling still, and I'm old and old and sad and old, waiting for life's last wheeze to rack my lungs and whisk me off to hell's welcome where I'll have to accept my damn damnation once and for all, oh Marta! I'm sorry! these petty pointlessnesses I filled my days with, I misunderstood everything, this short samba of my life was a wasted moment, and I'm scared of the other side, Marta! Marta! Marta! I'm just a bumpkin, I don't deserve any pity, but it's here, I hear the Ilha wind rustling the palm trees and there you are, and everything is getting soft and slow and bright, like your eyes, oh Marta, all these evenings, ours, remember me sweetly, oh I feel the waves lapping at our feet, let's just close our eyes for a short while, and let's sleep.

ON MY FIRST day off in weeks, sick with sleeplessness, I was in the passenger seat of a car, headed to the airport. My mom, who I'd been in
contact with all week, who had been shockingly and suspiciously kind
and ingratiating, had sent me money and told me to hire a driver to
go pick her up. I hired a man named Alexandre, who was blabbing
nonstop about everything, from his wife's gout, to his hundred year old
grandmother's death, to seemingly every incident he'd ever seen on the
news. I was trying to be nice and attentive, but I was exhausted. Last
night I had a fight with my grandma. We never fought, ever. But when
I finally told her about my mother's return, she was furious, and she
snapped back a sharp, vituperative reproach.

—Grandma! I said. I couldn't believe she was yelling at me.

—I'm sorry, Lucia, but I won't let your mother back into this house.
Not after everything that happened.

—This isn't your house, grandma. My father bought this. This is our
house. It's my decision as much as yours.

—Your father! That man was no father to you!

We both got silent.

—She's coming tomorrow, and I'm going to bring her over here. She wants to see us. She feels bad about everything, grandma. I think she's genuinely sorry.

I felt pathetic, going out on a limb for my mother, who until this week couldn't have cared less if either of us dropped dead. But I believed her. I thought there was a genuine reconciliation in her tone and, foolishly maybe, I was willing to risk getting burned if it meant having my mother back. I was upset at my grandma too, we'd been on unsure footing since our conversation on my birthday. Plus, her whole moral core was bound to a principle of endless forgiveness and unconditional love, yet here she was, doubting her daughter's intentions, casting all her words with an uncharitable pallor, and then, to cement her victory in our argument, she tells me she's been having dreams of her old friend Gloria from the Ilha issuing vague fiery warnings, and that she's seen grandpa's ghost wandering around the house.

—Something bad is going to happen if you let your mother into this house.

What was I supposed to say? You're crazy, grandma, there's no such thing as ghosts! Which I wasn't sure I believed. She talked about her visions with such conviction. Sometimes, when we were young, she would have people come to the house, and she would give them messages from their dead siblings and parents and lovers. I saw the startled surprise on their faces often enough that my skepticism was well softened. There was nothing I could say to her in response. I just went to my room, without even saying goodnight. Marta slept with her, and I stayed up all night, tormented, wishing the conversation had gone differently, feeling eerie and spooked by her warnings.

But she wasn't going to deter me. Rottenly and with anguish, I missed my mother. I hated her for leaving, as much as I tried to dispel hate from my life, and I used her as an easy blame for every bad thing that had ever happened to me, but if she changed, I could change. I was open to it. I could understand why she left. My father never married her, never gave her the life she really yearned for. She wanted a comfortable material life, and she wanted to escape the childhood she endlessly complained about, a country she despised. That was easy to understand. She found an american who gave her what she wanted, and she took the opportunity. Oh Lucia, he's so smart. He's a professor. I think you two would get along! Both of you love your books.

She never even told us about him until she was ready to marry and move. Apparently they had a whole secret online relationship for months and months. He's from Ohio, Lucia. You have to come and visit me! Are you staying there forever? What about us? I never asked. She flooded us with her future glories and all we were allowed to do was smile and support her. Time passes. She must feel some guilt about it, but those feelings congeal and get hardened by inertia, they become a little frozen block inside of you, impossible to break. She needed a sharp pick to start to shatter it, and that's what my phone call provided. I could understand her. I wanted to be good, I wanted something beyond the clumped calamity of my family's choices, and I felt like that started with having a relationship with my mother. Couldn't my grandma understand that? What else was I supposed to do?

There wasn't the slightest sliver of rancor or viciousness inside my grandma, until it came to Maria. The topic of my mother, one we avoided unremittingly much as I often wanted to broach it, would evaporate her saintly aura in a feral instant. My grandmother was irreparably wounded, she loved me and Daniel extremely, and she would never forgive my mother for what she did. And of course, there was Nara. My grandma firmly believed, though we only talked about it maybe twice, that my mother snitched on Nara and got her arrested, and Antonio killed.

It was a grave charge that I took as scripture in those early years after she left. But the more I thought about it, the less likely it seemed. My mother met this Larry guy on facebook months and months before that day, and he was the real reason why she left. Nara's arrest just pushed her over the edge. Anyway, it's not like the feds weren't already looking for them. How much could my mother even have done? That was six years ago to the day. New Year's Eve. Maybe my grandma just thought it was a bad sign that she was returning today. I didn't think she'd turned Nara in. It would've taken a truly evil person to do that. My mom might've been negligent and unwittingly cruel and narcissistic, but she wasn't evil. I hoped.

—Did you hear that? Alexandre said.

—Hmm?

—Crazy huh?

—What?

—There's been riots all over Jacarezinho. Yesterday the cops found those kids who murdered that family at the Christ, and there was a shootout, and they killed the two kids and a few other people. I think one of the cops died too. And since then it's been chaos! More shootouts, they've been setting cop cars on fire. It's a mess.

—Oh my god.

—I know! You just wait. One day this violence is gonna spill out from the favelas. We're gonna be in trouble.

I didn't respond. Flippant talk about violence and policing and poverty, all those impossible problems, left a hopelessness perched on my heart that was hard to remove.

—Anyway! You got plans for New Year's?

I told Marta that this year, I would take her to the roof to watch the fireworks. It was my little secret spot. You could get up there through the staircase on the thirteenth floor. I used to go read and sit with the vultures under the full blaze of the sun, looking out at the Christ statue, his arms open in wide welcome, the shadow of his heft covering the colorful waves of the Cantagalo homes.

—I would avoid going to the beach, I'll say that. Looks like it's gonna storm anyway, probably won't even be able to see any fireworks. Plus, I don't know. Betcha there's gonna be lots of problems this year. Thieving! Thuggery! I wouldn't risk it if I were you!

I thanked him for the advice. The last two years I didn't go to the beach. Back when I was still partying, I'd go with my friends and get trashed while my grandparents stayed home with Marta, soaking in somber remembrance of Nara's arrest, and Daniel would go out and do whatever he did. He called me yesterday, bizarrely. He sounded hammered and was going on and on saying he was sorry, begging forgiveness. I guess it was rectification week in the Cunha family. I told him that he should come by the apartment tomorrow afternoon. He said he would be there, but Daniel's word was as flimsy as a cheap plastic cup. There was infinite proof. When I first started working at the restaurant, I was saving up to buy a pair of Nike running shoes, and I would pass this store on Nossa Senhora and see them in the window, salmon pink with bright blue flashes. They were four hundred reals, an extravagance, but Daniel told me he knew this dude who sold them for way cheaper, so I gave him two hundred reals, my first month's salary. For weeks he told me, The shoes are coming, don't you worry sis! but the assurances slowly disappeared, and he finally stopped talking about it. Of all his petty offenses, I thought that one was the most flagrant because he knew how hard I worked and how much I wanted those shoes, and he swindled me without a second thought.

I didn't tell him that mom was coming back. I was worried. I didn't know how he would react to seeing her. Out of all of us, Daniel's reaction was the most explosive. After he came back from the United States, he grew into a moody, unpredictable teenager, prone to big flashes of rage. When our mother sat us down and explained that she was leaving, told us her whole incredible story of falling in love, Daniel screamed at her, screamed at her like he was a grown, pissed off man about to grab her by the throat and throw her into the wall. She calmed him down, but then he just sealed up and didn't speak another word to her until she was at the doorstep prested to leave. She said, I love you Daniel, and he said, Fuck you bitch, earning gasps from my grandparents.

That was the last time he spoke to her until about eight months later, during a period when I was still speaking to her. She called to talk to Daniel on his birthday, September 1st. I answered the phone because he wouldn't, and she begged me to get him on the line, to get him to talk to her. I had it on speakerphone, and he was listening in. He refused. She said that she was planning on coming back to visit us. He snapped. He screamed, If you ever come back here, I'll fucking kill you! It was teenage, masculine bluster, but still startling. My mother was at a loss for words. He stormed off, and I said weakly that he didn't mean it. We ended the conversation awkwardly and she didn't call much after that, so the threat was still suspended in the ether, unretracted, though of course, Daniel was no murderer, but he was immature and untamed, and having him around our mother would make my peace project exponentially more difficult.

ALEXANDRE DROPPED me off at the entrance of the airport, and he told me to text him when we were ready to get picked up. I reached the door at the same time as a very old man with wet weary eyes and a hunched, labored gait, and obviously I thought of my grandfather, so much so that I couldn't stand looking at him for more than a second. I opened the door and he walked in at a turtlelish pace while I thought about the fact that my grandfather did not exist anymore, and that my last memory was of him lying feeble on a stretcher with the awful distance of death in his eyes. A young airport worker walked by.

—Damn! I didn't know we were hiring baddies to work the door!

I looked up and I was holding the door for nobody, the old man was nowhere to be seen, so I walked inside, my sleepy weariness tugging at me sinisterly. I went over to the information desk, and the guy told me the flight I was looking for was delayed, it would probably be another hour. I stifled the urge to scream and strangle him, which would've been a severe misplacement of my impatience, and I thought, uncharitably, that my mother would take glee in me having to wait around, she liked when the world revolved around her inconsiderate clock, when she left a deep indent on the fabric of events.

I bought a pastel and a coffee, and I found a table way in the corner where I could sit alone and sulk at the stagnancy of time. I pulled out my phone. The curiosity about my mother's husband that I stamped down for six years was pushing back at me, and I realized I hardly knew anything about him, so I looked up his instagram. He taught at Franciscan University in Steubenville, Ohio, and he toured the country as a christian motivational speaker, whatever that entailed, but his big success was with these youtube videos where he blathered on about God and faith and life with the creepy smarm of a cool priest. Fifty three thousand followers. Pretty good for a niche that I didn't know anyone had any demand for. His feed was lame mostly, clips and long grateful posts after his events, not much of my mother on there. Only one picture I could find, from Thanksgiving, where she was standing with her arm around him smiling, two blond girls and a golden retriever at their side, everyone in matching clothes. That picture gave me a dreadful, jealous feeling, and I clicked out feeling dull, old, and rustcovered, traded for sheeny, better versions of me. I googled him. I scrolled down, and one result, deep down the page, caught my attention. Larry Johnson Exposed. I clicked it.

It was an anonymous post on a catholic blog. They were sharing this girl's story. She posted it on facebook and then deleted it, but they were preserving it here. Her name was Ellen Maguire. She wrote that two years ago, when she was attending Franciscan University, Larry was appointed as her spiritual advisor. They began meeting weekly and quickly developed a rapport. Larry was kind and funny and knowledgeable. They started to open up to eachother more and more. Larry told her how his first wife died of cancer and how he doubted God, and Ellen shared with him that she had been sexually assaulted, and he was supportive, but as their friendship developed, he grew increasingly inappropriate, texting her that she was beautiful, and that if he wasn't married and she wasn't a student they could be together. She batted down those comments discreetly because she valued him as a friend and an advisor. He started asking her to hang out outside of school. She thought it was weird, and she mostly rejected the offers, but one night she accepted a dinner invitation, where Larry started making overt physical advances, and feeling enormous pressure, she went with him to a hotel and they had sex. She was shattered and felt like Larry took complete advantage of her, and she reported it repeatedly to the university, but they ignored her. Word got out and the other students ostracized her. She ended up dropping out and moving back to Pennsylvania, where she lived with her parents, depressed and jobless.

Oh my god. I tried to look up more information, but that was the only post about Larry that mentioned anything of the sort. Ellen Maguire's facebook was deactivated. Oh my god. I was sick. I wondered if my mother knew. Was that how she needed to live, overseen by dangerous men? I felt bad for her. I hoped she wouldn't bring him, but I knew she would. But what if this was the whole reason she'd kept away for so long? Because this man resented her and wouldn't allow for her freedom? He'd snagged his brasilian trophy and clutched it close. Still, I was horrified. What attracted my mother to these baleful shadows of men who razed and ruined all the supple life in their path?

I put my pastel down half eaten. I walked to the bathroom calmly, stood over the toilet, and made myself puke, something I hadn't done in two years, but the pastel wasn't sitting right, and then I sat there, frustrated. It didn't mean anything. I still had control over my actions. But it felt appropriate that I was here puking out a pastel, the way I did on the night my mother flew off to the United States without saying goodbye. Why didn't she say goodbye to me? Did she not love me? Or was it just too difficult to leave? There were a million interpretations to every action. Why did it have to be so complicated to know anybody! There was a secret life happening behind everyone's eyes that would always remain mysterious, and all you could do was guess.

I washed my hands, took a deep breath, and recomposed myself. I looked at my phone and I saw that I missed a text. My mom's plane had landed fifteen minutes ago. I walked out of the bathroom and it felt like the energy inside the airport had changed, everything was dimmer, as if an immense storm had rolled in and dark blotted the daylight. I went and stood amidst the waiting throng of signs and smiles, watching for my passenger, my body stumped by a heart shaking dread. I couldn't account for any passing time. I didn't know how many people emerged, how many shouts and reunions I didn't notice, but reality outran apprehension, and I knew the moment had arrived.

There she was, bending the close knit fabric of our collective attention around her like a planet. She was dressed in all black, her eyes covered in black sunglasses, her loud heeled steps reverberating in the silence like a drum beat, the wavy rivulets of her nightblack hair falling down her head and chest like a funeral veil. My mouth went dry. Here was the defining absence of my whole life, suddenly springing out of the void like a statue molded from a molten vat of lost moments and lost words and abandoned hope. It was as if my fear's monster forged deep in the earth burst free from the dirt when I least expected it and took the form of a pretty middle aged woman, who, spotting me in my frozen state, granted me a faint blossom of a look, nearly a smile, revealing her new shock white teeth. Her whole grim aspect affected me so powerfully that I didn't even notice, trailing behind her, a big dopey looking man in a sweatdarkened dress shirt that was buttoned all the way up and tied with a thick red tie. He was tall and burly and had blue eyes. He didn't look unlike my father. He was dragging two suitcases and looking already finished with Rio de Janeiro. They appeared in front of me like a nightmare.

—Lucia.

She wrapped her arms around me, and I couldn't help but hug back, noticing that she didn't smell like my mother, she smelled acrid and bitter, like the house of a strange cousin, but whatever commitment I had to coldness and making her earn back my love dissolved, and I was a little kid, pining for her affection. I didn't say anything.

—You look beautiful.

I was staring at her, struck dumb like a biblical character.

—This is my husband, Larry.

—Nice to meet you Luchia!

He reached out to hug me and I put my hand out to shake, very unbrasilian of me, but he was the last person in the airport I wanted to touch.

—Hi.

The first word I spoke, and it was to him. I was desperate for spontaneous combustion. I didn't say anything else, and they were looking at me like I was malfunctioning.

—The car is waiting for us outside.

—Thank you, Lucia. I appreciate you coming to get us.

She touched my arm. She had a glazed, newly christian look, one of glossy kindness that kind of freaked me out, because maybe she really had changed, and like the freshly converted, her past sins were nothing more than a few potholes to be paved over and ignored, but I was no inquisitioner, I wasn't here to press and punish. Larry walked toward the door, and me and my mother trailed behind. She hooked her arm around mine.

—I'm sorry about grandpa. I'm sorry I wasn't here.

—It's ok.

—No, it's not okay ! I missed too much, Lucia. I missed too much. I'm sorry.

Was I stupid? She sounded so sincere. I didn't say anything, and we walked outside, into the diffident day, cowering in the blistering December sun. Larry, the target of the sun's invidious assault, was standing there ooofing, heatworn, his unsunscreened face beginning to burn purple. Serendipitously, Alexandre pulled up to the curb, and it hit me, like a splash of cold water, that his car was the same exact car that Antonio used to drive. An inconspicuous, shabby black Fiat. It jolted me like a bad omen, a pigeon smashing against a closed apartment window. My mom never had anything nice to say about Antonio, in fact her malice and resentment was so heavy when she called him a thug and a favelado and worse that the only reasonable explanation was spurned love, but if she recognized the car, she didn't say anything. We crammed the luggage into the trunk and I got into the backseat next to her, Larry in the front. There were so many words burbling up that I just wanted to spill to see what stuck, but I didn't want to speak english, it felt unsafe, almost, with that man in the front listening, I wanted to use portuguese as a sanctuary where I could speak with my mother, honestly and unbothered, but she led, in their language.

—How is Daniel?

—He's good. He said he might come by later.

—That would be so great. All of us together again, won't that be nice? Maybe we can go see the fireworks tonight.

—Yeah.

—How's your grandma?

—Fine.

—I tried to call her a few times, but she didn't answer me. I wanted to give her my condolences about grandpa. I'm sure she's heartbroken.

—You called her?

—I've called her a lot over the years, Lucia. She never wanted to speak to me.

Grandma never even told me my mother called her. In fact, she said just the opposite, that the barren silence between them was mostly my mother's fault. Had she lied to me?

—Can you turn on the AC? Larry asked the driver.

Alexandre met my eye in the rearview mirror like, What did he say?

—It's broken.

—Too bad, Larry said, beads of sweat flying off his face.

WE DROVE until traffic accumulated around us. Kids walked through selling biscoito Globo and water. Larry's window was wide open, but when a kid leaned in and yelled, You don't want no cookies turista? he jumped back and tried to roll it up quickly. My mom handed him twenty reals and asked him to buy a water. He waved the money around in the air like a matador shouting, Water! Water! and a kid came over, snatched the bill, and gave him a bottle. Larry was exasperated.

—Water costs twenty bucks here?

I almost laughed. I thought it was very strange how foolish and ridiculous he seemed juxtaposed with the awful darkness I knew he was capable of, and not only that, he was a rich american, so he was likely the most powerful person in this traffic jam. I wondered how much my mother really knew and what she silently tolerated, and I wondered what this landscape looked like through Larry's eyes. He must've seen it akin to how my father did. The North Zone spread out scabrous and unkempt, kids playing in trash heaps and sharing puddles with skinny horses, but when you were a man like him, this was all an opportunity. You could be a savior. Maybe you knock up one of those poor broads, put them up in a nice apartment, dip out shining and heroic, make an occasional visit. It was like an investment, if it didn't turn out as lucrative as you hoped, no skin off your back, on to the next one.

I stared out the window and thought of Marta. She was really shaken up by what we'd witnessed the other day. Her nightmares, already persistent and intense, had amplified. I had to hold her especially tight. What good was that? Sometimes I thought about how little I was prepared for such serious, significant duties, keeping a child safe, when everyone I knew personally who was thrust into that role failed and absconded. Well, Nara and Antonio didn't have much of a choice in the matter. Or did they? From what I knew, Antonio could've quit, but instead he grew his business, he branched into gambling, the Jogo do Bicho, knowing the threat he and his family faced from dangerous competitors, and of course the police. And then there was Nara.

We visited her in prison once, four years ago. It was a disaster. Me and Daniel and Marta. We took an all night bus to Paraná to get there. Marta didn't sleep, she was so excited. I was giddy too. Childishly, I expected the gracious, smiling Nara who was everything my mother wasn't, supportive, nurturing, kind, but when we arrived, the woman we saw in an orange jumpsuit was not my aunt. She looked like a woman cut away from the stake, fire wasted and emaciated, a haggard, skellein shadow of the Nara I had loved. My heart ached seeing her like that. She wouldn't stop talking, and she had a lone, obsessive matter she wanted to discuss: my mother was a snitch. She wouldn't be in jail and her husband would be alive if it weren't for Maria. We were all complicit. We all chose my mother's side. It was an unbroken tirade. Marta begged her, Mommy, please stop! until she started to sob. I listened to her solemnly. Daniel was convinced. But how can you trust a person like that? Someone who's been so beaten and battered, their perceptions all slip toward that dark abyss where chance has wronged them. It was chance. Wasn't it? The slings and arrows of outrageous fortune. The monstrous fact of a ruined life has its own gravity, it pulls everything in and skews it, everything becomes a reason why. I tried to change the subject.

—Nara, this isn't why we came to talk to you.
—Then leave!
—There's nothing we can do anyway.
—Then leave! I never wanna see any of you ever again!
—Nara, please.
—Goodbye.

She walked away and that was the last time any of us spoke to her. Marta and I cried on the way home. Daniel said, She's right you know, about mom. I didn't think so. I saw my mother the night of the raid. Her and Nara were both in their white dresses looking beautiful, off in the corner, laughing like old friends, and it was like they turned a corner in their rivalry. Maybe because my mother was comfortable, happy even, chatting online with a man who wanted to marry her, and I think she was ready to put all their old enmity aside, but then the police broke down the door and blew up our lives.

—What are you thinking about? my mother asked me.
—Nara.

She bristled at the mention.

—Wow, Nara. What is it, six years today? she asked me in portuguese.
—Yes.

—Sometimes I think, if that hadn't happened, maybe I wouldn't have left, she said with trepidation, like she was dusting off her carioca accent.

—What?

We were interrupted by the sight of the ocean as we emerged from the tunnel into Copacabana. Woah, the gringos in the car said, faced by the impossible immensity of the Atlantic, stretched out like a fallen sky. We didn't return to the subject I wanted to discuss. We passed the statue of the princess, and Larry inquired.

—Who's that?

—Princess Isabel. You know what she did?

—Sewed the flag?

—She freed the slaves.

—Like Lincoln!

My mother giggled. We turned onto the Avenida, and I felt angry and strange. What did my mom mean when she said she might've stayed? I was angry on behalf of a different Lucia, years ago, tiny and diluted in her mother's unsaid goodbye. But she said Nara's name wistfully, like she cared, when before she had only spoken of her with temerarious condemnation. Was she playing some sort of game with me, or was she actually different? Simple and smooth and saved. I was uneasy. My whole life I'd constructed myself in opposition to her, on the foundation that she was cruel and irresponsible, a construction enthusiastically affirmed the day she left, but now the edifice I'd constructed was wobbling in the gale of her ostensible change. I didn't know what to think. I realized now that I didn't want to forgive her, I didn't want her to change. It would've all been much easier if she returned brandishing her garish nastiness proudly, like she used to, but I felt the furnace of my judgement cooling, underfed by the charred fodder of her old sins.

We pulled into their hotel. They were staying at the Marriott. I must've not noticed when they told Alexandre. It was the hotel my dad always stayed at when he came to town, even though there was room in our apartment, he could've stayed with us and slept in my mother's bed, but he didn't want to, so my mother would pack a suitcase and spend the few weeks he was in town holed up in his room. I would barely catch sight of her. Many nights they would invite Daniel over and the three of them would go out to expensive dinners, but I never even stepped foot into the hotel lobby. Our apartment was literally directly behind it, so I would stare out our window at the back of the hotel, pathetically daydreaming. After my father died and we needed money, my mother worked in this hotel as a maid. It was a hilarious failure, after a month of daily, ceaseless complaints about her terrible toil, she was fired. So my associations with the hotel were overwhelmingly negative. It felt like a subtle taunt, that she was staying there. But. It was extremely close to our apartment. Maybe she accounted for that. Maybe she expected to be seeing a lot of us.

We got out of the car and Alexandre helped with the luggage. We said our thanks and goodbyes. Larry gave him a big fat tip, and I was frustrated. I couldn't securely account for the morality of an action as small as that. Alexandre likely needed the money and he was beaming gratefully, but was Larry just flexing his power, forking over an amount that was functionally meaningless to him? I stared at him. He was a bad guy, I felt like I knew that, but where were the markers? There were no horns on his head. He didn't breathe fire. Though if there was one often repeated mistake in history it was thinking any exterior appearances corresponded with an inner truth, but I was in sore need of a sure grip on the world. This was a man my mother seemingly loved. A person that she chose over our family. Why? Because she wanted to be wealthy and american? She would tell us when we were kids that she would stay up on the Ilha and watch the planes take off from the airport, dreaming of the United States. It seemed like she would've taken any means to that end. Any Larry could've been Larry. Yet this specific man, the whole woven web of his individuality, sins and all, was the one she chose. Was she complicit in everything he did? I didn't know anything.

In Grande Sertão, the narrator, Riobaldo, spends the whole book ruminating on the existence of the devil. He was a jagunço, cowboying around, roaming the backlands, where justice is arbitrary. He kills a lot of people. But there's this man, Hermogenes, who leads another band of jagunços that ends up killing Riobaldo's former boss. Riobaldo is out for revenge, but there's one thing that scares him. He's certain Hermogenes made a pact with the devil. So what does Riobaldo do? He goes out and tries to make his own pact. He goes out at midnight in the midst of the lone voice of being, pure dark, where the cricket chirps and bullfrog ribbits all blend and rise into a pervasive single sound. He yells for Satan. He hears only silence in return. What's silence? he asks. It's us ourselves too much. But soon he's more powerful than he could ever imagine. He becomes chief of a band of jagunços and leads them on their plundering, pillaging path to a final battle where Hermogenes is killed and his revenge is complete. But during the battle, the love of his life, Diadorim, is killed. Was that the devil's price? he wonders. Did I actually make a pact? He concludes that, no, there was no pact, and there is no devil. All there is is human man. But devil or no devil, there is evil isn't there? Evil has a dateless fame, and you didn't have to look far to see the scars it left in its wake. But I didn't know if I could recognize it, and if I did, what power would I have in its presence?

—Lucia.

—What?

—We're going into the hotel to put our luggage away and change. And then I was thinking, why don't we just go over to the apartment? See grandma.

Ok, I said. I would wait outside for them. I didn't want to step foot in that hotel. Honestly, I didn't want to do anything. My mother was being sweet. She touched my hand tenderly as she spoke to me. There was nothing I could do now, I was stuck in this path. I was going to bring my mother into that apartment, simply spitting in my grandma's face. But wasn't I doing the right thing? Marta would be thrilled to see her aunt. There was a real possibility that for the first time in my life, I was taking the right steps to have a positive relationship with my mother, and she seemed contrite, maybe we could actually get past everything and heal. Despite all that, despite weighing the facts of everything that had happened this week, everything my mother said and did, I had an overwhelming, irrevocable feeling of doom.

I waited in the shade, staving off a panic attack, breathing through it until my mood broke into a weird, agitated happiness, like I had too much caffeine on a beautiful day, until they came back outside. My mom was still dressed in a suntaunting all black, manifesting the appearance of mourning, but she'd exchanged her heels for a pair of flip-flops, and her designer purse for a canvas bag. Larry was in a more casual shirt and had dropped the tie, but he looked dumb in his hard shoes. I led the way, and they walked holding hands. The three of us walked toward my apartment, looking like a cardboard cutout of a family.

—What's the deal for New Year's?

—Honey, don't speak english so loud.

—Is it really that dangerous here?

—Nothing bad happens in Copacabana.

—Weren't tourists killed here the other day? Was that close by?

—That was at the Christ statue, but anyway, there's more to that story, they were trying to buy drugs. It's complicated. But we're safe, sweetheart.

The romantic little nicknames nauseated me, but then my mother smiled, bringing me in on a little joke, like look how worried this turista is, and that gesture, a little insider brasilianness, cozying herself up to my team, my side, softened my heart, and I smiled back. I was feeling myself change, and it frightened me.

WE WALKED until we passed a man who frequently begged on the corner of Santa Clara. He was rail thin and obviously in need of money, but he was a little bit of a scammer, moaning in pain and shaking his head back and forth and feigning muteness, though he was a neighborhood mainstay, and I knew many people who'd had totally normal conversations with him over a pastel and a beer. This was the first homeless man we passed and Larry said, Oh my gosh! We have to help this guy! and he pulled out a five real bill and stuffed it in his cup. All of a sudden I heard, Ayy! coming from behind us. It was a guy I recognized who was really, seriously homeless. He dragged a stained, sopping mattress around the neighborhood as the police booted him from corner to corner. He would lay there, naked, often masturbating, and invite passing women to come spend the afternoon with him. It was horrifying, but honestly, pretty funny. Now he approached, angry and cloaked in a dirty comforter.

—E pra mim porra? Tu é rico eu sô pobre então, hora de pagá branquelo!

Larry looked spooked, his eyes flicking from me to my mother for enlightenment. My mother looked like she wanted to walk away, so I translated.

—He said you're rich and he's poor, so you owe him money.

—Ohh, well I'm not rich. I mean, I don't have anything. That was my last bill.

—Falou que não tem, I said to our toga'd nuisance.

—Mentira! Mentira! Mentira!

—He says you're lying.

—Larry, let's go, we can't keep talking to this guy.

They started to walk off, and I shrugged apologetically, but he wasn't even looking at me, his gaze was burning a hole through Larry's back.

—Toma cuidado gringo! Você vai pagar de um jeito ou outro!

He stood there pointing and snarling as we walked on. Larry leaned in and asked my mother what he said.

—He says you'll have to pay one way or another.

Larry threw up his hands and they both laughed. I wasn't crazy about ominous warnings, no matter how deranged the source, so I did not laugh. Maybe I was superstitious, but I was a product of my grandma's raising, and so I took omens seriously, which made me want to stop this whole enterprise, turn them around, go to their hotel for some opulent shitty meal, say goodbye and divest myself of my mother for good. But we walked on. And soon we were standing in front of the building. The Donas and Seu Zé were chatting out front, and their faces lit up when they recognized my mother. She always had a knack for accruing ardent affection from the people who would never know her well, if anyone ever would know her well. Seu Zé and the Donas cheered, Maria! and dove over eachother to give her a hug. My mother fielded condolences about my grandpa and smiled, then exchanged some quick catch up with them about the residents of the building. She could court good will in a chillingly dexterous way because she always knew what to say to draw out any effect.

They confused Larry for her former american, whom they hadn't seen in over a decade, and greeted him like an old friend. Larry was about the same height as him, but his hair and eyes were a different color. Plus, my father carried himself more menacingly. He wore his power and influence like a gun in a holster. After the chatter dissipated, we walked in, and up the stairs to the third floor. In front of 302, the 30 in gilded blocks and a faded outline where the 2 used to be, like it was plucked away to a better life. My mother pointed to it.

—When did that happen?

—A long time ago.

She touched my back gently, and we all stood around. I realized I'd been waiting for her to open the door. I'd reverted to little kid mode, waiting for mommy, but I had the key. I could end this now. I didn't have to go inside and face my grandmother. But I wasn't brave. I opened the door. My grandmother and Marta were sitting at the kitchen table. My grandmother with her back to the door. There was a white urn with a Vasco sticker on it between them, my grandpa. Marta saw my mother and gasped. To her, this was a character in her drawings come to life, she didn't have any real memories of her, but it was like a missing link to her mother. She jumped up and ran to give her a hug.

—Aunt Maria!

—Marta!

My mother picked her up and spun her around. This was the same Aunt Maria who, when Marta was born prematurely and interned in the hospital for several weeks, refused to visit and did not allow me or Daniel to go, and said that if little Marta died, it was what Nara deserved. Thankfully, time had grooved a canyon through the solid rock of my mother's brutality. Or. There was a trick being played on me that I could not comprehend. My grandma turned around and was looking at us sternly. My mother walked over and said, Hi mom, and gave her a kiss on the cheek, then she touched the urn prayerfully and sat down. Marta sat on her lap. My grandmother still had not said anything. Larry was standing uncomfortably. He stuck out his hand and said, Hello Mrs. Cunha. My grandma touched his hand with the opposite of ardor.

—Is there a bathroom around here? he asked.

—First door on the left, my mother said, pointing his way out of the kitchen.

I sat down. My mother and grandmother stared at eachother. Marta wouldn't take her eyes off my mother, searching her face as if it was a cure to her neglected childhood.

—Oh Lucia! my mother said in english. I forgot. I got you something.

She pulled a small box out of her bag and handed it to me. I opened it. It was a golden necklace that said Lucia in small letters. I never wore any jewelry, but this necklace was simple and not at all tacky, it wouldn't be out of place around my neck.

—There were just so many emotions when you called me that it slipped my mind to tell you happy birthday. I know you don't like gifts, but I thought you'd like this.

I could literally not remember a single time my mother got me a birthday gift, so I was astonished, speechless. There were so many different stories I could tell myself about what was happening that I couldn't get a handle on anything. Who was this Maria? What did it mean for this Lucia sitting across from her? It was like being rolled by a wave and as soon as you felt the clear air of relief, another wave thrust you back down. Marta grabbed the necklace from me and cooed at how pretty it was. And then my grandmother spoke up.

—What are you doing Maria?

—What do you mean?

—You know exactly what I mean. Why are you here?

—My father died. It was time to come back.

—You missed everything. You should've just stayed away.

—Mom, please. Don't start this now, okay?

—You abandoned us! You abandoned your children!

—I didn't abandon anyone! I did what I had to do.

Marta wasn't smiling anymore. My grandmother was shaking her head, angry and in disbelief. I didn't know what to do.

—Marta, go to your room, I said.

—No!

—Marta! Now.

She stood up, her eyes watering, and left the kitchen. I'd never barked so harshly at her. I wanted to follow, curl up in the bed next to her, soothe her tears, but I was frozen in my seat.

—And you bring this man into my house. Are you mocking us, Maria? That's the man you left everything for?

—You always had a problem with me. Everything I did was always wrong. Do you ever think maybe that's why I wanted to get out of here? Because of you and dad criticizing everything I did? You think I'm a bad mom? You were a bad mom!

—Mom. Stop.

—You should be ashamed to be back here, my grandma said, totally ignoring me.

—Ashamed?

—Yes! Ashamed! To be back here, hugging Martinha after what you did to her. Her parents would still be here if it wasn't for you.

—Oh my god, this old story. Is this what she tells you too, Lucia?

—It's the truth! You betrayed Nara.

—You act like that woman was a saint! Everybody acts like she was

a saint! She wasn't Nelson Mandela. She was a drug dealer. She married
a thug, and they dealt drugs and destroyed communities. Why do you
think there's so much violence in this city? Because of people like them!
My god, mom. She didn't need anybody to turn her in! She was bad.
She broke the law, and she got what she deserved.

—She was a good person, Maria. She was a good mother and a good
daughter. A better daughter than you ever were!

My mother laughed. I was scared.

—Lucia, do you know what your grandmother did right after I was
born?

I didn't say anything.

—Maria, don't tell her this.

—She left your grandfather and she moved in with this janitor who
lived way up on the hill. She left your grandpa to take care of me all
alone. I got so sick I almost died. Grandpa was so depressed he almost
killed himself.

—Maria!

—No, she needs to hear this for when she's pushing for your canon-
ization. She came back, but guess what. She was pregnant with Nara.
Do the math on that timeline please, Lucia. Did that ever come up in
one of your late night talks? Grandpa wasn't Nara's father. Her father
was some poor bum named Marcelo, and the only reason your grandmother didn't stay with him is that she couldn't stand what other people
would think. So we just tucked ourselves up into our little lie.

—Grandma. Is that true?

—Yes, she said, putting her hands on top of mine.

I pulled away. I stood up. Nara and my mother looked different,
sure, but not that different. I never thought. My grandma didn't tell me.
She lied to me. She lied to me and my mother was telling me the truth.
I didn't know anything. I couldn't trust anything. There was a knock on
the door. I walked over to it, dizzy like I'd been punched in the head. I
asked who it was.

—Daniel.

I opened the door. He was raggedy, sand spotting his hair like lice. He had a black eye and was wearing a shirt that said, Don't Mess With Texas. He asked who was here. I just got out of the way.

—Daniel!

My mother ran over to give him a hug and he held his hands stiffly out in front of him, pushing her away. When I opened the door, he looked nice, he smiled when he saw me, but now his face turned dour, he looked like a mean street dog ready for a fight.

—What the fuck are you doing here?

—Didn't Lucia? Um. Your grandpa, Daniel. I had to come back.

Just then Larry walked back into the room.

—Do you guys have a plunger? I think there's an issue.

—Who the fuck are you?

—The famous Daniel! How's it going?

Larry stuck out his hand and Daniel didn't even react to it. He glared at him with an evil glaze over his eyes.

—Who. Are. You.

—Daniel, this is my husband.

Daniel laughed. I caused this whole situation. I should've never come back here with them. My grandma was crying at the table with her head in her hands. Who was she? Whose side was I on? I didn't know anything.

—You shoulda never come back here.

—Daniel, please. I miss you!

—Hey calm down, buddy! Why don't we go have a beer? Start the New Year's festivities a little early.

Daniel was biting his bottom lip, pacing around the kitchen.

—Yeah! You guys should come out with us. The girls would love to meet you.

—The girls?

—My daughters. Rachel and Olivia.

—They're here?

—They came down last week.

—What? Daniel said.

—Uhh. My daughters are here.

Daniel laughed, loud and maniacally. He was doubled over, laughing like a lunatic.

—Rachel huh? She got some good pussy.

—Watch your mouth!

—You oughta ask her where her mouth has been.

—Don't you dare talk to me that way! Have some respect!

Larry roostered up. Daniel stared him down.

—Say some shit to me man. Say it. I dare you.

I watched Daniel stick his hand in his pocket and pull out a switch-blade. He was hiding it behind his back. I don't think anyone noticed. I was frozen with dread.

—Daniel, please, calm down. Let's just talk.

—No. No talking. I told you to never come back here. I told you!

—Don't talk to my wife that way!

—Fuck you! he said and the rare certain dread that somebody was going to die fell on me like a twelfth floor air conditioner, exactly like on that day six years ago, sitting in Nara's apartment, when, Policia! and the door came crashing down. Daniel, stop this right now! Make me stop, you motherfucker. Daniel pushed him and Larry pushed him back. Daniel showed his knife. Daniel no! The cops dove on Nara slamming her head against the cold floor. They ran back to Antonio's room. He's got a gun! Brrrapbrappbrap! Marta crying so loud it shook the room. I told you not to come back! Daniel pushed him so hard he slammed his back against the refrigerator. No! my grandma yelled. No! They hauled Antonio's mauled body out in a bag while Nara wept. Daniel cocked his hand back and all of a sudden there was no knife just his fist bashing into Larry's chin and he fell stiff on the ground like a corpse falls I was dazed the room was spinning my only thought was death Lucia! all of a sudden looking up at the ceiling Lucia! dark figures floating around my sight like stars.

part two

inferno

ô morena do mar
sou eu que acabei de chegar
ô morena do mar
eu disse que ia voltar

—nara leão

january 1

DANIEL! SHE SAID looking like the goddess of the sea in her white dress and flower crown. Those savage green eyes sparkling with my day-dreamed futures. My lost futures now that I committed myself to this doomed present. Daniel! The statue of Princesa Isabel watched as she kissed my cheek and sat down at the beerstrewn kiosk table. Mateus bumped up his wild stage batucada and the crowd densed up around us like a forest of white trees. Eu moro num país tropical!

You have a black eye!

I laughed and shrugged. Everything was funny and nice and cute. Haha! Little did she know how clear I saw it. After I dropped her nothing father in that kitchen that stunk like peace. I wandered angry in my all alone wilderness, thinking I should've stabbed him. I was gonna stab him! Why didn't I? Because I realized it wasn't him who deserved it. What was he worth to me? He was just another useless dope used by my mother. It was her. I fell on the street like I was hit by lightning. And I saw. Her blood on my hands like it was my born fated purpose. Revenge!

He's really good!

One more song!

The sky started to close up above us, thunder thumping against a hard black dome. Even the military police gathered around to listen. Thirteen of them in their battle uniforms, big dark guns held calm at attention, like in the seconds just before a war. Burumbum! The rain started to drip, dotting the white shirt I stole from Lojas Americanas after the plan came together in my mind. I wouldn't be no sad mope no more. I felt all the good drop dead from my life like a shot criminal, and I was ecstatic. I stole a phone charger and tucked myself clandestine in the busy supermarket where I charged my phone and ate crackers, feeling a hot madness burble up inside me. I was gonna do it. The act that could redeem my life once and for all. I wanted to laugh and puke and scream!

I was gonna do it.

Mateus was done, soaked in sweat and rain, the applause rising up like steam from our bodies. The military police whooped and hollered and then walked away phalanxed up, prepped to pop a wayward reveler on sight. I was rooting for it. I wanted chaos. I was in an untamed stupor, drunk and giddy and doomed to hell. I was about to cross an evil threshold, and I felt order and decorum melt away.

Mateus came and sat with us, basking in his love. He kissed Rachel on the cheek and slapped my hand. The crowd cheered for him and sent over drinks and we poured back shot after shot of cachaça in the swamp heat of the beach night. I needed them here. Mateus would say that everything was normal, he was with me the whole time. We were fucked up, but it was New Year's! A body would fall in the shrill mayhem of the fireworks and the storm and the crowd, but it would be like nothing happened. And the rope would be cut to the past that pulled at my life like an anchor. Rachel was here to take me to them.

You talk to your parents?

I texted them a couple times. I've been avoiding them since they landed. Always so much drama! But they asked me to meet up with them over by our hotel. You wanna walk that way?

What do you think Mateus?

Bora!

We stood and set off on our steep and selvic way. Mateus pulled out a huge joint and handed it to me. I lit it with my hands cupped against the raindrops and took a deep hit. I looked around at the sprawling lives that surrounded me. Drunk and loose and stumbling to the music, damned to die. Maybe drugs would stop their hearts, or a knife. Or maybe the sun would explode and all the buildings and statues in Copacabana would liquify and any life left would burn, blistered in the boiling river.

My mom brought me to Copacabana when I was a little boy. I must've been six years old, and I was used to the Engenhoca beach and little waves that nipped at your shins. Mom let me go into the new beach by myself and I felt the true power of the ocean, how it could pull you out any second and strand you to glug your lungs done. I was so happy playing in that water. She told me dad might move us there. They were gonna get married. But as she was sitting on a beach chair, ignoring me while I tried to build a sandcastle, here comes this man who blocks out the sun.

There you are, Maria.

Daniel, I need you to sit right here, ok? I need you to sit right here and be good because mommy has some things to do. Don't move an inch!

And she went off with that man and left me there, her word my utmost command. I sat on a canga for hours watching the waves swell and recede. Straining sand through my fingers as beach vendors came to check on me. You ok kid? Want some biscoito Globo? A popsicle? Drink this water. Don't worry kid, your mom will come back.

She didn't until the beach was dark and empty and I was terrified.

She materialized like a ghost, that man by her side.

I'm sorry Daniel, we just got a little caught up.

I watched her kiss him on the lips like I thought she was only supposed to do with dad.

Say goodbye to Uncle Antonio, ok? Say goodbye.

I didn't say anything. I wouldn't even remember that moment until years later when Nara introduced him to us and the memory fell on me like a body from a building.

My dad was right about her. Wasn't he?

But I was like her. Nobody could trust me. She dug a grave and tossed her dirt on me the moment I was born. I was a liar and a cheater, and that's why Leticia didn't want me. Because of her. Because of the path she set me on. But as soon as I got rid of her all that shit would be done. I could still save myself.

Bururubam!

That thunder is crazy!

Rachel held my hand as we walked. Her hips bumping into mine. Her lithe body. I could throw her down right now. Is that all we are? Yes! I would embrace my strength. I was tired of being weak and scared. Subject to my mother's constant whims. I never wanted to leave. I never wanted to go live with my father. She sent me on that mission. It wasn't about me and my life. It was about how to save her.

This is your chance Daniel! You have to convince him we're his family. Me and you.

What about Lucia?

Don't worry about her. It's me and you.

All the shit that happened was because of her!

Now my steam was building, I was ready. I couldn't keep a smile off my face as we walked. Mateus said, My aunt is right up there! Let's go say hi. We snaked our way through the shoulder to shoulder muvuca. Everyone bordered by police stares. Anitta bumping distant on the main stage. The rain increasing slowly. The intense packed crowd heat. All the chittering and music and laughter like a gnashing howl. The night spiraling toward its explosion.

Where was my mother right now? Probably holding hands with that man and laughing about her delinquent son. Why was she back? What was her plan? She got what she wanted, didn't she? When it should've been me. I should've had that life there locked up, all mine. I didn't want it at first, but I was there. There was a certain cushy splendor I got used to. Even though they made me sleep in that cramped closet room. Where I would stay awake hearing her voice.

Save me! Save me, Daniel!

So I desperately tried to mount a scheme. I learned to pick the lock to my father's office. I would sneak in there when he left in the morning, looking for anything that could be a small gateway. And one day, I discovered his computer password on a notecard. LillianDiana, his daughters' names. His fucking daughters who looked at me like I was a cockroach. With their hoity outfits and their braces. My crooked teeth.

Can I have braces dad?

Don't ask me again!

For months I pored through his emails every day looking for anything that would give me leverage. But I found nothing. I turned surly. I hated my life. I couldn't understand why my dad brought me over to do chores and yell at me. Everyday he ordered me around like he was trying to scrub out my carioca laziness.

I didn't belong anywhere. Not with his daughters. Not with the gardeners I mowed and mulched with, who talked shit about me in spanish I could barely understand. Not with the kids at school. Who I wasn't allowed to hang out with anyway. Anyone I tried to see was a hoodlum and a bad influence. But I would sneak out and go to parties where girls would mock my accent and my crooked teeth. Just to get berated the next day by my father.

That house was like a pressure cooker, and I was ready to burst.

So, feeling lost and overcome with rage, I snuck out of my room in the middle of the night. I took a can of gasoline from the garage and the lighter I kept in my room to smoke my secret joints, and I snuck across the monstrous cosmos of that house. One of those awful girls was gone, at some dumb bitch sleepover. I went into her room, her huge room overpacked with stuffed animals and clothes and books. All the shit I thought I'd get once I broke the border of my shithole country into paradise. I poured the gasoline over everything, overjoyed! I crumpled a page out of that girl's journal sitting on her desk. I lit it and tossed it on the heap! But just as the room was about to spark and blaze, someone yanked me down by my hair and I heard the fire extinguisher. It was Mrs. And it was over.

My rebellion stamped out like a cheap cigarette.

They were gonna send me home. I was angry and frustrated and I hated that house, but my mother gave me a strict mission. Find some way to get me and her to live in the United States. And the mission wasn't complete. So I decided to give my dad's office one last look. His guard must've been up before. Because now I got into the computer, and he was logged into a different email, a secret one. I found what I was looking for! There was a long thread with this woman named Vera, gushing loveydovey bullshit and explicit pictures. She looked young, she sounded young. The emails started to get mean between them.

Then! It turned out she was pregnant! And a senior in high school!

I waited around for him all day brimming with excitement. He came home. I asked him if I could talk to him in his office. He sat down, and I said, I know everything. This was my chance. I was gonna do what my mother wanted me to do, carve our names into this american tree. I was doing everything for her, her, her! I gave him my demands, and he laughed in my face.

Go ahead. Tell everyone. You can't hurt me.

It was like beating my fist against a concrete wall, I couldn't make a dent. He just walked away. I was frantic, pleading. Don't worry, he said, this won't matter soon. Two days later, he drove his car off a bridge. In clear daylight, no traffic, on a route he drove everyday. He killed himself because of me. Because of her. Because of what she made me do! That sun in the blazing constellation of her sins. That's why I needed this revenge. To snuff that shine dark for good. Soon it would be time.

Bararababum! The pitch black clouds flashed, the lightning trying to escape.

I looked up. Mateus and Rachel were looking at me.

You ok?

Sitting in front of us with a weary smile on her face, next to a styrofoam container with refilled water bottles and beer, was Dona Isabel. She had been like a mother to me for the past six years. Now she was staring at me. That half smile giving way to a look of pure condemnation. Like I betrayed her.

I stared right back at her.

I wouldn't spare her the smallest swell of kindness.

From that moment on, all my thoughts were bloody.

I STOOD there looking at her. Mateus gave her a big hug and introduced Rachel. He grabbed a beer for each of us out of the container. I couldn't stop staring because all I could see was Leticia's face. Leticia! All I wanted was for her to be next to me. I missed her so much already! All I wanted was to go back to that day before I left to live with my father. We spent the whole day on the beach basking in the sun, hands held, getting stoned as the sun faded. That night, under the moon and the busted streetlights, we laid out a canga and I felt her body, all mine for the first time. Her brown eyes shimmering in the dim night. Her soft moans like the waves kissing the shore.

Do you love me?

Forever Leticia.

Then don't leave.

I won't.

You promise?

I promise.

Of course I lied, that was all I was good at. All I ever knew was lies! There was a plot behind every one of my mother's words, every smile. How was I supposed to be different? But tonight was the last night. I was gonna free myself. Leticia would take me back. She would have my child! I knew it. I could see tenderness tucked beneath her snarls.

We would be a family. The knife was in my pocket. There was only one thing I had to do.

Are you guys having fun?

Yeah tia, just having a couple beers.

Take a few more. Be careful, ok? This storm is going to make people crazy.

Obrigada Mrs. Isabel!

Cavalo! someone screamed.

A police horse, bucking wild, burst loose and ran through the crowd. Chaosing the people into mad wayward stumbles, trailed by shrieks like clashing armies. It came charging. I leapt out of the way. Banged my head on a sharp cobblestone. Wet seep on my skull.

Dona Isabel fell, her container contents spilled all over the ground like squished animal intestines. I stood and reached my hand out to help her up. She looked me dead in the eyes. I scowled. Don't do it, Daniel. Don't do it. Talking like we were sitting in her tiny kitchen and I was zoning out to one of her long lullful stories. But I would listen because I loved her. I loved her daughter. I loved her nephew.

Don't do it, Daniel. Staring at me, her eyes as black as the night.

Barababoom!

The sky was even blacker now. It was like my feet were on the floor of the ocean and all the noise was pressing on me like water and I couldn't move. Don't do it, Daniel. Earsplitting screeches like a throat flood of water ripping my lungs.

I was in Dona Isabel's kitchen standing right in front of Leticia screaming at her. You're cheating on me! No I'm not I'm not! Then why are these pricks liking your instagram pictures! I can see my hand on her throat. I'm Cabral with a dark black beard shoving my claimed woman against the trunk of a gnarled tree. You're a whore! Why don't you love me? I do love you! Why don't you love me! Fuck! Please Daniel, please. No, I know the truth about you. I know the truth! There's my mother shoved up against the refrigerator like a frightened animal trying to shield herself from a blow. I was in my apartment. She was in front of me. I banged her head with mine. No! I didn't mean to do that! It wasn't my mother, it was Leticia. Missing gaps in her front teeth blood pouring out her mouth. You hurt me! I didn't mean to.

Braap! Boom! Crraak!

I was Leticia and there were bottles flying at my head the glass smashing the walls, I was shielding my eyes from the shrapnel. I was looking at me. Daniel! I looked like evil. Daniel! Are you ok? Daniel! I didn't mean to throw it at you! I wasn't trying to hit you girl I love I love you. It's too late! Cuddling Leticia. Her broken betrayed eyes. Her soft body sweating in her bed. Smell of coconut oil. Girl I love you. She's not breathing. Oh no. Deep slashes all over her stomach. Fuck! No! No! No! Dona Isabel at the front of the bed staring at me, her eyes like pools of blood. Don't do it. I will never forgive you. My fist bashing into her face. My knife going into her throat. No! Bararabababoom!

Daniel!

I opened my eyes.

Mateus and Rachel were standing over me. My heart was pounding.

Holy shit dude, are you ok? That horse almost killed you!

They helped me up. I was woozy.

I'm good! I'm ok!

They laughed. Mateus and Dona Isabel were smiling at me. Rachel looked worried. A small crowd of revelers had stopped to check it out, hoping maybe I was dead, something exciting to report to their friends. But when I popped up they walked away.

I was feeling strange. Euphoric almost. Different.

Rachel stepped forward and wiped the blood off my hair with a napkin. Dona Isabel handed me a cold beer to press against my forehead. My head was aching.

Mateus was laughing hard.

Dude if you had died like that, oh my god! That would've been embarrassing.

I cracked up. Rachel laughed.

I told you to be careful! Dona Isabel said.

Let's keep moving! I don't wanna miss these fireworks.

We said goodbye. Dona Isabel stood and hugged me tight. I could feel Leticia's warmth through her, and I knew I'd been wrong. Imagine if Leticia found out what I was planning to do? The horror would turn her against me forever. Because my mom didn't deserve to die. She was just as pathetic as I was. I'd still be mired in the same cycles of bullshit. But there was a clear villain. A bitchass wannabe conqueror cavorting in my country. Fitting my dad's mold.

Someone was going to die.

I was right the first time.

It was him.

We walked off.

Moving slow through the thick crowd stagegathered for Anitta's performance.

I can't believe how many people there are! Rachel said as I held her hand tight.

The rain was falling harder. It was hot and pleasant. I was calm. It was like I was seeing everything from above. I saw us singlefiling through the crowd, Mateus leading the way. The distant dunchedunche and dispersed chatter floating like a foggy miasma above our collective heads. So much english being spoken everywhere. English and french and german. Europeans and americans everywhere with big drunk smiles plastered on their faces. They could come here and do whatever they wanted. Splash around in our ocean. Fuck our women and dip out.

That's why it had to be him.

I saw my father with his bloody beard and squinted beady eyes. His slick talk. Flashing a roll of dollars to some easy fooled broad. That was my mom. He scooped her up. Sculpted her like clay. It wasn't her fault. She followed the paths laid out for her. I couldn't be angry with her. She was naive. I had it all fucked up, twisted. She didn't have no agency with this. That was the big trick of fate. The phony, I choose! You didn't choose nothing. Your steps were engraved. My knife was stuck in Larry's heart already.

Poor Rachel, smiling pretty. She just had to lead me there.

I have to go to the bathroom!

Mateus, you heard the girl, take us there!

She would lose a father, but I heard what she said about him. She would thank me. I lost a father too. I didn't have any choice in the matter. I was an orphan already. Why did my mom come back? She was him now. She was an extension of him. So long removed, she wanted an american romp. She wanted to see what it was like from the other side. Once you flipped that switch, once you crossed that threshold from helpless to powerful, you could never go back. I felt it for that brief moment I was the ambassador's son. How the world could look like a barren moon just waiting for you to plant your flag. But my mom would pay for that.

She should've never came back. I warned her.

This would be her last time in Rio de Janeiro.

There was a row of portapotties on the other side of Avenida Atlántica. We pushed through the crowd and walked over there. It was still packed, but less dense, open space to maneuver. I was so serene and set in my purpose, I didn't mind a delay. But I needed to be drunker. I chugged the two beers Dona Isabel got for me as we walked. Mateus lit up another joint and we smoked. Everything felt as smooth and nurturing as coconut milk. I grabbed Rachel's ass. She was sexy and I wanted her, and maybe with her father out of the way. If she didn't know how it happened. Then. No. I would have to remove her too. She was part of the malevolence that dragged me down. America sunk me. Sunk my family. I was gonna get my revenge.

I'm about to pee my pants!

We hustled toward the disgusting conglomeration that stunk like a sewer. The rain was steady now, and the way the ground was sloped here made the water accumulate. Trash floated around us. My flops were soaked. It was gross. And laid out in the putrid pooled muck, getting circumvented like a rock in the stream, was an obvious turista with a smile on his face and his arms splayed like a cross. He was unconscious, or dead. We bypassed him and Rachel beat a lagging brasilian to the only vacant portapotty just in time. Me and Mateus stepped up on the curb, under the cover of a big street clock that read 23:39. It was almost time. We passed the joint back and forth. I felt like I had to tell him.

Are you ok man? You fell pretty hard.

I'm feeling good bro.

What the hell you wanna go see her parents for?

I got a plan.

A plan?

Burumbum!

I'm telling you. Just follow my lead.

Whatever bro, but I'm not getting arrested for you again.

We laughed.

Rachel approached. What are you laughing at?

That was fast.

That was the worst bathroom I've ever seen!

We laughed. Everything was nice and funny and normal and nice! It was New Year's Eve!

I looked at Rachel. She was smiling at me. I nuzzled up to her, kissed her cheek, and she blushed. Her cheek was red and shiny from the rain. There was a version of this night where the three of us walked away from here and turned left toward the main stage. We would watch the concert and dance in the hot rain. Inaugurate the New Year with big booms and I would kiss her. We would find someplace to fuck. We'd say goodbye and she'd leave Rio and maybe I would see her again. But that storybook version crumbled like a collapsed bridge. I made my choice! Rachel was dead to me. This would be our goodbye.

The turista who was laying in the streetmade bog suddenly stood up. He started screaming.

Ahhh! O Brasil tá fudido! O Brasil tá fudido! O Brasil tá fudido!

He was chanting like he thought it was gonna catch on with the crowd.

But it did not.

People looked at him like he was crazy and fled in the opposite direction.

What does that mean?

He's saying Brasil is fucked!

O maluco tá certo!

Huh?

Mateus said he's right.

We laughed and walked on. The air smelled like piss and rain and smoke. I needed something to drink. The sky was rumbling serious and the night was getting darker by the second. We cut through a sudden forest that was in the median between the avenues. The trees were warped and sickly, shortwick partyers hung off the branches like laid out laundry. There were homeless people passed out around the trunks like fallen fruit.

I spotted an almost full bottle of vodka next to an unconscious dude. I snuck over and snagged it and we ran. As we got back on Avenida Atlantica someone yelled, Cavalo! and I saw the horse gallop in the opposite direction, toward Leme, stomping revelers in its wake. It was being chased by the military police, their guns drawn.

Oh no!

We gotta keep walking.

Bararararabababoom!

The thunder hit with a bang muffling the sound of the fallen horse, the deep, hurt whinnies, and the rising complaint of the crowd.

Come on! We gotta find your parents. The fireworks are gonna start soon.

YOU THINK that horse is okay?

Rachel asked as we walked on. Now the storm was starting to fall with full fury.

A fervent catatau like a pot of boiling water being dumped over us.

Eu acho that the horse is ok!

The rain made the tide of people swell and it was getting harder to move. I saw the Marriott, clear and close, and I was starting to get nervous. My purpose was set. But my belly felt invaded by a buzzing hive. I was getting weak with chills.

Are you okay, Daniel?

Rachel handed me the vodka and I took a long, long drink that burned my throat and set me back at ease.

I'm good!

I wasn't gonna let no silly nerves unmoor me. We walked. The rain bucketed us again.

Essa tempestade tá crazy!

My clothes were soaked and I could feel my flipflops squeak but I couldn't hear it above the total noise.

We were about to climb down to the sand. There was a wall of people there unmoving. Police officers trying to orchestrate the traffic. Rachel's face was close to mine and I kissed her in the short visibility. Her lips were pulling to quit my mission. Telling me this could be a wrong-headed walk toward disaster. Maybe I should just chill. No. Leticia. I needed to kill this pest to kill my past. And then we could be together.

She was waiting for me, I could feel it. She was waiting for the big act that would win me worth. Make me husband and father material. She wanted a family with me. She had to, right? What a woeful power that was. She could snap a thing in and out of existence. Like my mother did. I wasn't, and then suddenly I was. And she didn't even have to care. She didn't care. I was only good if I was good for her. And when I wasn't, I was worthless. What a sick, destructive tie a mother has. That umbilical cord never dissolves.

Easy for a father isn't it? The link doesn't even exist.

Every father, every father, every father failed. That was the nasty fact. As soon as the progenation was done you could abandon all hope of success. Isn't that all I had seen? My grandfather reared two daughters who hated his fucking guts, and then he pissed blood and shit himself until he got burnt to dust. My own father. What did he do? He spilled his seed like he was planting damn apple trees. Didn't even stick around to see a bloom. Wouldn't even claim Lucia. And I was complicit in all that shit too. I abided by his rules. Maybe he was right. Maybe Lucia wasn't his. But then who. Antonio? Antonio didn't even get a chance. He became a bodybag in front of his little daughter. Because of my mom! When she finally bucked up to act, it was that. Her hands were covered in blood. Poor Marta, cute like a mouse.

I was fucked up. I was just like all them, bad. But that would end today. There was a perfect target clomping his dumb steps toward his end. He was everything I wanted to kill and it would be a perfect revenge. My mom would finally exit my life for good. My father's ghost would vanish. No more looming haunts. I would be free. Free to finally be a man. The real man this family needed. Who cared for his sister and grandma and cousin. Who raised up a kid, good and careful and kind. Who was good to his wife without no violence lurking around the corner. It had been a damn mess. A blathering of errors. But I was finally gonna do something right and clean. Trovarraraboom!

There was a huge bang and a flash.

Lightning hit the Leme rock and lit up the whole beach.

Woah!

Everyone screamed.

Caralho! O ano novo é foda!

Now we were moving. We stepped off the sidewalk. I could feel the wet sand burrowing into my flipflops. I was in a supreme agitation now. I finished the bottle of vodka and launched it into the crowd. Daniel! Don't do that! Vai tomá no cu porra! someone yelled and flipped me off. Hey! police officers yelled from far away.

The switchblade was burning a hole in my pocket.

Wooo! I screamed. Rachel and Mateus laughed and screamed with me.

The rain poured down on our heads.

There's no way we'll find my parents in this mess. I can't even pull out my phone.

Let's just keep walking, we'll see the fireworks anyway!

The sky is totally covered up, how are we gonna see anything?

We'll hear it at least!

I had no doubt I would find them. It was my destiny!

We walked as an almost contiguous mass, connected to the people in front of and behind us. A big white blob bobbing back and forth moving slowly toward the ocean. The beach was like a cosmic feijoada about to be cooked by this lightning. There were more and more people pouring down off the sidewalk into the sand causing us to stumble.

It was almost time.

I heard someone far off behind us yell, Fuck! in english. They took my fucking phone! He was way back on the sidewalk, but word was traveling fast, person to person in portuguese. Keep your shit close! There was an arrastão down there! Don't pull out your phone.

What does that mean?

They're stealing, don't pull your phone out. Just keep walking, we'll run into your parents.

Barababarabum!

Porra!

The rain fell even harder. My feet walked on without me. I knew they were close. My knife was out in front leading me.

I slipped away, pushing farther through the crowd.

Daniel, tá indo aonde?

Slow down!

There was loud samba playing on the nearest stage. The speakers must've got fucked up by the rain because it sounded harsh and discordant. Every noise in the raucous, impatient crowd was blurred into the same flat cacophony. It was hellish, horrible. But I wasn't thinking nothing. I was just moving through the crowd. A single focus.

I was gonna kill that man. I was gonna kill that man.

My revenge was coming!

My whole body was burning. I felt like I was scalding in a pot. Each breath I took scraped at my lungs. The rain felt hot like acid. But every feeling faded in the unstoppable movement of my feet. I knew they were here. I could smell the blood about to be spilled.

Bararabababoom!

The peopled knot loosened and I was on a bare patch of sand staring right at my sister.

Daniel?

Her hair and dress were drenched and she was wearing a necklace with her name on it.

What are you doing here?

I smiled. They were close.

Daniel?

I stared at her dark eyes. My sister. Was she?

We were back on the Ilha and it was New Year's. No mother or father around. Grandma cooking in the kitchen. We were sitting there laughing recklessly smelling the heat burn on the gas stove. We didn't have no mother or father. We were together in that. And instead of claiming that solidarity, I shirked her. I said She ain't shit to me! Fuck Lucia! I'm going to the United States! Fucking shoved her off my boat and let her drown.

I grabbed her hands. This was why. I was gonna do this for her too.

My purpose was set!

The rabble tightened again and got loud. I pushed away. Shoving forward.

I knew it was time. I knew it was time.

Daniel! Where are you going!

Slow down!

I could hear Mateus and Rachel's voices behind me. I couldn't see nothing but the north star of my knife pulling me along like a reeled in fish. Bababdakaboom! The dam of the sky burst. The rain was dropping in sheets. Where did Daniel go? I can't see anything! A scream rose up from the people, a scream that soured my stomach like an enemy goal sweeping through Maracanã. Oh shit! What was that? The knife was in my hand. The countdown was starting. Mateus grabbed my shoulder. Dude, where are you going? I shook him off. Ten! Hey stop pushing kid! Nine! Revenge. Revenge! The knife in my hand. Eight! Daniel slow down! What the fuck man. Happy New Year! Not yet! Seven! That guy has a knife in his hand be careful! Six! It crashed down on us like a wave. Arrastão! Five! Kids with knives and guns all around me. Pushing people to the ground. Grabbing phones out of their hands. Four! People started to run. And there in front of me. Daniel? My mother and that man. Three! My knife was ready. Rachel? Daniel what are you doing! Come on don't do this. Two! A kid ran up. He had a gun. The rain stopped for a moment. One! Boomboomburumkarakaboom! Happy New Year! He pointed it right at Larry. Oh my god! Give me your shit now turista! The knife was in my hand. I couldn't do it. I couldn't do it. I lunged. My knife plunged into the kid's leg. Porra! Boom! Boom! The gun went off. No! Dad! Dad! Dad! No no no no. Larry! Holy shit that guy just got shot! My face was on the ground. Wet sand in my mouth. Mateus grabbed me. Dude what the fuck did you do? We gotta run! I looked back. My mother was gone. He was on the ground. Rachel was standing over him screaming. I did it. I didn't mean to do it but I did it. My mouth was dry and I wanted to pass out. Run dude run! Boombababoom! All the rain dropped from the broken roof of the sky. I couldn't see nothing. I couldn't hear nothing. We ran toward the sea through the mud sand in silent horror like it was the end of the world.

LUCIA IN HER new white dress, with the necklace her mother gave her glinting in the streetlights, marched in doomed step with her turista troops as if anchor fated to the blood dark sea, Lucia and the drunk jittery multitude like an army in white uniform, her mother and her father and her sister by her side in rapturous felicity. Wait. Not her family, no. It was obvious she didn't fit the picture, like black paint slurred on a museum canvas. Where did she belong? Lucia had no answer, lonely in the turbid throng, the black clouds watching her like vultures on a rooftop.

I didn't know who I was. I was taking swigs from a vodka bottle after two years sober, after a life spent watching how alcohol slackens your holds, turns you into a loose prickly creature prone to catastrophic lapses. You might headbutt your daughter. Or, worse, tell the truth. Where could I find the truth about anything? It certainly wasn't here with my mother, her mouth perverted into a perpetual smile, and her husband, who earlier today, with his christian acuity, diagnosed Daniel as a sinner and absolved him immediately. I can't be mad at him for punching me! What would Jesus say? Though I'm sure somewhere in his

155

heart, Daniel was tied to a breaking wheel and Larry was bashing him up with hammers and clubs.

Where was the truth? Hidden behind the eyes? If we flayed someone open, could we find it? It wasn't with this girl, Olivia, and her floppy blond ignorance, shrilly proclaiming in her american tone, Let's be friends! the second she saw me. You're so pretty, Luchia! The c catching with an awful clank. Was I pretty? Was that my value in the precise economic geometry that shaped our skeletons for purchase? I fainted in the kitchen, and when I woke, my mother wanted to take me on a shopping spree. Let me buy you a new dress! You don't have to pay for anything when you're with me, Lucia. She bought me. I traded my worn flipflops for elegant new sandals. I was wearing her dress, her necklace. I ate dinner in their sumptuous, ridiculous hotel and spoke english while the waiters gawked at me suspiciously. I laughed at Larry's boring, unpleasant jokes. My mother dragged me into her world. Wasn't she mocking me? See, Lucia, even you have a price. The only moments she was ever partial to me were when Daniel faltered, and I basked in it, and now I was the one who accepted her new husband, so she rewarded me.

Marta sat on the bed watching silently while I tried everything on.

—What do you think?

—Lucia, didn't you say you were gonna stay here tonight?

—I'll take you to the roof some other time. Ok? I promise.

—It's gonna rain! You won't be able to see the fireworks anyway. Stay home!

She begged and I snapped at her. I was annoyed. My mother puppeted me so perfectly that I was her living copy, rebuffing Marta like she used to do to me. My grandmother heard and came into the room.

—Lucia, don't talk to her like that. She just wants you to stay. We both want you here.

—You lied to me grandma! I can't ever trust you again.

—Lucia, I'm sorry. Let's talk about it.

—No. You hurt me!

She started to cry. I stared at those weepy brown eyes, and I didn't flinch, I walked right past her and out of the apartment, as if that was courage! Why? Because she lied to me about the thing she was most ashamed of? No. It was deeper than that. She was the only model I had for goodness, the only inviolable life I could point to, the only standard I could judge myself against. There was no more certainty. I didn't know anything about anything. So later, when I was with my mom in her hotel room, sitting on the bed while she put her makeup on, just the two of us, talking and giggling excited about how I looked in my new dress and the wonderful day we spent together behaving like mothers and daughters were supposed to, I didn't know what to say when she brought it up.

—Lucia, have you ever thought about coming to the United States?

—What?

—You're only twenty one. You could still go to college. You know, Larry can get you free tuition at his school. And of course, we have room at the house. It's not forever. You can always come back. Think about it! It could be a great opportunity.

I smiled. That's what I did. I didn't think about Marta, or my grandmother, or anything, all I imagined was Lucia in a college library reading and studying for tests, walking in a college graduation, choosing her own life freely for the first time. Hadn't I spent so much time deferring my own life? I deserved better. I was smart and capable, I deserved opportunities, those denied me because of rotten facticity, opportunities Daniel had and squandered. I deserved, I deserved. What was more spurious than merit? But I understood the thinking now. My mother brought me into her arms and hugged me, and I could feel the cleanslate power of a new conquerable world revealing itself, as if my caravel landed on the empty shore and all I could see was an impossible verdancy to claim and cut through. What were love and duties to me? Dusty trade pieces, shackles to shuck. Wasn't it time to be a whole new Lucia?

We were almost on the beach and Olivia handed me a pill. You like percocets? Mommy and daddy were out in front of us, holding hands and laughing, and I took it and remembered a haze of brutal vomit covered mornings and dawn walks home, despair rattling like rocks in my brain. Marcus. Who, lucky Lucia! chose me out of all the bodacious avistable women, and I got a taste of what it was like to romp permissively around this city, served at places I served at, finally elevated to the vaunted realm my mom spent my childhood celebrating. All it took was submission. When he choked me past pleasure and said, I own you! I could give myself up because the return was so worthy. What was it worth being me, being free, if it meant a paltry, meager life? But when he returned that last time with his sure swaggering thunder and asked me to marry him, to live under his thrall and be thrust into that vile realm of motherhood where everything you do is a failure, I couldn't do it. I could see my grandma and Marta, brokenhearted at the door watching me leave, and I couldn't do it, because I was certain which side I was on, that I wouldn't be my mother under any circumstances.

But now. My mother was offering me an opportunity that had nothing to do with submission. Maybe her absence had transformed her into a mystic, malevolent force that only existed in my head, maybe she earnestly cared about me but her material concerns got in the way, she was diverted by a petty selfishness, but now that she was comfortable, she wanted to prop me up to free myself, to break the sullen bars of this soft brasilian prison. And this freedom could be generative. What could I do for Marta if I stayed here? What kind of life did I want to live? One like my grandma's? My mother was right about her, she didn't have the courage to live the life she wanted, she didn't even love my grandpa, she endured her flat, weary, unprofitable life, heaping misery on misery as time chewed its nails down to the quick. But I wanted to live! I wanted to live, but I wanted to be good. Good! What did that even mean? Grandma lied to me. I was so harsh to her about it, but it was only one lie. A lie that lied beneath all these foundations. Because if Nara wasn't grandpa's daughter then that drew a straight line to me, didn't it?

My mother lied to me for twenty one years. I remember she dragged

me to church the week before she left, and I sat the whole time, pum-
meled by stultifying boredom, staring at a striking painting of Saint
Sebastian, eternally fleched, arrows gored into his chest and neck, and I
remember I read that he was tied to a tree and shot with arrows but he
didn't die, and I thought, Wow, that's what having a father is like. God
was his daddy, and no matter how vicious the world's scourge became,
he could endure it, because he had a stable, strong, encompassing love
to catch him if he fell.

On the way home, I asked my mother for the last time.

—Who's my dad?

—Lucia!

—Seriously, mom. I don't care. I just wanna know.

—Your father is your father. God rest his soul. Enough, ok?

That was the same story I had to hear from Nara, who I trusted like
the sun, even though when I would look closely at Antonio's face, I
could see little resemblances. I was so naive, thinking that if it was true
someone would tell me, even Nara, because if it was true it would mean
Antonio wasn't the person she thought he was, right? Nobody is who
we think they are, there are real lives teeming under ground you can
never breach no matter how hard you dig, you're stuck trusting the long,
lying, soil sprouted stalks. I was Lucia, floating around untethered, un-
begotten. I would never have a father. Unless I chose this man, in front
of me. Who kissed my mother on the cheek and then jumped back
horrified when a big bellied man skipping through the crowd stopped
and yelled in his face.

—O Brasil tá fudido né mano?

—Ohbreegado! Larry said, and then tried to keep walking, but the
guy tugged on his shirt and held him there.

—Ué que mulher linda hein, é tua?

—What did he say?

—He said that's a beautiful woman, is she yours?

Before he could answer we heard someone scream, Cavalo! and
the multitude lurched in tandem and sent the drunk questioner down

headfirst on the cobblestones, where Larry would've fallen too, but I stepped in, unthinkingly, his big wet head thumped into my chest, and I caught him.

—Good catch Luchia!

He got balanced back on his feet and thanked me. Luchia, Luchia, Luchia. Maybe I was part of this family now. I could be like Olivia, who squeezed my arm and joked that I must be stronger than I look. Olivia who frolicked boundlessly, she didn't have to know anything, she didn't have to do anything because she had a doting father whose wealth shined on her, so she could prance around my carioca garden stomping all the flowers, forever consequenceless. Why couldn't I have been born like that? Olivia. I could wear her name like this dress. Try on that life. I could take my mom's offer, and I could have that. How fast would I change? How true was the me entombed in this lucialike body? There was nothing natural in a name, it was like clothes, a daily habit, you wore it to hide the nothing you were born with. My mother recognized that and she put on a new outfit. A sharp horror shuddered through me as the thunder cracked above, and I realized, there was nothing stopping me, I could leave all this behind.

BEFORE WE walked down to the sand, Olivia asked her father if she could go to the main stage to watch the concert, bringing me along of course. Larry looked out into the roaring multitudinous sea of soaked people dressed in white, drunk, screaming, and stumbling.

—I guess so. But be careful girls!

—Text me updates, okay?

I thought my mother said that to Olivia, but she was looking right at me. I didn't have my phone, but that gesture shook me. Did she care? It felt like suddenly there was an anastomosis between the rended, diverging streams of our lives, and I felt, as a shock even to myself, that I could ignore the initial separation, treat it like a tossed rippleless pebble in the riverrunning flow of time, and move on. The hot rain hit my face, and I was happy. I hugged my mother goodbye, and when Larry held his hand out to shake mine, I hugged him. I thanked him for taking me out to dinner and I said it was very nice to meet him, and I walked off with Olivia, feeling the rumblings of a potential sisterhood.

I was corrupted, but everything was corrupted, everyone here wearing white, foolishly aping a forgotten candomblé ritual, turistas heading shoreward to toss their white flowers in the ocean as an offering to Iemanjá because it was a Thing to Do on a travel guide. This storm felt like a judgement. Xangô banging his axe on the world's roof. Maybe it would rupture and release another earthwiping flood, but with no Noah this time because nobody was sinless and nobody deserved to survive. Rio de Janeiro would be left to rot and ruin, extinguished by perpetuity. My death would mean nothing to time, it would keep rolling on, immense beyond imagination, it would be around long enough to see even the world's skeleton tossed on the bone pile. Why not live now? Live for me? My finite material reality was a truth I grasped everyday. If I lived for that, I couldn't fail. Or I could be my grandmother, living for her saviors and paradises on behalf of whom she paragoned an impossible virtue which she failed to uphold. It was all failure, death, and lack. Maybe goodness was an error. Maybe sin was invented to implement domination. Maybe it was time for Lucia to live for herself.

—I'm trying to meet up with this cute girl I met yesterday.

We were in the middle of the closed down, peopleful street. Olivia was talking to me.

—I gotta text her to see where she is.

—Oh.

—Her name's Rita.

—Rita?

—Isn't it pretty?

It couldn't be my Rita. I didn't say anything. We kept walking. I led the way, pushing through a gargantuan mass of men who swayed over me like rickety buildings. The path cleared a little, and we were in a space with more breathing room. Olivia had her phone out trying to text, intermittently wiping the rain off with her shirt. She looked up and spoke to me.

—I mean, you're a lesbian, right?

—What?

—Sorry just a vibe I got. I'm drunk.

She pulled out a flask from her shorts and handed it to me, and I took a long swig. Everyone was always trying to tell me or ask me who I was, but I didn't know! I felt tyrannized by ascriptions, I was crumbling under the weight of a named and categorized Lucia. I hadn't had sex in two years. I loved Marcus. I loved his body and his strength and his unexpected moments of kindness, but it was nothing like what I felt with Rita. Those long nights in her apartment with a cramped fan sputtering as we talked and held eachother until sunrise, those full ample curves and the dizzying plunges deep in a soft pink pleasure. There were others too. Nameless nobodies who took what they could from me when I was addicted to sundering myself from my actions. I loved Rita and I told her so, but I couldn't be with her because of preponderant responsibilities I had, over and above romance and pleasure, I needed to look after my dying grandpa, my fading grandma, and my little orphaned tamanduá, Martinha, my cousin daughter sister, and I needed to figure out who the hell Lucia was. Two years of dutystuck asceticism and I was more lost than ever. I felt like my limbs were amputated and scattered, left to crawl disgustingly toward a wholeness that was never really there. I needed a thunderbolt to scalp me down to my soul and melt my flesh and maybe the charred remainder would reveal the truth. If there was any truth at the core.

Olivia was holding her phone out tauntingly. I almost warned her, but at the moment the thought occurred to me, a little kid like a bolting blur nabbed it out of her hand and took off running, navigating the crowd as expertly as a rat.

—My phone!

—Thief!

—Ladrão!

—Policia!

The multitude, like a mob, started to run in his direction. You could feel them teem with a hungry frenzy as they sought to stamp out the furtive flame of the quickhanded kid. I had no choice but to go along with them, my sandals slipping and splashing in the street puddles. Olivia was raving angrily.

—There he is!

A burly man snatched him by the collar of his worn Vasco jersey, the kid dangling there by the scruff like a bear cub, and the crowd circled, shouting nastiness in english and portuguese and spanish, a cosmopolitan scolding. The kid looked scared, his eyes dark with a silent sadness. I thought of Marta, languishing at home tonight, unprotected.

—I didn't take nothing.

—Liar!

—He took my phone, I saw him!

Three military police officers shoved their way through our ring of vigilante justice.

—What's going on here?

The civilian bystander let the kid go.

—This kid stole her phone!

—It's a lie! I didn't take nothing!

—Give it up kid, don't waste our time.

The kid looked like he was going to protest again, but the thunder roared so loudly that attention on him wavered for a second and he tried to squirm away, before one of the cops grabbed him by the back of the shirt and pulled him back so hard he fell and hit his head on the cement.

—You're gonna run away moleque? Show me some respect!

He pulled out his baton and whacked the kid on the stomach. He retched in pain and curled onto his side like an armadillo, but when he turned, Olivia's phone slipped out of his pocket and landed in a muddy puddle on the concrete.

—The phone!

The crowd exploded. The cop hit the kid again with the baton and he started to cry, he sounded like Marta crying, and the crowd cheered as the cop beat him and Olivia grabbed her phone and stood next to me, yelling provocations, but I could only think of Marta, this was a little boy, so what he stole a phone! he was a little boy and he was getting beaten on the concrete and everyone was just watching, infected by rabid lunacy, like this was a normal thing. I couldn't stand it anymore, all my drunken opioidic warmth was replaced by a stiff panic, and I screamed and dove down and embraced the kid. The cop almost brought the baton down on top of me but stopped short. I could feel the kid trembling underneath me, panting terrified like a trapped dog.

—Get outta there girl!

One of the other cops came and pulled me off. I was crying, repeating, Don't hit him don't hit him, between sobs. The crowd booed.

—Porra garota! Stop crying!

The officer put his baton away and simply handcuffed the kid and walked away, dispersing the inflamed vigilantes.

—Fun's over!

I was still crying. Olivia grabbed my face and made me look at her.

—It's okay ! The kid's fine! I got my phone. Don't cry.

I pushed her away from me and turned around.

—Jesus Luchia. Get a grip.

—That's not my name! My name isn't Luchia! It's Lucia! With a soft fucking c!

—I'm sorry geeze what got into you?

—You did! You almost got that kid killed over your stupid fucking phone!

—I'm just supposed to let him steal from me?

—You don't get it!

—I get it. He's a poor kid who needs a phone. It's mine though.

—You don't understand anything!

—Chill Lucia. I thought we were having a good time.

—You're just a dumb american! Fuck off!

—Oh my god. I didn't do anything!

She was standing there looking bewildered. She really didn't get it! She would never understand. I threw my hands up and walked away, pushing through the dense multitude.

—Lucia come back!

I made the wrong decision. I should've stayed home tonight. Marta! She was all alone. And I was the only one who could really protect her. Instead I followed my mother out here, I entertained her temptations, I made the wrong choice, but that's the great illusion, that we have anything to do with what we choose. This lucialike boat was caught in the turbulent currents of all the lives preceding mine. My great grandmother's choices, my grandma's choices, my mother's choices accumulated in a torrential flow that left me paddleless and listing, about to crash into whatever dangers appeared in front of me. I couldn't stop if I wanted to. I wouldn't know if I wanted to! What was me, and what was a ripple set in motion decades ago by a rock plopped into a random river? We were all swept up in the same old water. How could that kid say, I will steal that phone? How could my grandma say, I will cheat on my husband? How could my mother decide to leave? Nobody had a choice.

What would I do? If it was my fate to be just like my mother, there was nothing I could do. We were all sick trees planted in a sick soil, everyone in my whole family from the very beginning, all we did was hurt eachother. It's these entanglements that sink us. I needed to be perfectly alone, where there was nobody to harm, nobody to betray, no reason for me to be Lucia, I would be as pure as the wind and the air, and then finally I could be good. But there was no leaving this web. We were jumbled in this muddle forever. Was it really all oblivion? Just terror and torpor until your coffin is sealed shut? It couldn't be. What about those grinning mornings spent listening to my grandma's stories and hearing Marta laugh? Love was anguish when you were in the dark pit of it, but then the pretty sunshine peeked over the horizon and you forgot. How could you just live for yourself? That would grind you down to a nub of a soul. It would be an emaciated life. I didn't want to spend my brief drama of flesh in spiritual penury. I didn't want to be Lucia if it meant being comfy and cozy, relaxed on some american couch stuffing my face, with nobody to hurt, nobody to truly care about. I wanted to be bad if it meant I could be good! If it meant I was really loving. Existence was a putrid, overflowing dump, filled with all these dumb idiots shouting and getting in my way, but I wanted all of it. Because if the storm scalded it all to bones and dust, the seasons might keep passing quietly, but it would be missed. I wasn't flung into this wild concatenation choiceless. I was free. I would be the Lucia I wanted to be. It started now. I had to go back home and apologize to Marta, but first I needed to tell my mother that my life was here. I made my choice.

THE MUVUCA tide was rising. Everyone who was hanging around the street was now pushing their way to the beach to watch the impending fireworks, and I was in the middle of it, being slowly pushed along, unable to cut my own path through the crowd. My brief euphoria now seemed like an effect of the alcohol and percocet and I was at the bottom of a valley, tired, with a dry throat, and getting even more drenched by the increasing rain. The multitude around me made me nervous. People were tense, shoving, and the nearest stage was emitting a sound like train gears creaking in hell. I was still sure about my love for the world, but superiority to my fate was seeming like a more difficult thing to gain.

But I needed to see my mother, and I needed to tell her that I didn't want anything from her, anything at all. Honestly, I was getting angry again. Why did she think she could come here and brandish these luxuries in my face as if that was going to make up for everything she ever did to me. Oh I'm sorry Lucia! Here's a necklace. Here's an expensive dress. You like that? How bout you come to the United States and we'll pile a bunch of gifts up and you can sit on it like a throne? Will you love mommy now? It was phony bullshit! Wasn't it? She was putting on a good mother act in front of her stepdaughters and Larry. Why the hell would I believe any of her promises? She was sowing discord to try to get me on her side, that was what she always did, so why would she be different now? She told me the truth about Nara and grandma, but that wasn't for my benefit, she was trying to tear the remaining threads of my family to shreds! I was mad now, I was really mad. Lucia was a sheep! My mother had pulled the wool over my eyes again with another nasty fraud. Look at me. I was lost now in this lousy night being batted around by turistas and drunks when I just wanted to be home and dry and safe with Marta and my grandma. Daniel's reaction was right. I should've screamed and punched and clawed and put a middle finger right in Larry's face! No! No! I didn't know! Violence was always destructive, all those impulses, rage and envy and hatred, they just sucked you down into their noxious whirlpool, and if you ever got out, you were left crippled and coughing blood.

You had to forgive and be kind and merciful. I needed to forgive my grandma. I could understand why she wouldn't tell me, the link between me and Nara was just so clear, and our lives were safely covered by the delusion that my father was the pernicious american, it couldn't be anyone else. My father, who pulled up to the Ilha do Governador, left his caravels floating in the Guanabara Bay and found a world he was ready to remake in his image, a woman who would do anything to be his. Maybe he really was my father and he chose to treat me the way he did because he wanted to punish my mother, for cheating and what exactly? Did she even cheat on him? Anyway, he had another family! My mother wasn't allowed to have boyfriends?

Or I was the grievous fault. A child born to another man, a burning shame living under his roof. I could think of it so many different ways. Maybe my mother was the great victim, her man stolen and her dreams usurped by her sister, beaten and belittled by an american who wouldn't marry her, and so skewed up in her moral compass that she thought it all right to abandon her kids and move away. Or, she was a villain, and she lied to me my whole life about my father, got my aunt thrown in prison and my real father killed, and flew off without an ounce of love for me or Daniel. Thinking was a losing proposition, anything could become true. You just had to choose your convictions and keep them. My mother was evil.

I stepped down to the muckslop sand, and there was more space to maneuver. I knew where she was going to be standing, straight in line with the Marriott well before the shore, around the same spot we stood the few times we celebrated New Year's here as a family, and I walked that way, longing to be a kid again, safe in my grandmother's arms as she shushed away the firework cacophony while my grandpa teased me playfully. Don't be scared, safadinha! There would be no new year for my grandfather, his history was vaporized in a crematorium, all his hopes, loves, crimes, and humiliations a pile of indistinguishable ashes. His fading photograph would remain to remind us of violence and error, as if that was all there was to him. We would be judged by our worst acts because really that was all that mattered, a lifetime of good graces could be wiped out in a single instant. But was the opposite true? Could you eliminate a bad life with a good act, a few positive steps? Was my mother doing that? No. I needed to prove she was evil. I needed to look in her eyes and confront her and prove it to myself once and for all.

I was in an area with real space, finally. I could reach both my arms out without touching anybody for the first time tonight, so I stopped. I needed to breathe and compose myself. I was distressed and nauseated, whatever substances I consumed at the vapor dreg end of their effect. I felt like a gnawed cob of corn tossed in the trash, bare and useless, but I needed to keep going, finding my mother would be much easier than pushing my way home. I turned to look at the Marriott which had the time displayed on its façade. It was 23:54. And suddenly I saw a figure barreling through the crowd like he was hellbent on a mission. A shiver went down my spine, I knew it immediately, as soon as I saw his head bobbing through the multitude. He was right in front of me.

—Daniel! What are you doing?

—Lucia!

He grabbed my hands. It was Daniel, but it wasn't. His eyes were crazy, burning with some faraway fire, and the way he was grabbing my hands was scary, full of perfervid purpose.

—I'm gonna do it Lucia! For us! For the both of us!

—What are you gonna do?

—I know they're around here! I'm gonna kill him!

—No Daniel! Don't do that!

—For us!

He let go of my hands and took off, walking fast like he knew exactly what he was doing. He was going to kill Larry. Oh my god! That would be the worst thing he could do. For us. Us, he said. He never ever did anything for us. I remember the day I found out my socalled father died, it wasn't until Daniel came back. I didn't even know he was going to come back, and one day he was at the door, glumpy and irascible. I had to press everyone for the information, why was Daniel back? What happened? Until finally my mother told me, Your father killed himself. I didn't know for a month! He was dead? So he would never want me, there was no chance, it was over. I sat at the kitchen table and cried inconsolably, hysterical. Daniel walked into the room and thumped me hard.

—What are you crying for?

—Dad died.

—Don't be sad! He wasn't your dad!

He walked away laughing. He's right, I thought, I don't have anybody to cry about. I was alone and low and alone. He wasn't my brother, he never thought of himself as my brother, and now he was going to murder someone on my behalf! It was insane. What was I going to do? I couldn't stop him. I couldn't move, I was stuck again in the crowd. And then I heard a far off commotion, screaming, but not goodtime screaming, it was noise like an unexpected alarm. It was swelling with the sound of the countdown.

—Ten!

—Nine!

—Eight!

—Seven!

—Six!

—Five!

—Arrastão!

The people around me started to run. I ran too, clumsy in my new sandals. The fireworks were booming overhead and everyone around me was fleeing terrified. It was getting harder for me to run because the sand was bunching up underneath my foot, pushing it out against the sandal strap, until finally the strap broke and my loose shoe tripped me. I was on the ground shielding myself from the stampede. People were leaping over me, tripping, stepping on my feet and my stomach, but my head was well tucked and covered. I heard someone fall right next to me and I peeked out behind the cover of my hands.

—Lucia!

It was my mother, fallen right there. She stood up quickly and grabbed my hands.

—Lucia! Lucia! Get up!

She helped me up. We were getting trashed around but she held me steady.

—Lucia! He's dead!

—What?

—Daniel killed him!

Oh no. We ran toward the calçadão. Oh no. If Daniel killed him. It couldn't be true. The fireworks were still booming and people around us were falling, all the horrid sounds bursting agonized and clear. Larry was dead? There were going to be two more fatherless girls in the world. How terrible! I hoped Daniel didn't kill him. The way my mother looked when she told me made me feel like I was wrong about everything, her sorrow was so extreme and unmistakable. My poor mother! Misfortune hit her hard in the heart again. I held her hand and we ran. On the steps to get up to the calçadão, people were pulling and pushing eachother off, rough and careless, but a man helped us up and we were on the safety of the sidewalk. It felt like everything cooled. I hugged my mother tight and she cried against my chest. But then I saw a teenager sprinting down the street and military police officers charging after him screaming, Stop! Stop! The kid stopped and pulled out a gun and shot at them, this wasn't even a block away, the bullets were flying random through the crowd and the cops drew their guns and released an onslaught. No! I couldn't see if they hit him or not because everything turned to chaos everyone started running again it was a full riot I grabbed my mother's hand and we sprinted toward our apartment I was barefoot I didn't even realize I lost my shoes the cobblestones stabbed into my feet and all the sounds around me flattened into silence and we ran and ran and ran and I was afraid.

MARIA! A LIGHTNING crack like a booming voice woke me. I sat up in the dark room. He was still there, paunchy in his sleepy slab. His sleep apnea machine chugging. Fuck! It was a dream. His body on my homeland sand, knives sticking out like porcupine quills. Think of my despair. Knowing he was still breathing. That I was still rapunzled in his deadwife decorated tower. I went back to sleep. Back to my spoon shovel freedom dreams. How would I ever slough my doughy yoke? Larry. It turned sour so quickly! Back when I was grasping godward, looking for something to plug the emptiness, I found his videos online. Those steel blue eyes and that smile. I had a spark of life for the first time in years of dour days and nothing nights. I sent him an email. Soon we were swapping lusty ardent letters, trading confessions. He told me about his cancer eaten ugly wife. I told him about The American. We'd spent hours on skype in the middle of the night when my children made themselves delightfully scarce. I would get naked on the camera and touch myself, feeling like a teenager again. His face would get all red and prudish and we would laugh.

One day he said, Marry me. Come live in Ohio. It was the proposal I'd been waiting for my whole miserable life. Yes! Yes! But I should've done more research. I didn't know he was holing me up in bumfuck nowhere. Stupidville, Ohio. Where he would take me to excruciating, eyegougingly endless dinners with his insane religious friends, and he would mummify me in these long puritan dresses and drag me to church. When we got home, he wasn't the man from the emails. There was no fire. He was stuffy and churlish, weird about sex. He didn't like to kiss, or caress. He didn't go down on me once! Ever! He would stick his little chode in, gyrate twice, and come like he was holding in a sneeze.

How was it for you?

Sure, I had a walk in closet. Sure, I had shoes and purses and all the shit I imagined came with an american life. But at what cost? Not to mention his cunty, spoiled daughters. Who spent their weekends drugging and carousing with their phony catholic friends while he thought they were at sleepovers. He was a fool. Then I found out he was worse than a fool. He bamboozled some greasyhaired girl with pimples and bad parents who taught her to trust manly authoritative airs. Whenever I would walk into church the women would whisper, rumor, whisper. As if I didn't know. He embarrassed me. I could ignore his predations on weakwilled students. I could endure him clipping my wings and caging me. But I would not be humiliated. I wanted him to die. I started fantasizing about it. A few drops of arsenic in his bland morning cereal. Or maybe I would nag him into a heart attack. Cut the brakes on his car. I prayed for sudden diseases to befall him. Something rare and quickly fatal. Every night he would lock the doors and check and recheck the security cameras in his bumbling anxious fright. And as soon as he was sound asleep I would undo everything. Hoping some thug from a bad neighborhood would tie him up and fuck me right in front of him and put a bullet in his head.

All I needed was for him to die. My name was on everything. And I was in love again. One of the university donors who would come over for dinner. He was six foot six and sturdy, hard everywhere Larry was soft. Jim the surgeon with the dowdy wife. We would meet in Weirton motel rooms and he would thrill me and tell me he loved me and that he wanted to be with me. But Larry wouldn't allow me to leave. Wouldn't allow himself to be humiliated. He would cause me problems, with my citizenship, everything. I needed a clean, easy break. A break that would leave me independent financially.

That's when the dream started to infect my mind like a tumor.

He died in different ways everytime, but it was always in Rio, and Daniel was always there. Of course, Daniel's last words to me would play over and over in my head. I'll fucking kill you if you come back! He was brash and rash like his father, and he held a grudge like any good Cunha. I knew he would do something stupid. He didn't have the guts to kill me. But maybe Larry. I knew all I needed to do was get him there and he would die. The trouble was how. Everytime I even mentioned Brazil he laughed his stupid laugh and said, Too dangerous for me! But I started to plant little breadcrumbs. The girls wanted to go somewhere on vacation.

How bout Rio?

We were thinking like Paris.

But Rio is so fun and hot and cheap!

I never spoke about that infernal city, but I started to mention it more and more. I started to tell Larry how much I missed it. I softened his fear. Let him know that the danger was in the media portrayal. That everything would be fine. The girls booked their trip, but he still resisted. I thought they would come back with rave safe reviews and then we would go. But I saw a news report that sent a shockwave through my body. I almost yelped with pleasure. American tourists decapitated at the Christ. Yes! It was a sign. The universe was on my side. Two days later, the rotten fruit of my womb calls me up and lets me know my father died.

Larry! Larry! My daddy died!

Tears and tears and tears.

I have to go back. I have to see my family.

Okay, honey. Let's do it!

What I didn't expect was Lucia. In my mind, she was still the ugly gloomy teenager with knobby joints and jutty ribs like a crack whore. Obsessed with my horrible sister. I thought my mother's influence on her would be too detrimental. I thought she was just going to be another one of them. But we talked on the phone a few times, and I actually liked her. She was smart and mature. She would throw passive aggressive jabs at me like she really was my daughter. I couldn't believe it! Daniel was always my favorite. Daniel was so handsome. Built just like his father. He had a conqueror's ease. There were no obstacles in life for men like that. But of course, he turned into a fucking loser. The limpdick genes from his pervert father and cuckold grandpa were just too overpowering. I thought he would be the one to save me, but just like every other man, he failed.

I thought Lucia would always be worthless. She was conceived in a blistering March of confusion. Her very existence ruined everything with The American. But then she comes to get me at the airport. I hadn't seen her, not even a picture of her, for six years. She was beautiful! Grown into a real woman! I couldn't believe it. My dark ugly duckling transformed into a swan! She was courteous and bristly and funny. I saw the hateful gazes she shot at Larry. My affection grew by the second. I knew I could save her from her grandma's evil clutches. From Nara's hagiographied ghost. After Daniel wreaked his brief havoc in the kitchen, I knew for sure. I could take her to the United States! Save her from the mudshit life she'd be doomed to if she stayed, forced to look after my mother and that fucking slum girl.

The thing was, I never wanted to be a mother. The American tricked me. He led me to believe that Daniel was my bridge out of here. Instead, what did I get out of it? A third floor apartment in Copacabana. The third floor! When I knew how much money that bastard had. We should've been living in a Leblon penthouse. I would never be free like I wanted to be, stuck with my parents and shackled to those strange things that popped out of me. One minute you could control them, they would do what you say and rely on you. The next minute they had their own lives happening behind the eyes. It was creepy. I never got used to it. Even despite the few blips of joy. My gigglesome pair with their milk-teeth all loose, piled on our bed in the Ilha. I would get the flashlight out and make shapes on the dark wall. We would make up stories and voices for the bunnies and elephants and tigers.

What's the bunny's name mommy? Do it again!

Weren't they the most precious things in the world with those unstoppable laughs? I loved their smallness. Their warm little tricks and mean cozy turns. All the greedy gushes out of their small souls. The lazy leaks down their brash bodies. They would turn into dirty unwashed beasts after playing at the beach all day. Tracking sand through the house while I yelled at them. But after they showered and changed we'd go down to Blockbuster and pick a movie. The three of us would tuck under the same blanket, Daniel on my right, Lucia on my left. These things that I created! They lived inside me!

Those moments with them were the highest peaks of love I felt in my life.

But it was over too fast. They wanted too much. They were little leeches sucking the life force out of me. I couldn't be free and still love them. Why did it have to be me or them? They grow into these frightening monsters you can't hope to control. So I chose me. I would've been better off if my mother left like she wanted to! Instead she stuck around and sunk me with her rancor. I saw it in her eyes. She looked at me like the reason she would never be happy.

I wanted my children to be better off. To choose their own freedom. So I left!

But now Lucia was past mothering. She wasn't some needy suckling destructive force. She was a real person. We could be friends! I could give her the opportunity I chased for years and years. We could have a real relationship. I saw the vision spill out in front of me as soon as Daniel arrived in his frantic state as the tumult raged around us on the beach. Daniel too weak to accomplish his mission!

He wanted to kill me.

He wanted to kill Larry!

But instead, he stabbed his knife into an innocent thug's dirty leg and my mission was accomplished. It was exactly how I dreamed it. I almost felt bad. Seeing the shocked face that would serve as Larry's death mask. I didn't care. I wouldn't miss him. Too many of my men had died for me to make a big stink about it. His girls would cry! They would weep and weep and weep. Especially when they found out who got all the money.

I wore the panicked grief and ran.

No, no! Daniel killed him!

I fell right into my girl.

Lucia!

We ran as the populace exploded and turned this shithole into a nightmare.

But at that moment I knew, Lucia was mine and Rio was dead to me.

MEMORY IS a mosquito. Dengue filled, yellow fevered. The first time death sunk its claws into me, I was a little girl. My grandma came to die in our house. My grandma who never came over even though she lived in town. Life dug trenches in her face, it was wrinkled and wound tight. I never saw her smile. Her chin slunk toward her chest and she shuffled around the house quiet and hunched. She had a brain tumor. A pumpkin growing in the soil of her skull. My mother, always wanting to spare my awful sister life's worst brunts, put up a cot in the kitchen for her to sleep alone. While my grandmother eroded every night next to me in bed. She would wake up screaming and nobody would come help her. She'd hawk her talons into me like she was trying to give me her pain. I would stroke her head wondering if I could pop it if I pressed hard enough.

I watched her gaunt face wither away for three months.

One night, she screamed herself hoarse. And it stopped. There was a rattle and a huff and she was gone. Leaving bulging eyes and a skeleton head on the pillow next to me. I didn't sleep and I was too scared to get anyone. Her corpse was cold by daylight. We plunged her into the ground with no fanfare, no waterworks. But death was on me. Like slick poison from a dart frog. Her screams were lapidated in the caves of my ears. Nara came back to share my bed after that. I always expected to wake up to her corpse. Instead, she'd wake me up with her piss stained nightmares. Maria don't tell mommy, ok? I would have to clean our sheets in the middle of the night while she stared at me with her pouty bottom lip. She looked like a mangy street mutt. Nara, my lifedrain. She stalked me like a filthy seagull squawking reminders of my hodunk life.

It felt like real life used to pass over me in airplanes. I would sneak into the movie theater to watch old american movies and drool. I wanted to be Marilyn Monroe. Beautiful, blond, and American. I felt like if I could get to Los Angeles my life would be made! I wanted a lavish, powerful life. Which I got a glimpse of when we went to see my aunt in Copacabana. I wanted a mansion like that. Diamonds and jewels. She was an old hag and all she had to do was suck the dick of a fat oaf to keep that up? I thought that sounded pretty good! But there were strictures on my life.

I lived in a shitty house with two jokes for parents. A cuck and a witch. And the cuck would give the witch all night earbeatings where he'd maledict her, slutwhorebitchcunt! while I shivered awake in the adjacent room. The next morning he'd rise from the scummy pond of his stupor, syrupy and sorry, full of empty promises. My mother redirected her cowardly impotent rage from him to me. She would dress me in rags, but when she got a little extra money, Nara suddenly stepped out in a brand new dress. I was the oldest! It should've been me! I had no privileges. I was fat and ugly. The Island bumpkins used to jeer at me. They make those Cunha girls extra thick! I thought my beauty would never bloom. I was fifteen and an eyesore. Meanwhile my younger sister, who got grown tits and an ass at thirteen, flaunted her goods all around town. Enjoying the leers and the dark attention. She got popular, invited to all the parties. My mom would taunt me.

Why don't you go out more, Maria? You should be like your sister.

You mean the Blow Job Queen of Ribeira?

If I gave it up like she did I'm sure I'd get some invites!

But one summer, my beauty bloomed. When I turned seventeen, I grew up and thinned out. I was the one getting gawked at when we walked down the street. My sister was already haggard and used by fifteen. That's when I met him. In all his sand lambuzled glory.

I happened to stop on the beach to watch a soccer match.

I hated sports, but I saw this boy, shirtless and rippling, golden in the December sun. He scored on a bicycle kick and I couldn't help but cheer. He saw me and smiled. After the game he came walking up to me, wiping off sweat with a tattered Vasco jersey.

I'm Chico. You're pretty.

I'm pretty. I mean, I'm Maria.

I was shy and embarrassed. A boy had never liked me. Out in the open, unashamedly.

Suddenly Chico had his fingers laced in mine and nothing mattered. Time stretched and faded and nothing else meant anything to me. I didn't have to think of going home to my awful house that reeked of failure. I didn't have to worry about my father starting his drunk sloppy fights. I didn't have to worry about carrying him home from the bar slumped on my back like a flaccid cross. I didn't have to endure my mother's endless self righteous babbling. Or my sister's envy. My toes were in the sand and my head was snug on my boy's chest. I was Chico's. Forever. I would stay awake dreaming of his eyes. I would bury my smile into my tattered pillow and burst with private joy.

Chico!

I didn't want to go to school. I didn't want to go home. I was obsessed. I wanted Chico's body from morning until night. I wanted to consume him completely. Pour his smell all over me. Be buried in his skin. Some nights we would stay on the beach fucking until dawn. He

would play me songs on his guitar and sing to me. He was going to
be a famous musician. I was going to be an actress. As soon as we got
enough money, we were running away to Hollywood. He would pound
me with his huge vibrant youth and I would see our future written out
in the abundant stars. I would spend every night emparadised with my
heart's lone thought.

But one night, my sister caught us.

She was coming home from some late night whoring.

And I heard an awful sound while Chico was on top of me.

Maria! I'm telling mom!

What did I care? My life was split from theirs as soon as I had real
love.

I walked home in the clear morning glowing and confident.

My mother was waiting for me at the door.

Where were you all night?

Nowhere.

Your sister told me. Who is this boy?

Nobody.

Tell me who it is.

Nobody.

Tell me now, Maria!

It's Chico. Seu Marcelo's son.

She smacked me across the face.

I was seventeen. She never hit me before. I laughed.

You can't hurt me.

You are not allowed to see him again!

Fuck you, mom.

I laughed again. She kept talking but I walked away. She had no
control over me. Her slaps and scolds were like little pebbles thrown
against a fortress.

She was puny and weak and pathetic.

But I didn't understand exactly why. Nara was allowed to slatter it
up with every Jorge, José, and Gustavo who threw a nickel her way, but

I couldn't have my love? I thought it was because she hated me. Which she did, furiously. Since I was a little girl, I never received a tender look, even a kiss on the head from my mother. I didn't understand. But it all came together two weeks later. Chico told me he was going to visit some family in São Paulo for the weekend. A whole weekend without Chico! I bawled. But the next morning, my sister came running inside.

Oh my god Maria, I have terrible news.

What happened?

I don't know if I can even tell you.

Tell me!

You could almost see that bitch smile, delighted to report the worst thing I ever heard.

Chico and his dad died in a car crash.

What?

They ran headfirst into oncoming traffic. My friend said the whole car blew up. Their bodies were burnt pretty bad. Too bad, I know you liked Chico.

Liked Chico! My body was sawed in half. I couldn't feel my hands or my feet or my head. I spent the next days in a numb constant weep. I was flattened. I couldn't stop crying but I didn't even realize I was crying. I wasn't thinking. My clothes were soaked in tears and snot. The strangest part, my mother acted like my mirror. She was broken, devastated. At the towncrowded closedcasket funeral that my father refused to go to, my mother ululated like a widow.

The truth hit me like a brick on the head. Marcelo. That was why my aunt said what she said. This was why our family was a joke around town. I always knew in my heart me and Nara weren't sisters. But I didn't really know until that moment. That's why she didn't want me with Chico, she was impeding me the life she was denied. I went to my father and asked him. He told me everything, how she left him. How she betrayed him.

My mother the saint! She really was a witch.

Finally, I confronted her.

Marcelo is Nara's father. I know everything.

No, Maria! Your father is Nara's father.

Stop lying to me! I know everything!

Maria please. Don't tell your sister.

I have no sister and I have no mother.

Don't say that.

You're dead to me.

And she was, from that moment on. I graduated high school and started working hard in the city. I was determined to leave my soul sucking provincialism. I had three jobs at a time. I was auditioning for plays, tv shows. I started getting work as a model. I was saving money and I had a plan. I was going to the United States, and I was going to be a star. I was going to be rich and famous. I was so beautiful! My mother's and my sister's eyes were green seas of envy when I came home with my nice clothes and good makeup. I didn't even speak to them. There would be no paradise where they encroached. They had to be gated out of my bliss on bliss.

I was so close.

And then thwarted!

By a god glowing in the Copacabana sun with a dragon tattooed on his arm. Of course there were plenty of men after Chico. I would take the long dull bus ride into Copacabana every Saturday, and I would find some foolish tourist who wanted a Brazilian model on his arm for the day. I got good. I could guess which hotel they were staying at with one look. I got to know all the different types of rooms at the Palace. But there was no love. I thought it would never happen again. I thought Chico's death took that away from me forever. But then one day right on the boardwalk.

Where you going girl? Not gonna stop to talk to me?

Who are you?

Antonio Bala. This is my beach.

Tchau tchau, Bala.

You ain't walking away like that. Spend the day with me, see what's up.

Nah, I got plans.

Those turista boys can wait.

He saw right through me! He had this wry smile and a sun soaked chiseled stomach. Everything he said was magic. He tromped around with an oozing swagger like he owned the world. He'd take me up to his hot little shack on the hill as if it was a palace. I was drowning in him. I spent three months of Copacabana weekends with him, and then one morning I woke up to a shock. I felt different. I knew something was wrong. It was like stepping in shit on the street. At this point, no words were passing between me and my mother. But she saw me and spit out a hex.

You're pregnant.

I knew she was right. I was pissed. I started to get fat. I was losing work. Antonio was thrilled about it, he desperately wanted a child. I wanted to abort it so bad, but I didn't know anyone who ever did that. I had no options. I tried to drink and drug it out of me. Me and Antonio would fight for hours about it and he would beg me not to do it. But I knew, if I had a child here, with him, it would fuck me forever. I would never have the life I wanted.

One morning, like a gift from God, I felt a pain so grave it shook my limbs.

In a few anguished hours it was over.

The whole bloody goo was gone from me and I could be free again.

I was euphoric. Antonio was furious.

Why are you so happy?

Because you're a poor loser and any child of yours is gonna be a poor loser too! I didn't say. I didn't say anything. There started to be a coldness between us. Even though despite myself I was still in love. But I knew Antonio couldn't give me what I wanted.

It all ended worse than I could've anticipated.

One day, my mother sent Nara to surveil me.

I was at a kiosk with Antonio and his friends and she found me.

Woah, this is your sister?

Don't talk to her. She's leaving.

Nah, I think she should stick around.

Oh yeah? Have her then. Fuck you both!

Maria, chill.

I stormed away.

Antonio was supposed to meet me at a club that night, and he didn't.
I knew it was over. While I was burning with fury in the middle of some
indigent dance floor thumping with brain rattling samba, there he was.
The American. In his shining ambassadorial glory.

You wanna dance?

We danced for two minutes, and then I was sucking his dick in a
cab on the way to his hotel. I was angry and foolish. He was in town for
a week, and after he left, I was pregnant and Nara was with Antonio.

I knew two things for sure.

I would have that child and I would get revenge on my sister.

TIME CURDLES like milk. All these dead clumps of feelings, like bugs
smashed on an Ohio truck windshield. I gave up my life and I was
a mother. My dreams melted in the Brazilian sun, and I became an
exhausted, emptied, cracked egg of a human. I thought Daniel would
save me. I thought he could be my palm tree planted in a rich soil, that
he would grow sturdy enough to provide a home for me. Then it didn't
work. His father didn't want me. So I had Lucia. She was conceived in
a muddled month of murky margins. He already didn't trust me. Lucia
became the ultimate thorn in our relationship.

I loved The American bitterly for thirteen years.

Years of solemn waiting. Years of piled disappointments. My joy
would crest when he came. He'd play the jocular father for ten minutes
and lapse into wallshaking rage fits. He was like a fire that consumed
everything around him. Thirteen years and I never stopped hoping that
he would marry me. That he would love me back. I sent him our son,
thinking maybe, maybe if he lived with Daniel. Daniel who was strong

and handsome and looked like him. Maybe if he lived with Daniel, he would realize we were his real family. And then I received a phone call that crumpled my heart and threw it in the trash.

It was a shrill bitch of a voice that I'll never forget.

Is this Maria?

Yes.

You need to make arrangements for your son to leave our home.

Why?

My husband is dead.

What?

He died. Make arrangements for your son to leave as soon as possible.

You fucking cunt!

She hung up on me. He was dead. I didn't even cry. I resigned myself to the truth that I would never get what I wanted. I would never be happy. Death would hound me until the last instant of my life. I fell into a stagnant vacancy. I didn't want to do anything. I didn't care to exist. My parents were fading futile like broken appliances. My father's drinking turned him into a late blooming lunatic. His attritious assault on me had its culmination when I was forty years old with a skull on skull eruption. That my children had to witness. My children who were morose and lazy and futureless. And my mother would just pray and make excuses.

I hated everyone in my house.

And then I had to watch my sister flourish with the man she stole from me.

I was happy when Nara married him and went to live in that slum. She couldn't conceive and their marriage was immediately rocky. She would go to work and Antonio would call me over to fuck him and listen to his complaints. But eventually, she somehow voodooed a daughter into being and Antonio stopped wanting to see me. They had their life now. And then my husband died and I was stuck with nothing. I wouldn't let anyone go visit them. I hated them both. But I was happy that they would always be poor, stuck up on that hill while at least I had my Copacabana life. I provided for my mom and dad better than she ever did.

But one day, Antonio transformed into a drug kingpin.

He had more money than he knew what to do with.

He bought a penthouse on Avenida Atlantica.

A penthouse! That was supposed to be my life. That was supposed to be my man! He loved me more than he ever loved my sister. She thrived while my life turned into a stale trash littered street puddle. I couldn't hold my allegiances. Soon Lucia was basically living with them. My mother was baking them cakes and spending whole days with Nara. Years passed. My desire for revenge festered. I hated my sister more and more everyday. The American's money ran out and I had to work. I got a job as a maid at the Marriott. It was a shitty job and it reinforced everything I hated about the world.

One morning while I was huffing off to work, my shoulders slumped by the weight of my strictures, I saw him walking toward me. He had an unmistakable gait. I remembered the gossip that my little Lucia let slip. That there was trouble in their top floor paradise. I hadn't seen him in years. I slowed down. He spotted me. I put some glitter into my eyes.

Antonio.

Maria? It's been a while.

Doesn't seem like it. You look like you did the day we met.

Nah, I'm getting old.

I touched his hand. I could feel his old animal ferocity flaring back up.

You know, Bala. I work at this hotel. I got keys to all the rooms.

What's that supposed to mean?

I gave him a lush, lascivious look.

Maria, I'm a dad now.

Suit yourself. You got my number.

Of course he texted me! The next day!

For a month, Antonio would meet me at the hotel, a shout away from my sister. He'd come up on me, darkly roaring. His great black shadow would pierce me rawly in my maid's outfit in the dim daylight of those tourist rooms. Between fucks he would brag to me. He told me everything about his operation, named names, took credit for corpses. Everything! As soon as he left, I would write it all down, and slowly my plan started to come together. He got off on being bad. I asked him for more and more information.

Tell me everything Antonio, it makes me come!

I was too loud. Trembling from our livid glee. Some other maid who was jealous of me came knocking. She charged in and caught us. My maid's skirt was pulled up and I was begging my brutish brother in law to bust inside me. I got fired. Antonio got squeamish about Nara finding out so we stopped seeing eachother.

But I had all the information. All I needed was the right moment.

Larry came along and I saw my escape route. I started accepting my sister's dinner invitations. I laughed with her. I played with my ratty niece. Lucia even mentioned to me, Nara says you guys have really gotten along lately.

Yes! Golly it's all so swell!

After Larry's proposal, when my future was sure, I typed up all the information I knew. There was this military police officer with a nasally voice and an awful walrus mustache who I used to hook up with. I gave him everything. I didn't regret it for a moment. Nara ruined me. She stole my mother's affection and she stole my life. It was only right that I ruined her.

The raid was set for New Year's Eve. I knew about it. I accepted Nara's dinner invitation, and I told my officer exactly where they'd be. Maybe it was cruel to show up. I didn't think it would be so brutal. My heart wasn't as calloused as I wished. Seeing Antonio get shot was more than I could bear. My three greatest loves were all dead. What did I have to show for it? Two children who didn't like me?

I had to leave and I did.

I lived my life with Larry, and now he was dead too. Everyone was dead. My cold mad feary father. Chico, Antonio, The American. Soon

my mother would be dead. Then Daniel, and me, and Lucia. Time's
pyre was undefeated. We would all get burnt up and go nowhere. We
didn't matter. Nothing mattered. There was a brief loud little flash
where you existed. Where the world was in front of you in its scabrous
discord and you played out these pointless loves, these useless losses, and
you ceased. We were worth less than dust.

You couldn't wipe away dust so easily.

Now I was on this beach as it descended into hell. Watching myself
as if from a far off vantage point. Running away hand in hand with
my daughter feeling something close to love. Maybe I had hope again.
Because I was going to go back to the United States. I would break into
Larry's skinflint savings, sell his house, and move away. Maybe Jim the
Surgeon would come with me. Or there would be another man. I would
love again. Be subsumed by that gluttonous needy feeling that at the
bottom was pure emptiness.

Everything was exploding into chaos. The fools around me tried to
stave off the truth about life, the vacuousness at its core, by rioting and
destroying, throwing fireworks into buildings, shooting, breaking. But
I watched it all like I was floating far off. Because I was safe. I would
live out my nothing plushly. Never hungry, never wanting. And now I
would bring my daughter with me. But as we were about to cross the
border into the lobby of the hotel, safe and free. Lucia said something
that changed everything.

Wait! I need to make sure Marta is safe! We need to go to the apartment.

I would go with her. But it was over. If Lucia was going to choose to
live her life wrongly, so be it. She could've chosen me. But instead she
was on my sister's team, my mother's team. Their poison was too deeply
embedded in her veins.

I went off with her, hand in hand.

But Lucia was dead to me.

What you know, you know. I will say no more.

—MARTA, I'M GOING to bed. I love you.

   —I love you too, Grandma! Goodnight!

My mission was the roof. If Lucia wasn't gonna take me, I would find my way there myself. I just had to wait until Grandma fell asleep. She slept early and deep and she was sad because of Grandpa and all the fighting today. I was sad too. Aunt Maria came and it was supposed to be happy. I was happy. I hadn't seen Aunt Maria for so long my memories weren't even true. They were from pictures of her. But she looked like Mom enough that when she hugged me, I could close my eyes and pretend. Her and Mom were sisters. Me and Lucia were cousins but we were like sisters. At least that's what I thought. I never told her that. I would've been embarrassed to tell her that.

Lucia yelled at me today. She yelled at Grandma too. She never did that. She called Grandma a liar. While she looked like a princess in her new dress. I wish Aunt Maria would've took me shopping with them because I never got to go shopping. I wonder if being prettied up made you meaner. If it made you mean, I never wanted to be pretty. But Lucia yelled at us. I didn't get it. And then she broke her promise and left. Was she mad at me too? I couldn't understand why she would ever be mad at Grandma.

—Did you lie to her Grandma?

—Ahh fofinha. She's just upset. Sometimes people say things they don't mean.

—But why is she upset?

She hugged me tight and started talking about something else. I always knew when there was adult stuff happening that they didn't want me to know about. They thought I was too little. I was almost ten! They could tell me the truth. Lucia always told me the truth. But she got weird because her mom was back. I could understand that. If my mom was back I would want her all to myself. No. I would want Lucia with us too. So they could've at least took me to the beach.

But they thought I was too little, too little for everything.

That's why I would go to the roof and prove them wrong!

I tippytoed to Grandma's room to check if she was sleeping. She was laying there dead like a rock except she wasn't dead. I know because I checked to see if she was breathing and her belly was moving up and down real slow. There were no blankets covering her and a fan was spinning around and it was very hot in the room. The windows were all open and I could hear the rain sneak in. The storm hitting the side of the building made it seem like there were ghosts in the apartment. Grandma was breathing though. That was all that mattered.

I was used to checking. Sometimes I would see Grandpa or even Lucia sleeping and they would look dead and I would get that feeling like when you find a spider on your arm and you didn't know it and you shiver and your heart runs away. I would yell their name and wake them up and they'd get mad at me. But I had to check.

People died all the time and it was scary.

I took the key from Grandma's door sneaky. I shut it, turning the knob slow so she didn't hear, and I locked it. Just in case. I didn't want her to catch me. Because I wasn't supposed to be leaving alone. Never.

If she did wake up I knew what to say.

—Sorry Grandma! I thought it was locked and I was putting the key there to unlock it!

But she wouldn't wake up because she slept so deep.

And I would be back in time anyway.

I was like a spy! I would accomplish my mission and be back before anyone noticed.

Grandma must not have nightmares, the way she sleeps all through the night. Because I got nightmares all the time. I wake up and I can't sleep again until Lucia shushes me back to it. My really scary ones would be of Grandpa. I would be in the kitchen and he would grab a knife and start running after me screaming, I'm gonna get you Marta!

But I'd wake up and Grandpa would be nice and slow like a slug and he wouldn't say much. He smelled like papayas and sometimes he smelled like pee. I never said that though. It's mean when someone says you smell bad. Ana at school says I'm stinky and have bad breath. I'll start talking and she'll fake puke and then people laugh. I know the people laughing aren't my friends because I would never laugh at someone like that.

I bit Ana and I was happy I did.

I knew I would get in trouble even though Lucia told me to.

Though I thought maybe if she told me to, I wouldn't get in trouble. She usually knows the best thing.

But I listened to her and I got in trouble at school. She got me in trouble. She yelled at me. And she left me all lonely at the house. It was scary at home when nobody was awake but the shadows. I would get too scared to even turn the light on because that would mean I had to walk in the dark.

But I was going to be brave tonight! I was going to the roof.

Without Lucia. I wanted to show her I wasn't just some little kid she could leave behind.

Because what if one day she really decided to leave me behind? What if Aunt Maria wanted Lucia to go live with her? I couldn't make

Lucia do anything. The only thing that would keep her with me is if she loved me a lot. Like she said she did. I believed her. But what if? I didn't wanna be so needy like a little baby. I only had her and Grandma. And Grandma wouldn't be around forever. Mom wasn't coming back.

I hated to think that!

And being mad at Lucia made me so upset I wanted to cry.

But there was no time for crying. I was on a mission.

I tippytoed out through the dark kitchen and grabbed a handful of rabanadas Dona Regina left for us. I usually liked them warm, but they were still delicious cold. I needed them in case I got hungry on the way. I stuffed them in my pockets and I was out the front door without a peep.

Now all I had to do was brave myself up to the thirteenth floor.

It was higher than I had ever been!

I heard people stirring all through the building like rats running around.

I couldn't let anyone see me. That's why I was barefoot and wearing my black shirt.

I was blending into the night.

For a second I thought maybe I should ask someone to take me with them, if they were going to see the fireworks. But they would just take me back to Grandma and tell on me. They would think I was just some little kid stupiding out on my own.

But I was a girl with a plan.

I ran up to the fourth floor as fast as I could. I tucked myself into the wall past the stairs so the people coming down wouldn't see me. I had to go one floor at a time and hide. That was the strategy.

It was Paulinho and his mom coming down. Paulinho was really old. He was like eighteen. Him and his mom were not nice. They never traded bom dias with anyone in the lobby. People said she was a widow. I asked Grandma what that meant and I felt bad. Because she was kinda like Mom and Paulinho was like me.

But I was nice anyway. I told everyone bom dia.

Even this morning when I was exhausted because Grandma woke me up so early. I was ooofing and grumbly and did not wanna get outta bed. It was bird chirpy early. Only birds and adults in their job uniforms were supposed to be awake.

But Grandma said we had to go get Grandpa. I said ok and we headed down to the street.

On my day off from school before I even had my Toddynho.

Ridiculous! But I would do anything Grandma asked me to.

Fifth floor. No sign of anyone so I went right up to the sixth. Noises from people coming all the way from the top. And I could hear Crystal, a beagle from the eighth floor, barking crazy.

I saw a dog when I was out with Grandma today. We were right by the Bob's that was next to the house. We had only made it like five steps out the door. You have to stop all the time when you're out with Grandma because everybody knows her. It makes you feel kinda famous. So I like it. Especially when people ask my name and I get to say it's like hers.

So we're walking by and someone yells.

—Dona Marta!

I look and it's this guy who's way older, like Daniel's age. He's living there by the Bob's on cardboard with his friends and a dog and his clothes are dirty.

Grandma walks over to talk to him.

—Nando! What are you doing here?

—It's been a rough couple years, Dona Marta. I just got outta jail and I got no place to go.

—Jail? What did you do?

—I tried to rob this guy. I needed money, you know. It went all wrong. I was only sixteen, and you know. It went wrong.

He did a motion with his hands and his face that made me realize what he meant.

He killed a guy! I felt grown up for realizing, but that shocked me.

He looked so nice. He was smiling and he was Grandma's friend. He had a doggy!

Why would he do that?

Like the kid the other day who hurt that man at the bus stop. That kid looked just like Henrique from school and Henrique would never do that. I couldn't understand why people who looked so much alike could act so different.

Grandma wasn't angry at Nando though, and so I wasn't either.

Eventually he asked for food. Grandma bought him and his friend and his dog some burgers and fries. It was expensive. Grandma didn't usually spend money like that. But they were so happy so I thought she thought it was worth it.

And I got to pet the dog! His name was Lucky. They said because he was almost dead when they found him so he was lucky. I thought he was too because his family seemed to love him. I wanted a dog so bad! We couldn't get one because Grandpa was allergic. But now. No. It felt wrong to get something happy out of something so sad.

We walked away.

—Grandma, who was that guy?

—His family is from the Ilha. His great grandmother was my friend a long time ago.

—What was her name?

—Gloria.

—That's a pretty name.

I didn't ask if she died because I knew how time worked, and I didn't want Grandma to think I would ask her silly things.

There were people in the stairway. I was stuck between the seventh and eighth floor with no way out. It was an american family. They spent Decembers in an apartment on the twelfth floor. They were big and loud. I had never talked to them. Dona Regina said they were nice and rich. I didn't know you could be nice and rich. In all the stories I heard about rich people they sounded mean.

Mom and Dad were rich. We had a big house when I was really

little. I don't remember it though. I knew the building from walking by on the calçadão. Lucia told me once and never talked about it again. It was made of glass and it was shiny. It looked like where rich people were supposed to live. We lived there and we were nice. It made sense.

The americans came down noisy and bumbling and laughing about words I didn't know. I only understood rain and beer from their blabber. I got stiff like a lizard on a rock and thought that might help them not see me.

They passed me and smiled and said boa noite and kept going.

Phew!

I liked them.

They could see I wasn't just a little kid. I was on a mission.

They weren't gonna stop that.

They were american. Like Aunt Maria was now. I guess Daniel and Lucia were too because their dad was. I wanted to go to the United States. I never said that around Lucia because her face would get sour. She had never gone either.

Maybe me and Lucia could go visit Aunt Maria together.

Unless. Lucia went and lived with her.

That' s crazy talk, Marta! Lucia wouldn't leave!

But she left tonight. Why wouldn't she wanna go live with her mom? I would wanna go live with my mom if she was here.

Mom was alive. She should've been with me but she wasn't. Maybe one day she would be. But it was sad, and thinking about it hurt. I knew Dad would never be around again. Because he wasn't alive. That was easier since at least I didn't hope he would be back.

Now Grandpa was with him. Maybe they were together.

It was sad that people had to go.

Where did they go?

Mom and Dad loved me. We were all living happy and then we weren't. I knew why but I didn't know why. It hurt like someone was poking me hard with a pointy stick.

I felt so lonely.

At least I had Grandma and Lucia.

But one day.

I didn't wanna think about it.

One time I asked Grandma why everyone had to die.

She said death is like a trip.

—You know how Aunt Maria is in the United States and can't visit us all the time? That's what dying is like Martinha. A separation. But nothing is ever separate forever. Eventually you'll find your way together again. This life isn't the only one. We all come back again and again and the same people who were with us before, we'll see again.

—But why does anybody have to go away?

—Because people make too many mistakes. We need to keep evolving. So even if you're bad while you're here, you'll always get another chance.

—So you think, um. That I'll get to see Dad again?

—Of course! Meu xuxuzinho.

I didn't know if she was just telling me that or if she really believed it. Grandma never lied. Well. I guess she lied to Lucia about something. Why can't adults just be good all the time! Maybe that's what Grandma meant though.

We have to live a bunch of times to learn how to do it right.

I was on the eighth floor and hungry. Oh! I put those rabanadas in my pocket. I pulled one out and ate it while I listened to Crystal the Beagle bark. I thought maybe I should break down the door and rescue her. So neither of us would be lonely while the fireworks happened.

But mean Dona Irene, her owner who never let me pet her, wouldn't like that.

I was really tired. My bare feet were dirty and hurting.

But I wasn't done yet! I just kept pushing forward.

By the time I reached the tenth floor, I heard the people who stayed home cheering.

Which meant the time changed.

I started hearing distant booms.

I was gonna miss the fireworks!

I had to hurry.

I MADE it. The thirteenth floor.

Which I'd never been to. Seu Zé lived up here with his family. I had only seen his wife once. Her name was Nilza. She was small like him and smiley. They had a son, Gabriel, who was even smaller.

One time I saw them all out on the closed calçadão on Sunday. The three of them were holding hands and strolling in the sun. It was really cute. I almost said oi but I didn't wanna bother him when he wasn't working.

He lived in the free apartment that most buildings gave to the head doorman. Daniel taught me that because his girlfriend lived in one of those in Leme. I only met her a couple times. She was really nice and really pretty. But Lucia was a million times prettier.

Pretty doesn't matter! Lucia always told me.

Being good and nice was more important than looking good.

But I wished Daniel would bring his girlfriend around more. Hopefully one day they would get married. I could go to the wedding! I never went to a wedding before!

I wished Daniel would just come around more anyway.

I didn't even get to see him today. He came by after Lucia yelled at me to go to my room. I could still hear most of what was going on in the kitchen. As soon as he showed up it was a big fight. I curled up on the bed and tried not to listen.

It seems like boys are always starting fights.

They're meanies.

Grandma told me what he did. He punched Uncle What's His Name. Punching was always bad. I understood why he was mad. His dad was replaced by another guy.

Imagine if Mom showed up with another guy!

I would be face red mad.

Aunt Maria was probably bummed Daniel didn't like her guy.

Maybe that's why Lucia left me tonight. She needed to cheer up her mom.

I didn't wanna think about it.

But so I made it. There was a little door at the end of the floor. It was the only door other than Seu Zé's apartment so I thought that had to be it. I went and pulled it once and it felt locked. I got sad right away. Like this was a dumb mission.

But I thought, I can't give up!

So I pulled it with all my might. Like I was an elephant or something really strong.

It opened.

There was a little staircase and all my tiredness from the trip went away.

I ran up as fast as I could.

There it was! Outside! I could see the roof. It was made of metal and looked wet and dark and slippery. I had to make sure I was careful. There was a little spot where it looked like I could sit safe. On a little patch of concrete. With a cover over my head to protect me from the rain.

Lucia's secret spot!

I could hear booms while I came up the stairs but I thought the fireworks were over now. The rain was slowing down too. I could still hear thunder rumbling and the clouds were thick and really dark. I sat down and my shorts got wet. It didn't matter.

Because I made it!

I could see the tops of all the buildings in the neighborhood.

The night was really, really dark, but I could still see thanks to the building lights. The city was so big. Every little apartment square equaled a bunch of lives. Millions of people! Like me! Living behind their eyes.

I knew that if I climbed farther out on the roof and turned I would be able to see the Christ statue, that's what Lucia told me. But that would've been really dangerous. And I wasn't dumb. I was brave but not dumb. The clouds were probably covering it anyway.

But I made it!

It should've been me and Lucia here.

But I did it!

And then I got sad. I sat just looking out into the night. I tried to think that I made it and I was here and I was brave. I tried to think of other happy things but it wasn't any use. I felt so lonely that I almost wished I was dead. I could hear the rain slowing and hitting the building and the hot wind whistling in from the beach. I could hear dogs barking inside and some bemtevi with his little song hiding out from the rain. They were all alone too. All of a sudden, I was so scared to be up here in the rain and the dark that I got a cold shiver. I heard the people down on the street celebrating but it sounded creepy and eerie. I felt so scared and low I almost wished there was a ghost here so at least I would have some company. Lucia told me that Grandma talked to ghosts sometimes. I wish I could do that. Talk to Dad. Maybe he's still around and he can see me. I love my family, I do. Lucia is my favorite there is. But it's still sad when you think of the way something could be and it isn't.

I was trying to tell Grandma that today while we were out. Like when we got Grandpa and he was just a box. He was just a box with a Vasco sticker on it. One minute my Grandpa was slothing around our house and then he was a box. It made me sad that we were all gonna be boxes. That we were watching the world and feeling the rain on our leg and thinking about Lucia and then we were dust in a box. I was trying to understand that out loud to Grandma, when we were downtown today because she wanted to stop at the place where she prays. The Centro. The place that gave her the answers about this kinda stuff.

—Martinha, nobody really dies. One day I'm not gonna be in front of you, looking like this and talking to you. But I won't be dead. You'll still be able to think of me. You'll remember what I said. And

I'll be alive to you. And then one day we'll really find our way back to eachother.

She hugged me tight and it didn't feel like she was lying.

It made me think of a story she told me once and I always asked her to tell. About when Mom and Aunt Maria were kids. They were almost like me and Lucia but closer in age. It was about when they went to Copacabana for the first time ever, to visit my Great Aunt, Grandpa's older sister. I never met her. I begged Grandma to give me her name because she didn't wanna.

Her name was Otacilia.

Which is a name that gave me scares just because of what Grandma had said about her. She was mean like an alligator. She yelled at everyone and she loved money and she kept fifty pet papagaios in cages. I never forgot that because it was the worst thing I could imagine.

Grandma told me she only went to visit her once.

Great Aunt Otacilia walked them around bragging until they finally got to the bird room.

Mom went to pet one of the birds, which I would've done too, and Great Aunt Otacilia hissed at her like a snake.

—Don't touch that!

Mom and Aunt Maria weren't just gonna let her yell at them like that, so they got in cahoots and made a plan. There was a big window in that room, so they tippytoed over and opened it. They waited until everyone was at dinner eating rich people food. Like giant fruits and poor little lambs.

When nobody was looking, they unlocked all the cages.

The papagaios squawked up a storm and flew off!

Free!

They pooped all over, Grandma says, just for good measure, so mean Great Aunt Otacilia would have some work to do. They were never invited back ever again. Grandma said they laughed the whole bus ride home. Even Grandpa who was mad ended up laughing too.

I knew it was a story. It probably didn't happen like that, but a story was different than a lie. But I thought that those papagaios were maybe like us when we were dead. We had all our pretty feathers and our talking but something stronger and meaner put us in a cage. Eventually someone would free us and we'd fly again.

I didn't tell anyone when I was thinking silly like that.

The rain was really slowing down. It was a drizzle now. Though the sky was still black and the night was darker and louder than I wished.

It was the next year now.

I could hear the people on the street celebrating it. They were being loud too. Yelling and I could hear stuff smashing and breaking. Little fireworks everywhere. I could see smoke rising up around the building in front of me. Lights glowing in the building.

They were having fun.

I hoped Lucia was having fun.

This was the first time I had heard the year change without her. I thought it was gonna be our tradition, to listen to it together. Because it was New Year's when Mom and Dad. Iemanja's day. There's a picture of everybody from that night. I found it in Grandma's stuff when I was snooping one day. I don't know if she knew it was there. But I took it and I kept it in my school backpack and never showed anyone.

Everyone was wearing white. Mom and Dad have the biggest smiles in the picture. Grandpa wasn't looking and you can see Grandma telling him to look. Daniel and Lucia were next to eachother. Daniel had his arm around her smiling. Lucia wasn't smiling and she looked skinny and a little sad. I was standing near her legs. I was too small to remember, but she was telling me to look up I think. I hoped that's why she wasn't smiling, and not because she was sad. Aunt Maria wasn't in it. So I guess she took the picture. I had touched it so much that it looked older than it was.

But it was my favorite.

I know what happened after that. The police came in and killed Dad and took Mom. Because they were evil. Which was just another part of life that was too big for me to get. They were never evil to me. And yet.

It didn't matter. I got too sad even thinking about it. I walked down the street sometimes and a police guy on the corner would smile at me. And I would think. But you? But just because someone seemed the same didn't mean they were the same. I thought.

I was trying not to cry up here because I was brave and I had made it but I couldn't help it. The smoke from the little fireworks was floating over to me, getting in my eyes.

The building in front of me was glowing different than the lights usually glow.

There was a different kinda loud on the streets than I had realized.

It didn't sound like partying. It sounded like something was happening.

The glow in the other building looked like fire.

—HEY! WHO'S up there?

That was Seu Zé's voice yelling up the little staircase. I got up scared and didn't answer.

He yelled again and I didn't say anything.

Then I heard the door close at the bottom. I ran down quick. My feet and most of my clothes were wet. The door was shut. I banged on it. I didn't have any words right now. I was scared. I banged on it as hard as I could and it opened.

—Marta! What are you doing here? Oh no. We have to go!

Seu Zé was standing in front of me in his people clothes. Not his doorman clothes. He had adult fear on his face. Adult fear made everything worse.

It meant something bad was happening.

He pulled me by my hand and we started running down the stairs. He was too fast and I lost my balance and slipped. I landed hard on the ground and hit my shoulder and my knee. They felt red. Seu Zé stopped and helped me up.

—Oh my god Marta, are you ok?

But I couldn't talk.

I could hear footsteps on the stairs like a bunch of animals running away.

Seu Zé picked me up and threw me over his shoulder. He was small, I was almost his height. I could tell he thought I was heavy by the noise he made. I could feel the sweat on his neck and head.

He started running fast down the steps.

When we passed the eighth floor I couldn't hear Crystal bark. I couldn't hear anything. I couldn't think about anything. I knew there was something bad happening and I knew Grandma. I started crying on Seu Zé's shoulder. But he didn't act like he noticed.

We just kept going.

It got hard to breathe by the sixth floor. And as we kept going down, the smoke got thicker and thicker. And I couldn't breathe or see. And Grandma. Oh no.

Everything went black.

I woke up coughing on the sidewalk. On Nossa Senhora. I could see our building from across the street. There were firemen going into it. There was a firetruck on the street and more rain was falling now.

Dona Celeste and Dona Dalia were over me talking. I couldn't hear.

—Grandma.

—Where is she, Marta? Was there anyone in the building?

—Grandma.

My whole body hurt. I couldn't talk or cry.

I couldn't. Grandma. And I had.

Oh no.

I walked out into the rain. I hoped Grandma would appear.

I hoped she would pick me up and scold me.

—Silly Marta, I had a key! I went looking for you.

We would laugh and everything would be ok.

Everything went black.

When I woke up again, everything happened like a dream.

Lucia and Aunt Maria were there. Lucia was crying and holding me.

—Marta! Are you ok?

I didn't say anything. I hugged her tight.

Aunt Maria wasn't crying. She was telling us to follow her. Lucia picked me up and carried me. I felt safe. I didn't think about Grandma because I knew.

I messed up. I messed up really bad.

We moved fast. The rain stopped. The people in the street were going nuts. They were screaming and throwing things and I didn't wanna look. I could smell smoke and I saw fires burning in other buildings. I tucked my head tight into Lucia's shoulder.

We went into Aunt Maria's hotel. Lucia put me down. There were a lot of people in the lobby. They looked wet and scared like we were.

Aunt Maria told us to follow her. We rode the elevator up and went into her room.

I was so tired. My eyes were fluttering open and closed.

Lucia sat down on the bed but I just stood there looking at her and Aunt Maria.

Nobody spoke.

Being in Aunt Maria's hotel room with Lucia for a sleepover would've sounded like the best thing ever this morning. But I had never felt so bad in my life.

Lucia took me into the bathroom and dried me off with a towel.

All she kept saying was, Oh Marta.

I wished she would say something to make me feel better, but I didn't know what could.

I walked out of the bathroom and Aunt Maria was arranging the bed. She looked at me.

—Marta.

She walked over and gave me a hug. It could've been Mom hugging me. That was the only thing that could make me feel better.

I was so tired. Aunt Maria took me over to the bed.

—Lay down darling. Get some sleep, ok?

I thought of Grandma and I started to cry.

—Don't cry little Marta. Everything will be ok.

But it wouldn't.

Aunt Maria gave me a kiss on the cheek and turned the lights off.

I closed my eyes and I tried to think of something good.

But all I could picture was a sky so black you couldn't see any stars.

part three

paraíso

vai meu irmão
pega esse avião, você tem razão
de correr assim desse frio
mas beija o meu Rio de Janeiro

—chico buarque

february 18

I GOTTA GET out of here, I was telling Mateus. We were sitting at the kiosk we always sat at. But there was no music playing. There was no muvuca. The beach and the day were dead quiet. Military police officers patrolled the calçadão. The statue of the Princess that always watched us from its perch between the avenues was gone. It got toppled in the riots after New Year's Eve, and while it was down, someone stole it. I don't know how they hauled that big ass thing off. When it came to thieving, cariocas were top notch innovators.

Mateus didn't say anything.

I sipped my beer. I was trying not to drink at all. But this was a special occasion! Mateus hadn't been in town for three weeks. He got a gig touring with this band. It was called Nonada, or something dumb like that. They had been all over São Paulo the last month. Now they were getting ready to do a big tour of the rest of the country. He was leaving tomorrow. I thought he was pissed at me, for a while. After all the shit that happened. We never really talked about it. Because it was totally fucked up. How were you supposed to talk about it? I kinda went nuts. I almost did something that would've ruined my life.

And still, that dude was dead.

It didn't matter that I changed my mind. That I tried to do something good.

I was trying to save him! I was trying to save my mom!

Was I?

It didn't matter. He was dead.

That whole night was torture. Me and Mateus sprinted all the way down to the Fort. It sounded like a war was happening on the calçadão. You couldn't tell the difference between the fireworks and gunshots. We were terrified. I was terrified.

All I could think about was Larry's dead body.

I caused that.

But we needed to get to safety. We needed to get away from the poisonous cauldron the beach was turning into. When I was a kid, I always imagined climbing up the Fort rocks and sneaking over the wall. I didn't think it was possible. Especially in a full on storm. It was a crazy idea. But we climbed! The rain slowed a little but the rocks were insanely slippery. We kept falling and scraping ourselves. Eventually we made it over the wall. All hurt and sore and exhausted. We started laughing. And then we looked at eachother and stopped.

There was nothing to laugh about. It was a cold, grim night.

There were no soldiers there, nobody. It was quiet. We franticked around until we found a covered spot where we could pass out. We slept there shivering, huddled together, wet to the bone. Two rainsoaked runaways holding eachother scared desperate. Clutching tighter tighter tighter with each thunderous clang. The next morning we woke up to the barrel of a soldier's gun pointing right at us.

What the fuck were you guys doing, huh? Kissing?

Before we could even answer he was like, Get outta here!

So we walked out the entrance to the Fort. The beach clock said 06:05.

There was always something pleasant about being up early, early on the first day of the year. A few times me and Leticia stayed up all night, just so we could see the sunrise and walk around on the beach. It would be covered in party debris. Can pickers and trash guys would be pecking around. It was a new year! You could smell the endless possibility.

This was not that. The sun was out full force and clear. There was even a rainbow stretching out across the water. But there was a nasty sewage smell in the air, and the trash all over the ground was different. It was shit people didn't wanna leave behind. Torn clothes and phones. Glass all over the street. It looked like shipwreck waste washed up on shore.

And then after we walked for a while, I saw the worst thing I ever saw.

Mateus was lagging behind me, perusing around slow and shocked.

I spotted it and said, Don't come up here man. Go around.

He didn't listen. He came up to me while I was frozen looking at it.

It was a kid. It was a dead kid. Right on the edge of the sand. Like he got killed on the calçadão and fell into his beach grave. His eyes were bugged out and there was a dry stream of blood on his chin. He looked almost blue.

What if this is the kid I stabbed in the leg? I thought.

What if this is my fault?

I didn't know what to do. I ran to the edge of the water and puked. All on the decapitated heads of white roses floating around like sea foam. I puked more. I must've thrown up everything I ever ate. And then I just sat there for a long time. Mateus came and sat next to me. There were a bunch of cruise ships still anchored in the water. I was hoping they would sink.

I felt totally rotten.

Eventually Mateus got me up and we walked. We walked all the way to my apartment where Seu Zé was waiting outside to tell me the news.

Oh Daniel. Your grandmother.

I couldn't even cry. I just shut down. I got swept up by the next seventy two hours. I know Mateus tried to get me to go home with him, but I refused. I couldn't face Leticia. I wandered all over town, lost and confused. That night and the next two were chaos. People busting up the street, setting fires, breaking shit. Clash on clash with police. I spent my days stealing cachaça and getting drunk. I smoked so much weed and cigarettes my voice croaked. I even tried huffing glue for a quick second, but it freaked me out and I didn't do it again. At night, I would sleep newspaper covered in the park. Not thinking about nothing. Just suffering the fire of the people in the city, their war. And on the third day, I got arrested for fighting in the park. I was so trashed I don't really remember it. But that woke me up. I realized I was being sucked into that deadbeat darkness. My wrecks and errors were all about me. That ructious rascality wasn't fun no more, it was harmful. I wasn't gonna be obliterated by my damn foolishness. It was time to be good.

When I got out, the city had cooled down.

They brought in an army's worth of police officers. They weren't playing games.

It was a true risk to be doing something crazy, so people chilled out. Accepted it.

I didn't have the nearest nudge where to go. I was blankslating. Randomly, I decided to go over to the Spiritist Center where my grandma used to pray. I only went there like twice, back when I was a kid. They helped me out. Set me up in a tiny apartment and had me do chores and etceteras for rent. Eventually I found a job busing tables and started reconnecting with my life.

I was happy now.

I was alright.

WHERE YOU gonna go? Mateus asked.

I don't know man. Portugal.

Portugal?

Why not?

What the hell you gonna do out there?

I don't know man! I'll figure it out!

Ok bro.

Shit, or maybe I'll be a groupie for your band!

Nah, you not pretty enough.

We laughed and sipped our beers. It was good to see him. He was starting his real life. He had shit he really cared about and he was going for it and it was working out. I was happy for him, but I was jealous. I didn't know what I was gonna do with my life. I didn't know what I was gonna do damn tomorrow.

But I knew it was gonna be something better than I'd been doing. Maybe I would leave. I just needed somewhere to go. Rio felt like a soft prison. I was worried I was gonna die here, my whole life nothinged, wasted. What was keeping me here? Just my memories. They were like sticky ass goo I could never wash off my hands.

Leticia.

A few weeks ago, after I cleaned up a little bit, when my home situation was stabilized, I decided I was gonna make a big move for her. I hadn't texted her or anything. No contact at all. Was living totally Leticialess for the first time in half a decade. And it sucked!

I knew for sure I loved her serious.

So I wrote a long letter. I never wrote a letter in my whole entire life! But I got a pen and I scrawled this paper covered with the most sincerest, leakyhearted, gushing, enthusiastic, I am your man and I'm gonna be better forevertalk anybody ever heard. I was hurt by the end of it. My hand was cramping and my heart felt like it got jumped in the street and beat up. I didn't realize, until I put it all down, how I'd treated her with an unright heedlessness. Whenever I was really confessing love, it was a trick to distract from some sordid shit I pulled. And now the guilt from recognizing the truth was making me honest for maybe the first time ever. I got tearyeyed just thinking about it.

After I finished I went out and asked the flower dude on my block for the most apologetic arrangement he had. When he told me how much it was, I asked him for the second most apologetic arrangement.

I think I only got Leticia flowers maybe twice the whole time we were together. That was a tough truth to get hit with. Relationships are all about numbers to a certain extent. How much of this did you do? How much of that?

The numbers didn't lie, I was a bad, bad boyfriend. I was a villain.

I would've dumped me too.

But the reckoning was the key! I reckoned with it. I recognized my badness. Now I was truly ready to change. I wasn't the same guy I used to be. New Year's Eve made me see the moral slime I could slide into. Before I didn't think the whole right or wrong fuss mattered. But life had serious stakes. I didn't wanna be playing around anymore. I had to express that to her.

I put on my best clothes, which meant a clean tshirt and shorts. I enveloped the letter, swaddled the flowers, and headed to her place. I was shaking nervous. To put all my feelings out bare like that and get rejected would be a painful setback. But I had to do it.

I didn't have another option.

I got to her building. I felt sure that this was gonna work. She would read the letter and her heart would flutter. She would cry and hug me. She would tell me she loved me. And then we would be together forever after that. Even if it didn't happen so fast, I was sure it would soften her enough to let me back in.

Eventually I would earn back her whole love and affection.

I was willing to earn it. I wanted to work for it.

Leticia!

I snuck past the doorman and went up the elevator. I got off at the tenth floor and decided to walk. I needed to prolong it as much as I could. But you can't procrastinate nothing forever. The moment arrived and I was right in front of her door, 1301.

I knocked and knocked, and knocked again.

The door opened.

It was Dona Isabel standing there. She smiled at me.

Daniel, what a surprise.

Hey. Is Leticia here?

Her smile gave way to a pained, sympathetic look.

Why don't you come in and sit down?

She offered me coffee, goiabada, fruit and cheese and sandwiches. Like she usually did, offering everything, trying to get me to eat. I said I would take a coffee. She sat down across from me at the kitchen table.

Leticia's gone.

What?

She moved away.

Where?

She's living in Uruguay.

I don't understand.

Dona Isabel grabbed my hands.

She didn't want to be here anymore. She had some friends there, and they offered her a job teaching portuguese, and so she left.

But she didn't tell me.

I know Daniel.

She didn't tell me anything. How could she just leave?

You know Leticia. When she sets her mind to something she does it.

I couldn't believe it. The flowers and my card were on the table like the stupidest fucking garbage in the world. I was angry. I didn't get it.

Uruguay! Uruguay! A dumb country like Uruguay!

She didn't tell you to say anything to me?

No. I'm sorry.

I put my head down on the table. I wanted to cry. Nothing. She didn't have a last thing to say to me. So she really meant it? She didn't love me anymore. All I wanted was one more moment! One more conversation! One chance to just cling and chat and cling to her. But she didn't love me anymore. How could she just stop?

Leticia!

Why couldn't she talk to me one more time? Doesn't she owe me that?

Daniel. You know how much you meant to her. But things change. Fuck. Sorry. This sucks.

I don't even remember if we kept talking or what. She offered me food again but I had no appetite for the rest of my life. I never wanted to eat again.

I hugged her and left.

When I got back out on the street to endure the hot, miserable, dreary day, I tore up the card and threw it in the trash. I threw the flowers in too. I walked a few steps and I turned around to look at the flowers again, to admire and wallow in my misfortune, and I saw a homeless lady digging them out. She had a big, toothless smile beaming at the bouquet.

At least someone would get some joy out of them.

I went home. I must've laid in bed for three days. I spent a lot of time googling Leticia. Her twitter was private. Her instagram was private. And I would zoom in and stare at the profile pictures. I even went so far as to create an account under a fake name, Ronaldo Valencia. Who I imagined as a suave spaniard, and I thought maybe I would catfish her. Then I would emerge as Daniel himself, and she would remember that she loved me, and that even through all the pseudonymous fooling, she could recognize me, the love of her life.

But that seemed like the most idiotic idea in the world.

I didn't even have the guts to follow her. I just deleted the account and sulked.

I looked through all our old pictures again and again and again. And I tried my hardest not to text her, but I did. A few long messages I immediately regretted.

She didn't respond.

It was a real, deep hurt. She pushed me right off into the abyss.

I got stuck with the way things were. Believing just because it was, it would be. I took Leticia totally for granted. I thought she would always be around to scold and tolerate me. It was impossible to accept that she didn't owe me love. That she had an independent life away from me. A mind and thoughts I had no grip on, no hold over. She had a different life. Different ends that had absolutely nothing to do with me.

She didn't want my kid.

That was that. She chose a different life.

I had a fantasy of the two of us and our children all family cozy, parading down the street on sunny Sundays, holding hands and laughing. That fantasy was dead. Annihilated. Forever! How? Why couldn't I have something even when I wanted it so badly? It didn't matter. I would have to accept it.

You hear from Leticia? I asked Mateus.

Nah man. Not for a while.

Yeah. Seems like she's doing her own thing.

You know, she's always on her own shit. She'll be good.

Yeah.

I looked at the beach clock. It was 14:05.

Dude, I gotta go. I got lunch plans with my sister.

You guys been talking?

A little bit. I haven't seen her in a minute though.

I drank the rest of my beer. I pulled twenty reals out of my pocket and put it under the glass. We both stood up. I clasped his hand and gave him a quick pat hug.

Alright man. Have fun on tour.

I will. Good luck out here.

Valeu Mateus.

I'll see you.

Tchau.

I walked away. I wanted to say more. I was realizing now Mateus was the only person who ever really stuck around for me. It didn't bother him how many bad decisions I made, how I fucked my life up. He was there, he was loyal. He was like my brother and I loved him, and I was gonna miss him extremely. If it wasn't for him, I would've been doomed.

But I couldn't say all that.
Couldn't lame sentimentalize his goaway.
He knew it anyhow.
Tchau would suffice.

I WAS meeting Lucia at this restaurant around our old apartment. It was this restaurant right next to the bar grandpa stayed drinking at. He would get so drunk sometimes that my grandma would send the two of us to pick him up and bring him home. Shit that consternated me way back then.

But now I missed grandpa.

I'd take a drunk, sloppy, passed out grandpa anyday, over one who didn't exist.

After the whole post New Year's chaos, after I got out of jail, I tried to call Lucia. I wanted to know what was up. What happened to grandma. She didn't answer. She didn't respond to my texts, nothing. I didn't know if she knew what I knew. I didn't know where she was.

But she didn't want nothing to do with me.

I was familyless, forreal. I always imagined myself alone. In like a romantic way, I was a tough loner. Scouring these streets on my own. I didn't need nobody. I was the only one I could rely on. But that wasn't really true. I was well and strongly supported.

But when that shit really became true, when I was left all bereft, it wasn't cute.

It was mean. It wasn't the way I wanted to live.

Suddenly I wanted to be duty bound by everybody. I wanted heavy responsibilities.

I wanted real love. I wanted my family.

But my life was the walls in my room, dishes to clean, and floors to sweep. I stopped even trying to call Lucia. Weeks passed. But yesterday, she called me. We didn't talk for long but she asked if I wanted to have lunch and I said yes.

I didn't know what to expect. I thought maybe I should get her something. What kinda gift expressed sorrow and regret for decades of bad brotherdom? I couldn't think of anything. And I didn't wanna have another flower debacle. But there was a kid selling candy, and I got five reals worth of paçocas. I knew Lucia liked those. If I knew anything about her, I knew that. We used to eat ourselves sick as kids.

I stuffed them in my pocket and hustled to the restaurant.

I pulled up to the corner of Siqueira Campos feeling hopeful.

Lucia was sitting there, scowl serious, looking like our mother. She saw me and waved.

I sat down. Tried to get comfortable in the flimsy plastic chair, scraping it all over the cobblestones. There was water on the table and I poured myself a cup.

Am I late?

No. You're ok.

Good. Hey.

Hey.

The waiter came over and asked if we wanted anything else to drink. I wanted a beer very badly, but I didn't wanna drink in front of Lucia. At least right now. I wanted to be wearing some semblance of change on my sleeve.

We said water was fine. I ordered picanha and rice and beans. She ordered a few cheese pastels. The waiter left and we sat there, looking at eachother, looking around. Unsure how to communicate. We were never really good at talking to eachother.

How are you?

I'm alright, Daniel.

Yeah? Good.

Look, can we actually talk?

Yes, that's what I'm here for.

I was pissed at you. Really, really pissed. I didn't wanna see you at all. That's why I wasn't answering any of your calls. I thought I was done with you forever.

But why? That's what I don't understand!

Do you know what mom said to me? I asked her what happened that night. She told me she watched you stab Larry right in the chest. She said you ran to them with that knife out like you were gonna kill her, and then you stabbed him. And just ran away. I believed her. I saw you that night. Do you remember that? You looked totally crazy. You looked like you wanted to murder someone.

I didn't do it!

That's what I thought, you know. I thought, Why am I gonna believe her? She lied about everything else. Why would that be true? But. He's dead. If you didn't do it, what happened?

Look. I don't know. I mean.

But you do know. You were there. Just tell me the truth.

Lucia, I mean. It was like. I was there. I was right in front of them. And like this kid came up to rob them or something I don't know. He had a gun. And suddenly I pulled out my knife, and I lunged at his leg. I don't know what I was thinking. But I guess the gun went off. I didn't know what else to do. I ran.

Why were you there, though?

I don't know.

Tell me, Daniel. I'm not here to judge you.

I don't know. I think I wanted to hurt him. I don't know. I wanted to hurt her.

You wanted to kill him, and he ended up dead. You got what you wanted, didn't you?

But I didn't want it anymore. After I saw them, I didn't want it. I saw the kid, and I thought, This is my fucking moment, you know? I'll be a hero. I'll save them, and it won't matter what I did. But. Porra. I'm sorry Lucia. I mean, goddamn. You know, his daughter called me. You meet any of those girls? Rachel. She called me like two weeks ago. I thought it was you from a different number maybe so I picked up. But it was her. She was crying and like accusing me. She said I was a murderer. And she told me to fuck off and burn in hell. Shit like that and she just hung up. She said I was a bad guy. That got to me. You think that's true? You think I'm bad?

You want me to say no. That's why you told me that.

No, tell me what you think, honestly.

I think a man's dead because of you and you're not gonna have any consequences.

But that's not true! I didn't do it. And now I gotta live with this shit. That's consequences. Anyway, who is this guy? I mean, what does he matter? He steals our mom from us and then he's just jaunting around like that in Copacabana? Fuck him. No. I'm sorry. I don't mean that. But what I mean is like, when am I gonna catch a break, you know? It hasn't been easy for me, Lucia. Maybe I freaked out. It was a mistake. But I didn't kill anybody.

It hasn't been easy for you? Sometimes you seem totally delusional! You act like mom didn't leave me too. She ditched us both. That guy didn't steal anything. She wanted to go. You acted like a big baby over it. You raged and cried. A good guy doesn't ignore his mother for six years and then come home and try to stab her new husband. Stab him! That's not what a good guy does.

I mean.

I know it's been hard for you because it's been hard for me too. And I never got half the opportunities you did. At least you had a dad. I didn't have that. I didn't get to go to the United States. I didn't get to go to college. I had to work and take care of people. You don't think that's hard?

Yeah. It is. I'm sorry. I'm starting to realize that now.

Are you though?

I think so. Like, I mean. It's impossible not to. Lately. Impossible not to realize all the ways I fucked up. There's a lot of things I just didn't pay attention to.

You haven't been a good guy.

I know.

But that doesn't mean you can't be.

You think that's true?
Yeah. I do.

THE WAITER brought the food over. We sat and ate without talking. I almost felt embarrassed to be speaking so upfront with her. I felt raw and vulnerable. I didn't have a shield anymore. That's what lying was to me. It was a safe cover. Because the truth hurts. That's some dumb shit people always said, but it was right. Lying was always easier. You didn't have to be yourself. Now the only way I was gonna move forward was being me. As fucked up and messy as me might be.

So what happened to you on New Year's? You were with mom?

Yeah. She uhm. She fooled me, Daniel. I wasn't supposed to be out that night but she was taunting me with things. She was buying me shit. And then she offered to bring me to live with her in Ohio. I believed her. I think I wanted it too. But after everything happened, she came running up to me and told me Larry was dead. We were running to her hotel through the chaos, and I just couldn't go in without knowing Marta was safe. We walked over to the apartment, and Marta was standing outside in the rain and there was smoke billowing from the building. Mom took us to her hotel and we slept there, all three of us on the bed. In the morning, she was gone. I thought maybe she was just. I don't know what I thought. I thought she would come back. But she didn't. I haven't talked to her since.

Porra. What did you and Marta do?

We were hopping around the building for a few nights and then everyone got a collection together and we got a little apartment downtown.

Where at?

Catete.

That's close to me.

Well, maybe you should come over sometime. Marta misses you.

Really?

Yeah. You've been in some drawings lately.

Damn. I been missing you guys.

Lucia smiled at me for the first time during the whole conversation.

What happened to grandma? That night. How did the apartment catch fire?

They think it was a firework. It came right through her window. And uh. Yeah.

Oh my god.

It was terrible.

Grandpa and grandma gone in the same week. That's crazy man.

I should've been there that night. It would've never happened if I stayed.

No, that's not true.

It is true. I promised Marta that I would take her up to the roof that night to see the fireworks. You know where she was when the apartment caught fire? Seu Zé found her on the roof. She locked grandma in that room so she wouldn't get caught if grandma woke up. So she was stuck in that room. Right where the fire was. It's my fault. It never should've happened.

You can't think of it like that, Lucia.

I can. Maybe that's another reason I didn't wanna see you. Because I didn't want you to know that. It's just hard to live with. You can make these mistakes that you can never take back no matter what you do. We gotta deal with whatever we did for the rest of our lives.

You know, I think she knew what was gonna happen, grandma. I know it sounds crazy. I don't really believe all the shit about talking to spirits and all that. But I was a mess the days after New Year's. I ended up in jail. And then I wandered over to the Spiritist Center. And they were like waiting for me. She went there on the 31st and told them that I was gonna show up needing help.

Really?

Yeah, it was eerie.

What does that mean. If she knew?

Maybe you couldn't have done any different. Maybe neither of us could.

I don't know.

You think we're stuck? Like I mean me really. You think I'm just fucked up and there's no way around it? It's not fair, right? Like we didn't ask mom and dad to be the way they were. We were just thrown into this shit and we didn't have a choice. I just don't know if I can be better, Lucia. That's what I'm scared of. That for the rest of my life I'm just gonna keep screwing up everything I try to do.

I don't think anyone is hopeless. I think you can change. You gotta want it though.

I do want it! I'm sorry! Forreal. I couldn't be more sorry for everything. I miss our family, you know? I miss grandma, I miss grandpa. I miss you. Porra, I miss mom. It's so stupid because I know it's impossible, but I just want it all back.

Me too. Now it's just me and you and Marta.

I'm gonna be better. I swear it.

Ok. I believe you.

Oh! I forgot, I got you something.

I pulled the paçocas out of my pocket and put them on the table. As soon as she saw them, she started cackling loud and ruthless. I hadn't heard my sister laugh so loosely since we were kids, staying up late in our shared room making fun of mom and talking nonsense. She was laughing so hard she could barely breathe.

What's so funny?

Daniel! I can't eat that. I'm allergic to peanuts!

Damn it. I knew it. Oh my god. I knew that.

I started laughing too.

That is officially my last fuck up ever, you heard? From this moment on, I'm good!

As soon as I said that, I felt a ploppy dollop drop on my head. Hot and fast and wet.

Lucia started laughing, hysterical again. I went to wipe my head.

It was pigeon shit!

Hey, she said, that's good luck.

WE FINISHED eating. I asked for the check, and I paid it. Was that what being good was about? I needed millions of little gestures like that, and then the habit would accumulate. It was about doing the right thing all the time. I would figure it out.

Lucia said she had to go.

We stood up.

I looked at her for a while and then I went in for a hug.

It was the first time in years that we hugged.

Thanks for meeting me today.

Of course. It was good. You gotta come visit me and Marta.

I will!

Ok.

I love you, Lucia. Is that corny to say?

No. I love you too.

Ok. Goodbye.

Lucia walked away. I had nothing to do today. I was off from work, and there were no more people who wanted to see me. My only plans were to ruminate on my shortcomings and failures. But I was in a good mood. It felt like I was taking steps in an unvillainous direction.

I walked toward the beach.

The sun was huge and blasting. The sky was clear, clear and blue, blue.

No schemes, no hustles, no girls to chase. Just me, myself, and my flipflops.

I was twenty three years old without much to show for it. Little knowledge and no talents. I didn't know what I was gonna do. Not the slightest clue. All I knew was that I had a lifetime of gunk and sin and grime to scrub off. But I was happy. Really.

I could see the horizon out in front of me. There was so much time.

There was so much I didn't understand. So many people I relied on, that I expected to be around propping me up sustaining me forever, were gone, gone, gone for good. I didn't get it. But it was true. You couldn't rely on other people to be trapped in your entanglements.

Nobody was ever gonna be an extension of you.

You had to hew headstrong to your own damn separate path.

You had to find your own way.

Other people did exist, that was a good thing, but you had to treat them as their own, offalone worlds. They weren't there for you to use and plunder for your own willy nilly whims. That was my mistake. I was always caught up in myself. Way too caught up. I didn't even see nobody else unless there was something I could take from them. I got that from my parents. But I couldn't just moan and whine about them forever. Eventually you had to let go of that shit. Had to forgive them.

I was trudging toward the water, flipflops slogged with sand.

Everything seemed so good. I was jolted jubilant by a new excitement.

I screamed, Yes!

Nobody was even paying attention to me. They were in their own peaces. I was finding mine. I walked and walked and made it to the edge of the water. I took off my shirt and my flops and I bundled them up and tossed them just out of the tide's reach. I needed to wash the pigeon poop out of my hair and take a long pensive soak. The roary waves were slapping my feet cold as ice. I didn't care how cold it was. I took off running and jumped right in.

Flooded euphoric as soon as my head was submerged.

I popped my head back out and took a deep breath.

I wouldn't be undone by these cycles and cycles of bullshit.

My life was mine.

It was time to live!

—HAPPY BIRTHDAY LUCIA!

Plump, stately, grown up Marta sprouted from the kitchen bearing a bright package on which a green and a yellow ribbon lay crossed and tied, pão de queijo she made me for my trip. Confident, assured, formidable Marta, who was sixteen years old and an excellent baker, as if my grandmother's name planted intuitive bulbs that were now in full bloom. She was smiling, happy to get the apartment mostly to herself for the week while I was in the United States, for the first time ever, ending an old, sad, old story. My mother, dying! come quick! had asked me to spend Christmas with her, but I delayed because I couldn't shun Marta the holiday we treated as our mutual, sacred ritual ever since grandma died, splitting a vegetarian meal and swapping books with long inscriptions. In the first few years before we left Rio, Daniel would tag along, and once, euphoric after a whole year spent working, he bought me the running shoes that were long overdue, which still sat now in my closet, the sole tread worn slip thin, but I couldn't get rid of them because I missed him. Where is your brother, Daniel?

—Get me something from there. A sweatshirt, maybe?

I said sure and gave her a tight presaudade hug, and I walked out into the chilly Lisbon night, feeling forever unused to an unscorching December, missing the carioca rip your head off heat, though I liked Portugal, I was content with my life now. I got on a bus to the airport. I was flying to Pittsburgh, and driving to Steubenville, Ohio, where I would see, once and for all, if America lived up to all my family promiselanded it to be, and more importantly, where I would see my mother for the last time. A month ago, I was sitting on the bus, scrolling halfheartedly through my emails, when a message came clanging in from a name I couldn't believe,

> Lucia,
> I have a malignant tumor in my brain I am not receiving treatment so I will die soon ..
> I want to see you before I die. christmas maybe?
> will pay for your trip from wherever you are.
> Come soon pls. i will be dead soon.
> I looove you. Mom.

after I hadn't talked to her in seven years, seven years of tangled, tortured thinking, which was slowly nearing something like acceptance, impossibly, when early on I clung to hatred like a treasure, waking and sleeping, loathing Maria. But I started working on my book, going around Rio, back to the Ilha, listening and recording stories from people who'd known my mother, Nara, and grandma, just trying to understand my family, understand my mother, and years of working meticulously chipped away at the coil of rage in my stomach and left me with hardwon sympathy for her, abstractly, at least, because when I saw that email and that misspelled declaration of love at the end, my cold waters boiled over. Screw her. She wanted me to come back and forgive her, so she could die peacefully absolved. No way.

But I thought about it, and I realized I would regret not going, and selfishly, if nothing else, the visit would provide me with the end to my book, so I emailed her back and told her to book me a ticket, and she told me she actually didn't have the money for that, of course, and so I had to book it myself. I decided to leave on my birthday and return on January 2nd. Now I was on the plane, headed there, ashamed almost that I wasn't coming from Brasil, as if staying there my whole life would've won me an agonistic triumph against my mother, but I couldn't stay in Rio any longer, I couldn't tolerate the tightfist, bastardized order and progress my country was promulgating. After Leticia moved to Uruguay, I was helping Gilberto run revista pau brasil, and there was this dissident political spirit being fostered, a fierceness that made us all feel radical, powerful. We would do these readings downtown, and, honestly, looking back without nostalgia, they were packed with phony posturing, meandering mordant screeds, and some of the lamest poetry I've ever heard, but still, there was a teeming atmosphere, and at one of them, I met Francisco. This floppyhaired boy who gave a powerful reading, recognizing that we weren't there to be razed down by boredom, he went up and delivered something intense, funny, vibrant, and alive. I was so struck I went up to him and introduced myself.

We clicked easy, and I felt murmurs, susurrations of love, maybe, or he was just tall and pretty and I was intoxicated by his performance. We started seeing a lot of eachother, he was brasilian american, and I got to know his parents, his father was a businessman from New York, and his mother was a fashion designer from Minas. I spent long days in his Ipanema apartment, even taking Marta over there, and it felt, not like a family, but it was warm and safe and comfortable. He was my best friend, and I felt flickers of fire my fear hid away, though we never said we were dating or anything, it was a romance, beautiful and intense, but brief because of his nonsense, well, in hindsight it was all nonsense. Him and his rich quixotic friends caught cheguevara syndrome, gussied themselves revolutionaries, started spouting quotes from books they hadn't read, and eventually formed a guerrilla group. I loved hearing them plot and scheme. It was exciting being mucked in a realchange fantasy. But I didn't think they were really going to do anything, until one day a police station blew up in Leblon, and two officers died.

Francisco wouldn't tell me he was involved, but he became paranoid and snappy, mean even, and one night, when it was just the two of us in his apartment, he cried in a frenzy telling me they were going to kill him, and I told him to calm down and he screamed at me and told me to leave. Unfortunately, his paranoia paid out because they came by and arrested him the next morning, silently, reportless, they just tossed him in a van, and weeks later there was an article, officially denied, reporting the whole case, detailing how he died. He was locked up in an air force base, confined alone, tortured, and eventually they tied him to the back of a truck and dragged him around the base, stopping occasionally to make him suck on the muffler fumes, and finally he died. I was shattered, of course, and angry. For a while I thought of him as a spoiled, idealistic idiot who thought he could do whatever he wanted because mom and dad would always bail him out, but that was wrong, that wasn't the Francisco I loved.

I would never know for sure what happened to him, I would never see his body, and that made everything worse. I avoided our mutual friends, his parents, and I decided my only option was to leave the whole country. There was nothing left for me in Brasil. Marta was my only family. I hadn't seen Daniel in two years, he went off to Uruguay chasing Leticia, and I didn't hear anything else from either of them. The only person around from my old life was Mateus, who I was never close with, but who was living nice and successful, and who I saw on cordial occasions. And so I went off to Portugal, where I hired someone to fraud me a college degree from UERJ, and I got a good job tutoring wealthy children, and I had a life I liked with Marta, with plenty of friends and joys, but with an irrepressible longing for Brasil that I would never shake.

THE PLANE landed and the etceteras proceeded until I was in a rental car on the highway with the windows down, sweating, surprised at the hot, arid pennsylvanian winter. I finally got my license in Lisbon, after a fraught process that would've been much easier if I wasn't a terrible driver. I didn't have a car, but sometimes I rented one so I could terrify Marta, driving around, unintentionally reckless, lost, on portuguese daytrips. Today the road was wide open in front of me, and I was charged by that vaunted, mythic american freedom. I felt like a cowboy, galloping past the dead, desiccated landscape, like I could slice forever through the cool, pure air. What I didn't know, as I crossed the bridge border into Ohio and took an exit to John Scott Highway, then up a steep hill lined by bare trees looking shy without their leaves, was what I expected from my mother. The last time I saw her was when she sheltered Marta and me in her hotel room after the reveillonic tragedy, and though I was numb from the skull bashing events of the worst night of my life, she came through like an angel, shimmering whitespread on the highest mountain peak of motherhood. And the next morning, she was gone. I was fooled again. Fooled twice. What if I came all the way here and she wasn't dying? What if it was just another ploy to enlunce me?

I entered Steubenville. It looked quaint, cars mozily drifting across the hilly, bucolic landscape, but the picturesque charm was cut through with tinges of terror, a rotted deer carcass on the side of the road that looked like jutty, maggoteaten mush, and a gun store, positioned like a welcome sign, advertising their Glock of the Week. This was the town my mother left me for? I drove toward the address she'd given me, 66 Lovers Lane. I passed a few gas stations and about a dozen churches, until I arrived at a short cluster of apartments across the street from what looked like a torrefied, postapocalyptic golf course, brown and ravaged, with even a rust pocked, abandoned cart flipped upside down for good measure. I turned into the driveway next to the apartment complex and found a parking spot, and I sat there for a second to steel myself, then got out and walked to unit number 2.

There were six units, and at the end of the row was a man in a threadbare tanktop drinking a beer and staring at me. I smiled and he didn't react. The housing clump was the color of muddy leaves, tattered, and unsturdy, missing bricks and chunks, and I could see two units with broken windows. My mother lived here? This couldn't have been Larry's house. What happened? I took a deep breath and knocked on her door. The door opened, and an old woman stood in front of me, with a grim, gaunt, sorrow grooved face, mascaraed and blushed and got up clumsy, giving her a clownish aspect that I would've found poignant on a stranger, but then I noticed my grandfather's unmistakable eyes, and the woman who wore them noticed me back and smiled, revealing lipstick smeared, gappy, yellowed teeth.

—Lucia.

She hugged me. She was so thin I could've crumpled her like paper. Coming in, I was determined not to hug her right away, to try to make her earn an affectionate gesture, but seeing her like this filled me with so much pity that I didn't have a choice. We walked inside, and I looked around. The apartment was unadorned except for a few picture frames on a small coffee table. There was a picture of her when she was younger than me, toothy and fulgent in a beautiful dress, and beside it one of her and a man I didn't recognize, but they were standing far from the camera and their faces were shadowed, so I couldn't deduct anything, and the last photograph was one I hadn't seen in many years. It was back in our house on the Ilha, and it must've been after grandma made a cake and let us lick the batter off the bowl because me and Daniel's faces were slathered in chocolate and we were laughing big, and my mother was behind us, touching Daniel on the shoulder and looking at me with a soft mix of admonishment and love. That was one of the three pictures she still kept. Did we finally mean something to her? I didn't know what to say, so I opted for chitchat, in portuguese.

—It's a nice town.

—I can't speak portuguese. The words just don't come to me anymore and it's too much of a struggle to get them out.

She sat down on the couch, which was the only furniture in the room other than the table, and had two open tears and others covered with fraying patches. I sat down next to her, and the couch was so scant of stuffing it was like sitting on a plywood board. Was this going to be my bed? As soon as I sat, she got up again and asked if I wanted anything to drink. I said water, and she came back with a cup of water and a bottle of liquor she was sipping from.

—Is that cachaça?

—Yup. They got it at the store here.

We sat in awkward silence swigging our respective drinks, and she lit a cigarette.

—I smoke inside now. They tell me not to, but what are they gonna do. Kill me?

The apartment did smell like stale smoke, and though it was tidy, it was dusty and creepy and quiet like an unperturbed tomb. I had literally no idea what to say to her. She tormented my life monstrously since I was a kid, and especially over the last seven years, I often thought about how I would get my revenge if I ever got the chance, but this person next to me was so overtly pathetic that it felt like any revenge would be pointless. I couldn't even hate the way I wanted to. How had she ended up like this? I had the impression she won the life she wanted, but all her capacious rapaciousness, her conniving tricks and betrayals, had stuck her in a shitty apartment in a nowhere town, lonely and dying. Well, I guess I didn't know if she was alone, but this didn't seem like a visitor friendly environment.

—How long have you lived here?

—Oh, a while. The neighbors get too loud sometimes but it's not bad.

I couldn't get used to her hoarse, strained voice.

—Lucia, I almost forgot! I got you something.

She went to her bedroom and came back with a limp present wrapped in christmas paper. She handed it to me, and I opened it. It was a plain black shirt, my size, and across the front, bedazzled in orange and red beads, it said QUEEN. I nearly laughed out loud. She must've been rummaging in a discount store, ran into this and thought of me.

—Thank you.

—I don't know what your style is now, but I thought it was cute.

She smiled at me, for the second time today, and it was so well meant and genuine, lacking the asperity of almost all our interactions since always, that I didn't find the gift funny anymore, it was so sad I wanted to cry. We spent the rest of the evening interspersing long gaps of silence with small talk, and eventually I got hungry and went scouring the desolate cabinets and turned up some expired pasta that I cooked anyway. My mom, still drinking and nonstop smoking, told me the only thing she could stomach was grilled cheese, so I made her one and we ate together on a table in the kitchen with only two chairs.

—Do you usually eat alone?

—Sometimes Gary comes by and keeps me company.

—Who's that?

—The neighbor. He's divorced.

He must be the lurcher who was leering at me outside. She seemed reluctant to talk about anything that would've given me a better understanding of her life right now, so I didn't question her. Eventually she drank herself out and told me she was going to bed. I was right, the only other place to sleep was the couch, and she gave me a pillow and a blanket and pointed the way. That first night, I couldn't sleep, not only because the couch offered such a wimpy excuse for comfort, but also because I could hear my mom crying almost the entire night, in waves of intensity, from very private whimpers to huge pained ululations. I didn't know what to do, so I just lay awake, feeling sorry for her, wishing I hadn't come.

THE NEXT day she woke up around two. She told me she was out of cigarettes, and I was eager for any excuse to leave, so I sent myself on a mission to buy her more. I drove out in the hazy steubenvillean afternoon, windows down at first until a putrid sulfury smell made me roll them back up. Eventually I pulled into a gas station convenience store with a big neon sign that read Smokey's, and I thought they must sell cigarettes there. I walked in and waited in line behind a burly tattooed man with a crazy booming voice that nearly spooked me out of the store. But after he left, it was just me and the cashier. A young guy in his early twenties, who had a friendly, sunny demeanor that reminded me of my brother at his best. I read my mother's order from the piece of paper scrawled out for me.

—That's what you want?

—Why?

—Well, there's only one person who gets that.

—I'm actually getting those for my mother.

—Oh shit! That's your mom?

—Yes.

—So you're brasilian?

—Yes.

—Me too!

—There are other brasilians in this town?

He told me that his mom was from Rio and we spoke to eachother in portuguese. He spoke like an american carioca, with a noticeable accent, but fluent and right. Apparently his mom and my mom knew eachother, but an initial acquaintance turned to straight animosity and now they didn't speak. Hardly anybody spoke to her anymore, he said, after what happened to her husband and the other guy.

—You know, some of the meaner people that come through here call her The Witch.

—Why?

—Are you guys close?

—No, I haven't seen her in a very long time.

—Well, I don't know if you know what happened. But she was married to this dude, kooky catholic dude who was teaching at the university. It was kinda scandalous when she came to town, people were wary of her, you know what I mean, foreigner in a small town, but people warmed to her, and one day she goes back to Brasil for New Year's and the guy ends up dead. Rumor was that she killed him. I was in high school then and that's what everybody said. Her daughters moved to

California to live with their aunt and never stepped foot here again. And your mom got the house and the money, which people weren't thrilled about.

—But what happened to the house and the money?

—That's the thing. I hate gossiping, but I oughta tell you this because she is your mother. While she was married to the professor, she was having an affair with this surgeon, some dude named Jim Gag, big time asshole. When she came back, he even moved in with her for a minute even though Jim had a wife, this dowdy woman that ended up moving to Wheeling kinda in disgrace because of what happened. So, Jim was a serious philanderer, women everywhere, hookers, everything, but his biggest vice was slot machines, he was totally addicted, like one of these real sick guys who'll play for a day straight. And he ended up fleecing your mom for everything, man, she had to sell the house. He emptied her. Lost like two million dollars in a year. Then it came out that he was malpracticing every which way, leaving tools in people. It was a mess. And just about when the police were gonna close in on him, he killed himself.

—Oh my god, that's horrible.

—I know. Now I hear she's got bone cancer or something bad. She comes in here all the time but don't say much. Not even hello usually. Gets her shit and gets out.

—Yeah, I don't think she's doing very well.

—Hey, I'm sorry I told you all that. I shouldn't be blabbing around.

—No, I'm glad you did. It was nice meeting you.

—For sure. Take it easy.

I grabbed her cigarettes and left the store, feeling beaten down by that story, depressed at how morosely life progresses for some unlucky people. Life was full of failure, grief, and misery for everybody, but there were certain people hellselected for an unstoppable battering, and I was starting to realize my mother was one of those people. I was getting more and more uneasy about holding her responsible for her faults against me, because you don't handpick the qualities you're born with, and you certainly don't have a say in your rearing, and if you did, I doubt anybody would choose to be invested with greed, wrath, malice, and an utter, cold disdain for the people they're supposed to care for the most. My mother had all those qualities in droves because of things outside her control, and it led her to an unhappy life, chasing an always fleeting paradise, and neglecting the people who might, possibly, give her a stable joy. Now she was old before her time, alone, and dying, and I was the only real thing she had left. It was all too much for me.

I drove back to the apartment. My mother was waiting for me at the door, surprisingly ebullient, and she gave me a warm hug. I thought about asking her the cashier's name because I was curious, but I didn't want her to think he'd told me anything, so it was best not to mention it. That night after we ate dinner, the same identical pasta for me and grilled cheese for her from the night before, I sat down on the couch with some papers that I brought with me. It was drafts from my book that I was reading through and editing, a book whose writing changed me, because excavating my family history, trying to make sense of everyone and everything that happened that New Year's Eve, made it impossible for me to think of all the people in my life as simply as I'd done before, everything was tremendously murkier than I ever expected. But I was almost finished, I had one more chapter to write. My mother was sitting next to me, and I randomly started reading out loud, from the second chapter, one I wrote in Daniel's voice, and even though my mother claimed she couldn't speak portuguese anymore, she was in rapt attention, laughing, smiling, enjoying the story. When I was finished she looked at me.

—That was Daniel.

—I know. I wrote it.

—I tried to find him. I wanted both of you to come here together. But I couldn't.

—I haven't seen him in years. The last time we spoke he came to say goodbye and told me he was going to Uruguay to look for Leticia. He left, and I never heard anything again. But I feel like I would've heard if he died. I think he's still alive. Probably. He knows how to take care of himself.

—Who's Leticia?

—He dated her for a long time. Don't you remember? Mateus's cousin.

—Oh. She had a kind of ratty face. Bad hair?

I laughed. My mother could find something bad to say about anybody, even in the throes of a brainwrecking illness. It was a bummer to talk about Daniel because I missed him so badly, but he felt near to me when I was writing, when I was thinking through his voice. The same way I felt about my grandma when I was writing about her. For years, I felt like my grandma's death was my fault, that if I hadn't left that night, she would still be alive, and while that was probably true, I had to unyoke myself from that guilt because that tragedy was due to happenstances freakly agglomerated. If that night played out a million times, how many times would the apartment have caught fire? How many times would she have died? It was impossible to know. What was in my control, and my biggest regret, was that she died thinking I was upset with her, that I didn't get to express how deeply I loved her and would forgive her over and over for anything, anything. But if she was right about the universe and eternity, wherever she was, she knew the truth about how I felt.

My mother stood up from the couch and told me she was going to bed.

—Goodnight, Lucia. I love you.

SHE LOVED me. I wondered if she really felt that, or if she had an inkling that nonexistence would be colder than she imagined, and so she was trying to cling to warmth while she could. She loved me. What did I know about love? Even the possibility of it troubled me because feelings were so fickle, and if my feelings changed, my opinions changed, often from one day to the next, what was capable of grounding a sustained, permanent feeling toward another person? Because that was love. It had to be permanent, or it didn't exist. Because death was permanent. And in the balance of being, only another strong permanence could counteract the dark lurking eliminator awaiting us. But you didn't have to do anything to die, that just happened. Presumably, there were people unworthy of love. Because didn't you have to earn love? You had to show up everyday, be good, and be worthy, and if you messed up, unfortunately, you were cut off. That didn't seem right to me because people were so falterable, and the kind of love that mathematized and counted comforts and culps was meretricious and wrong. You owed other people love, a kind that didn't waver, and you probably owed it to everybody in the world, and though that was impossible, if there was someone I irrevocably owed it to, it was my dying mother. She hadn't been good to me, that was true, but I did love her. I wanted her to be. Looking past every action and interaction between us, I wanted her to be. That was love, wasn't it?

I thought about all that as I lay on the couch and listened to her cry, and it was nice and good and abstract and fine, my philosophical commitment to loving her, but she was right there, suffering in the other room, and lying here thinking wasn't going to help her, so I got up, and I crawled into bed next to her. Wordlessly, she curled up nuzzly on my chest like a skeletal cat, and I stroked her head while she moaned in pain, and it was a reversal of all those nights on the Ilha when I would have a nightmare and knock on her door, sheepish, sorry to bother her, and ask if I could please, please sleep with her, and she would sigh and say come on, and all my nightmares would go away. She was like a kid now, skinny, frail, and frightened, and I felt so sorry for her that I cried too, and eventually we wore ourselves out and fell asleep.

The next day we woke up in the afternoon and had breakfast, a banana apiece, and thankfully I wasn't staying much longer, or else I was going to starve. She didn't mention the night before, and she never discussed what kind of pain she was in, nor did she ever allude to the illness, so I didn't bring it up. We talked about nothing and the weather, which on this day was clear and sunny, though subject to change at a split second. She suggested we go to the lake, The Lake, she said, like I knew what that was, and I said ok. We crossed the street and climbed a hill until we were on the selvic scorched field she confirmed used to be a golf course, but she didn't tell me what happened. We walked for a while, through weeds and briars, tall snakesneaky grass, and up and down endless mounds until I was sweating through my long sleeved shirt and wondering how my mother could walk so briskly unfazed, but eventually, after we cut through the thickest vegetation on the route, the shrubbery cleared, and in front of us there was a big green pond, reeking like fish and decay, bug clouded, with a few brave ducks floating on top.

—The Lake.

We sat down on a curt, rocky shore, and I stared at the landscape and the stagnant water and wished that this dumpy, meager pond would transform into the Atlantic Ocean, and that I could be sitting, sunblasted, on the Copacabana beach with my family, healthy, alive, and around, but that was doomed wishing, and I needed to accept and enjoy what I had here, my mother right next to me and this tranquil afternoon. I reached out and let my hand rest on top of hers, and just then it occurred to me that today was New Year's Eve. The wound I carried from my grandma's death was time mitigated and calloused, but the day made it feel especially close, and it made me think the biggest tragedy wasn't death, but all the tangibilities that dissipate with death, what it felt like to get a hug from her, what she smelled like, her turns of phrase and the timbres of her voice, all the precious stamps of her existence that were lost forever. I was about to cry when my mother graveled out a question.

—How is Nara?

I thought for a second and then realized what she meant.

—Marta is good. She's smart and confident and funny. I think you would like her.

—Marta. Do you have a picture?

I showed her a picture on my phone.

—She looks like her mother.

I didn't say anything. Marta and I had tried sending numerous letters to Nara, in the few years after grandma died, but they were all returned unopened. One day I called the prison, and they said that she had been released and they didn't know where she was. It was clear that she didn't want to have a relationship with me or Marta, but I searched for news of her nonstop, feverishly, and last year I found her obituary in a paulista newspaper. They didn't say how she died. I cared and I wondered and we cried about it, and I considered the boughs on my grandmother's tree. The failure and disaster she brought up strongly contested her hagiography, but I couldn't judge her because living seemed more and more like a slippery enterprise I would never grasp, but I was becoming ok with the mystery.

And in the name of mystery, I thought I'd ask, one last time.

—Who was my dad?

My mom looked at the ground for what seemed like ten minutes, and then she whispered.

—Antonio.

We let that hang in the air for a few moments, and then we walked back to the apartment. Later that evening, we ate the same dinner each of us had eaten the past two nights, but I drank cachaça and had two cigarettes and we stayed up until after midnight, talking and laughing. I thought about her answer to my question, which neither of us broached again, and I came to the conclusion that she lied to me. I don't think she knew the truth. But she thought that answering affirmatively would give me the solid foundation she'd denied me for twenty eight years, and, by saying Antonio's name, that little gesture could serve as the fine point all her sins could funnel down to, and she could feel forgiven, with the nebulous knife of her transgressions stabbed into a scapegoat. Or it was true. It didn't matter because I didn't care. I was me. Nothing would change that. Paternity was a fiction I had no use for. Me, me, me, I was Lucia, complete.

After hours of drunk gregarious reminiscing, we went to sleep, and I crawled into bed right next to her. It was my last night, I wasn't about to sleep on that boardhard couch. The next morning, I woke before she did and I tidied up the house, got my things together, and drove around until I found a store that was selling Steubenville sweatshirts, and I bought one as a souvenir for Marta. I stopped by Smokey's to see if my brasilian buddy was working, but he was off, and so I left my contact information with another employee, just in case, I don't know, I wanted some tether to my mother, to this podunk town. When I got back to the apartment, my mother was still in her room. I walked in and opened the curtains and flooded the room with light, but she did not stir, so I pulled the covers off her, and what I feared was true. Her eyes were closed as if she was sleeping, but her lips were chapped and white, and she wasn't breathing, and when I grabbed her bone cold hand to feel her pulse, there was nothing, she was dead. I called an ambulance and watched as she was bodybagged and removed, feeling faraway from the fear and hatred that defined my relationship with her for most of my life, but I also felt like my duties as a daughter were complete, so whether she would be buried at a barren funeral or cremated, it wasn't my business, I had a flight to catch, and my story had an ending, so that night, wearing the gaudy shirt she gave me, I got on a plane and sat in the very last seat, and when I leaned my head against the window, I was overwhelmed by an ecstatic heartache for my mother and for Rio de Janeiro, but more than that, I was confounded and awestruck by the love that moves the sun and the other stars.

THE END

acknowledgments

thanks foremost to my mother, my father, rhiannon, vovô, vovó, e stella, to whom this book is dedicated. thank you to gaby, ethan, sean, jacob, carla, franklin, ferdy, and all my friends in copacabana, steubenville, and new york. thank you to rivka galchen, chris clemans, jade hui, lauren grodstein, binnie kirshenbaum, margaret luongo, lindsay sagnette, and everyone who made this book possible.

Harold Rogers was born in Steubenville, Ohio, to an American father and a Brasilian mother, and grew up between the United States and Rio de Janeiro. He holds a BA in philosophy from Miami University in Ohio and an MFA from Columbia University. He lives in New York City, where he works as a boxing coach and a stand-up comedian.